SWIFTLY AND EASILY, HE BENT
AND SWEPT HER UP INTO HIS ARMS

"What are you doing?" she asked weakly as he carried her along the stream's bank.

"I'm going to make love to you," he said matter-of-factly.

"I—please," she said, putting a resisting hand against his chest.

"You knew I was going to, sooner or later," he said. "I just decided or sooner."

He put her down gently on a bed of pine needles, warmed by the morning sun. She felt dazed and frightened, and yet strangely exhilarated too. For a second or two she closed her eyes—then, wanting to know it all, she opened them again and watched him with the sun behind him and the blue sky framing his naked body.

He paused, about to toss his trousers aside, and said, "You ain't going to scream or fight me or anything, are you?"

Her lips parted in a tremulous smile. "No," she said, in little more than a whisper, "I'm not going to fight you."

He lay over her at once, insistent, searching and yet, as she had somehow known he would be, gentle . . .

A Westward Love

Elizabeth Monterey

WARNER BOOKS

A Warner Communications Company

WARNER BOOKS EDITION

Copyright© 1981 by V.T. Banis
All rights reserved.

Cover art by Jim Barkley

Warner Books, Inc., 75 Rockefeller Plaza. New York, N.Y. 10019

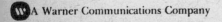A Warner Communications Company

Printed in the United States of America

First Printing: November, 1981

10 9 8 7 6 5 4 3 2 1

"Now I wish you to learn of one of the strangest matters that has ever been found in writing or in the memory of mankind... Know ye that on the right hand of the Indies there is an island called California, very close to the Earthly Paradise, and inhabited by black women without a single man among them, for they live almost in the manner of Amazons. They are robust in body with stout, passionate hearts and great strength. The island itself is the most rugged with craggy rocks in the world. Their weapons are all of gold as well as the trappings of the wild beasts which they ride after taming, for there is no other metal on the whole island."

Garcia Ordóñez de Montalvo,
Los Sergas de Esplandian

A Westward Love

PROLOGUE

London—1825

The window of the carriage crashed open.

"Why are we stopping here?" the woman inside demanded. "I gave express orders—"

"The horses, milady," the driver mumbled apologetically, "they must rest. There's water here."

"Oh, the horses! The poor horses, I hadn't thought—" Claire Hayes sighed and, opening the carriage door, stepped down by herself, to the dismay of the footman hurrying to help her.

It was just past dawn, the rising light turning the sky to stained glass. The driver hastily unhitched the horses and led them to a little stream that ran alongside the road. Claire could hear them drinking greedily while she paced to and fro behind the carriage.

The cool damp air smelled of the crabapples that bordered the route, and the freshly turned soil of the farmland beyond. By midmorning they would be in London, with all its stink and smoke, and there she would...

She paused, watching a nervous redwing lift from its perch in a bullace tree. What would she do once they had reached London? Continue a stupid quarrel with Richard, who was, so far as she knew, fifty miles behind at Everly Hall?

It had seemed the only thing to do last night. With tempers flaring and angry words falling like shards of glass between them, she'd leapt into her carriage and set out pell mell for London. Of course, Richard had been expected to follow her. It was doubly infuriating that he had robbed her of the roadside reconciliation she had envisioned. After all, she had hardly intended to end up in London alone, while practically everyone who was anyone was at Everly.

On the other hand, she couldn't turn back now, she told herself, furious with Richard for his obstinacy. I would be a laughing stock.

"Aren't those horses ready yet?" she demanded, coming around the carriage.

"We're just feeding them, milady," the driver said. "Soon's they get their wind..."

One of the horses whinnied, pricking up his ears. In a moment Claire heard it as well—the distant rattle of hooves on the hard ground. Someone was approaching, riding swiftly.

Claire smiled to herself and walked into the roadway, watching back the way they had come.

So she was to have her way after all. It was a triumph of sorts, though a hollow one, for she felt at the same time a disconcerting sense of disappointment; this would have been the first time that Richard actually stood up to her. She made an unconscious gesture, as if dismissing that idea out of hand.

The horseman rounded a bend into sight, slowing his mount as he caught sight of them along the road. He had reined to a stop and was leaping down before she saw in the pale light that it was not Richard, but his brother Peter.

"Claire, I've been worrying myself sick over your traveling alone."

"In the company of my servants." She corrected him. "Really, Peter."

"Yes, well, I've been praying every mile, just the same."

She smiled grimly. "I rather fear prayers concerning me are rejected automatically on arrival."

"You mustn't talk like that," he whispered, glancing at the servants.

"At any rate," she added, ignoring the objection, "as you can see for yourself, I'm quite all right—or will be, as soon as I'm on the road again. Aren't those blasted horses rested yet?" she demanded over her shoulder.

"I'll hitch 'em up now, milady," the answer came back.

"And Richard?" she asked, turning back to Peter.

"You haven't seen him then?" Peter looked surprised. "He left the same time I did, only he rode cross country. He said he could make better time that way. Not knowing the way, I thought I'd be better off following the road. My guess is, if you just sit tight here for half an hour..."

"Twiddling my thumbs?" she snapped. "Thank you, no. It looks as if we're ready to go at last."

She started for the carriage. Peter, pausing to glance back the way he had come, followed her. "If you don't mind, then, I'll ride inside with you."

She shrugged and allowed him to hand her inside. "As you wish," she said, sinking wearily back into the leather seat. She did not say so, but she would welcome the company; her own had proved a trifle unsatisfactory.

He called for a servant to tend to his horse, and then climbed inside. The driver larruped the horses, and the carriage jolted forward.

Peter had taken the seat opposite her. "I'll have you know you set the entire party on its ears," he chuckled. "They would talk of nothing else. Why did you decide to leave?"

Claire frowned, realizing that for the moment she could not recall precisely what it was she and Richard had quarreled about this time.

"Because I chose to," she snapped. "If

you're going to ride with me, Peter, *for God's sake—*"

"Claire, *please.*"

"Oh, I *am* sorry," she said, exasperated. "Though I don't know why you don't just take the vows if you're going to be all that dreary about a simple oath."

"My religion means a great deal to me," he said soberly, his eyes meeting hers. "And I think you know why I haven't taken vows."

Her gaze slid away from his. "I don't think you ought to talk about that," she said. "I am engaged to marry your brother, after all."

"Yes. I'd almost forgotten Richard." He turned to stare out the window.

She studied his face in profile, thinking, not for the first time, that Peter was better looking than his brother. She knew that he was in love with her. She thought of the passion with which he embraced the Church and its teachings; if only that passion were directed into other channels...

She blushed, smiling to herself; she could just imagine what Aunt Tess would have to say about her scandalous way of thinking. If she returned Peter's love, would his passion still be for the Church?

But there was no sense in such musings. Richard was an earl, the eighth Earl of Everly, and enormously wealthy, while Peter was only a second son, who must live on the allowance his brother provided.

Peter turned abruptly from the window,

and for a fleeting moment she saw something she had never seen in his face before, something hard and intense and almost frightening. She blinked, and it was gone, so completely that she could not be certain that her lack of sleep and the gloom of the carriage had not combined to delude her.

"I can't tell you how glad I am to have you to myself." He smiled.

"Your company has always been welcome to me."

"Has it?" he asked. To her surprise he leaned forward, clasping her hand between his. "Claire, I must know, if there weren't Richard...?"

"But there *is* Richard." She interrupted him, alarmed by the intensity of his gaze and the fierceness of his grip. She tried to free her hand, but for a few seconds he held it tight. Then some of the tension seemed to drain from him.

"Yes, there is Richard." He released her and sat back.

It was the last time that he touched her during the ride; yet, some hours later, when she alighted from her carriage before her aunt's house on Prince Edward's Square, it seemed as if her hand still burned from his grip.

"You must wake up, Claire!"

Claire reluctantly came awake. She opened one eye with effort and found that the midday sunlight still struggled to get through the closed curtains. It could have been no more than an hour since she'd crawled wearily into bed.

"Claire, don't you hear me? You must get up," her Aunt Tess demanded, shaking her shoulder. "Something dreadful has happened."

Claire's eyes, which had drifted shut, opened again. "What is it, Aunt?" she asked sleepily. "Don't tell me the house is on fire?"

"It's Richard."

That brought her awake. She sat up, giving her head a toss to dislodge the cobwebs inside it. "So he's finally come," she said with a grim smile, but the smile faded when she saw her aunt's face. "What is it? What's happened?"

"He's had an accident. They've brought him home on a stretcher."

The whole square was astir with the story. There had been a quarrel between the couple and, against all reason (as the story was being circulated), Claire had started back to London in the middle of the night. Distraught, and worried over his fiancée's safety, the Earl had had his horse saddled hastily. Too hastily, as it turned out, for somewhere in the countryside a girth had given, and the Earl had been flung from the horse. Stunned by the fall, his foot twisted in a stirrup, the poor man had apparently been dragged some considerable distance by the confused beast. The Earl's servants, hard on his trail, had found him lying in a ravine.

Richard's townhouse and that of Claire's aunt shared a corner of the square, sitting at right angles to one another, so that Claire's room actually overlooked the garden of the other house. By drawing the curtains, she could look down on the bedlam below. There had been a delay while a bed was made ready, the townhouse having been closed while Richard was at his estate for the season. As a result, it happened that Claire was at her window the moment Richard was carried across the garden by his servants.

Even at the distance, she could see the blood-soaked clothing and the ghastly, unnatural angles at which his legs were twisted. The sight, brief though it was, made her stomach turn. She had been twelve when her father died in a hunting accident. She had seen the grooms riding in with the strange, awkward bundle flung across the saddle of her father's horse. Unsuspecting, she had run out to see for herself the cause of all the excitement.

The servants were accustomed to paying little attention to her, and they were too caught up in the drama of the moment. No one had noticed a young girl staring as the still bleeding body had been laid upon the ground, almost at her feet.

Since then the sight of blood or a wound—even a scruffed elbow—was enough to make her ill. She knew that she must go to Richard, that it would be expected of her, but the very thought filled her with dread.

"They're saying you're to blame," Aunt

Tess wailed, wringing her hands. "Oh, what's to be done?"

"I shall go to Richard," Claire said, her voice quavering.

A short time later, those who saw her hurry down the steps of her aunt's house attributed her paleness to grief, for which they gave her due credit. Her coloration, in fact, had more to do with a sleepless night, and her dread of seeing Richard in his battered condition, but the firm tilt of her chin gave an honest indication of the courage it had required of her to make this visit.

It was Peter, however, who spared her the worst of the ordeal. She had found the house in a state of total confusion, the front door standing open and servants too busy rushing to and fro with cloths and basins of water to notice or much care who was about. Claire had started to enter Richard's room when Peter intercepted her.

"You mustn't go in there," he said, taking her arm. "The doctors are trying to set his legs. It's an ugly business, and anyway, he wouldn't know you."

She might have argued, but at that moment another maid came out, this one bearing a basin filled with bloody water. The sight made Claire's legs weak, and she let Peter help her to a chair.

"This is my fault," she murmured, echoing what others were already saying.

"No, it's God's will," Peter intoned.

There was such an odd note of satisfaction in his voice that she looked up at him, surprised, but at that moment he glanced away, so that she could not read his face. When he again looked at her, his was the anxious face of the concerned brother.

"I think you'd better go now," he said. "It will be a day or two, at least, before Richard will want to see anyone. I'll let you know how things are."

It was, in fact, the better part of a week before she saw Richard. The blame was not hers, for Richard had sent back a reply to her first inquiry, asking that she wait until he was somewhat better before she called on him.

She attributed the delay to his consideration of her, since he was acquainted with her aversion to such injuries, though it could not but make her look worse than ever in the neighbors' eyes. The accident had occurred sometime in the early hours of Saturday morning, but it was not until Thursday that Claire received a note from her fiancé, telling her he would welcome a visit from her if she could manage it.

Unconsciously she had dressed in black, which only emphasized the paleness of her complexion. She was not a pretty girl by ordinary standards; the planes and hollows of her face were rather too exaggerated, and her mouth, though full lipped, was not especially large. Her large, dark eyes, however, were expressive and arresting. They could smolder with anger or passion at one moment, and then, caught unaware, gaze at one with a child's innocence and vulnerability.

Her mother had died in childbirth. Claire had been more or less raised by her father, though his idea of the best way of doing that was to leave her as much to her own devices as possible. Still, he had tried to take some interest in her, and he was not entirely to blame if she had consequently grown up more comfortable in the company of men than women. By the time of her father's death, she could ride like a cavalryman and handle a rifle with fair skill, though she had never learned how to brew a decent cup of tea or mastered any of the other homely skills considered so essential to womanhood.

At her father's death she had come to live with her only relative, his widowed sister, Tess. The alliance between the independent and headstrong young girl and the flighty, old-fashioned widow had been an uneasy one. Aunt Tess had for the most part allowed Claire to do as she wished—which Claire would have done anyway. It was undoubtedly true that Aunt Tess' enthusiasm for her niece's upcoming marriage was greater than Claire's own.

Which was not to say that there was not a certain affection between the two, nor that

Aunt Tess, watching Claire pin a small hat to her pale yellow hair, did not feel a certain sympathy for her.

"Shall I come with you?" she had asked.

"Thank you, Aunt, but I think not." Claire had smiled gratefully. "The neighbors might think I'd only go on a leash."

"It would do you well to pay a little more attention to what the neighbors think." Aunt Tess had scowled.

"I'm never unmindful of it," Claire had replied, letting herself out the front door.

Though it was only a matter of a minute or two from her front door to Richard's, she was conscious of a number of curtains being discreetly edged back from windows, and of heads turning in the little park in the center of the square. She smiled with grim amusement and went straight across, looking neither right nor left.

At first she thought her fears had been excessive. It was true that there were several ugly bruises and scrapes to be seen, but she was able to avoid looking directly at these, and for the most part Richard's major injuries were concealed from her sight. He sat in a carved wooden chair, his legs covered with a plaid blanket. His hands and head had been swathed in so many bandages that he looked like an Egyptian mummy.

"It's a good thing the wedding isn't immediate," she said. "They'd take you for one of the gifts rather than the groom."

"I'm glad to see you taking my misfortune so well," Richard said, a trace of irony in his voice.

"I am sorry," she said, and meant it. "Sorry for everything, and especially seeing you like this. But it isn't forever."

"I'm afraid that some of it is," he said.

Her smile faded and her eyes grew wide. "What do you mean?"

Richard tapped with his finger at the plaid blanket covering his legs. "The bones were rather shattered. The doctors were able to set some of them, but not all."

"Do you mean you'll have to walk with a cane?"

"Yes," he said, adding on a lower note that she had to strain to hear, "if at all."

"My God," she breathed, rising from her chair and going to the windows. They were in the parlor, and from the garden outside came the scent of spring flowers, and not too far distant the *clip-clip-clip* of someone trimming hedges.

Richard, her husband-to-be, a cripple? It was something she'd not contemplated, though she now saw that she ought to have been prepared for the possibility. If only...surely someone might have warned her...it was so much to digest all at once.

"That's why I put off your coming, I wanted to think how best to tell you about—about everything," he said. "I'm afraid there's more."

She turned back to the room, trying without success to manage a smile. "I suppose I'd better hear it all, then."

"My face—it was rather banged up as well..." His voice trailed off and he was unable to meet her gaze.

"You're going to be scarred as well?" She felt the taste of fear in her mouth and swallowed hard.

"Yes. Permanently."

As if from a great distance, she heard her own voice saying, "I want to see."

He looked up with hope, but it was dashed by her appearance. Her skin had gone ashen white; one could almost see the veins and arteries beneath the flesh, and her eyes were enormous.

"I must know the worst," she said.

Richard was half-afraid she might faint, and if he had been able he would have gone to her to put his arms about her, but he could not. Her eyes met his with such unwavering intensity that at length he reached up and began to unwind the bandages that concealed most of his face.

She put a hand to her throat, all but strangling herself to prevent the retching that threatened. She watched, mesmerized, as the bandages came away to reveal the still raw, purple scars discoloring his skin. One corner of his mouth—that finely etched mouth she had thought so classical—had been torn downward, leaving him forever leering. He tugged away the last of the cloth and she saw that he had lost all but a remnant of one ear...

She turned once more to the garden. A bee, lured by her scent, came in to circle twice about her head before flying off again, humming his disapproval.

It was horrible to think that she must see this not just once, but over and over again, day after day, for so long as they lived. How could she endure it? If she had loved him the way some women were said to love their husbands, the way women did in those romantic novels of which Aunt Tess was so fond, perhaps it would be easier. But she had never pretended to more than affection for Richard; that, and the desire to be married to an earl, a man of wealth.

"I'm truly sorry," Richard said. "However, the doctors have assured me there's no reason why I shouldn't marry—" His words caught in his throat as Claire turned from the window. He saw the utter revulsion etched upon her face, scarring it as badly as his wounds had scarred his. "—and I, of course, have told them they are fools," he finished lamely.

"Richard—I..." She stammered helplessly, unable to conceal her feelings from him, and hating herself for what she knew he saw in her face.

"It'll never do," he said, slamming his fist down upon the arm of his chair. "I've known that from the moment they told me."

She forced herself, with more willpower than had ever before been required of her, to look directly at him: at the torn ear, at the twisted mouth, at the hideously colored mass of flesh that had once been a patrician face.

"Richard, I will marry you regardless," she said with a voice that threatened to break into a sob with each word.

"And I'm to bed a bride who looks at me as you do? My dear, you are incapable of concealing your true feelings." He seemed to smile. "Until today that had always been one of your charms for me."

"You must know that you have my affection and—"

"Damn your pity." He interrupted, his fingers clawing at the plaid as if he would like to tear his broken legs from his body.

There was a long moment of silence. She had closed her eyes, no longer able to bear the sight before them, but the tears streamed unchecked from beneath her lashes.

"Shall I release you from our engagement?" he asked in a dull voice.

When her answer came, it was but a single whispered word: "Yes."

"So be it." He nodded. In his heart he had known all along that this was the inevitable outcome, but yet there *had* been the hope... "I think you should go now. It's pointless to prolong something that's distasteful for both of us."

She gathered her hat and gloves, not

bothering to put them on, and started from the room. At the door she paused and would have turned back, but he spoke sharply, saying, "Don't look at me again, please."

Without turning, she said, "Forgive me," but her voice was so faint and tremulous that he did not hear her at all, and when he looked again, she had gone.

Her aunt was incredulous. "You must be mad! He's one of the wealthiest men in the city, scars or no scars. And anyway, who else do you think will have you now? This whole affair hasn't done your reputation very much good, you must know."

She was well aware that the last was true. The Hobbs sisters, who lived directly across the square, and had never quite approved of her anyway, had actually cut her when she'd passed them in the park a short while ago. She had always had a reputation, but her youth, and later her engagement to Richard, had provided her with a certain protection against gossip. Privately she railed against the conventions that allowed a man to do as he wished while condemning a woman for following her own dictates rather than those of the crowd, but she was no fool. She knew that the circumstances under which her engagement to Richard had been broken would harm her socially.

Public disapproval, however, did not weigh

upon her so much as her own judgment of her behavior. At the present time the latter was harsh.

Though she might agree with the wisdom of Richard's decision that pity would have been a tragic basis on which to found a marriage, it was hard not to feel guilty when she looked from her bedroom window to see the blanketed, bandaged figure taking the air in his garden. The sight of him filled her with shame and anguish and yet, as if to scourge herself for her weakness and her selfishness, she found herself drawn again and again to the window. She would stare down upon her former fiancé, rarely leaving her place until he had been carried inside by his servants. Whether or not he was aware of her presence she was unable to say, though once or twice he had glanced briefly upward as if he could see her through the curtains.

It was during this time of brooding that she received a most unusual visit from Richard's brother, Peter.

She was glad to see him, as she had had little company of late and was restless with her own. Moreover, she thought that perhaps he had brought some message from Richard. It would have eased her conscience a great deal to know at least that he forgave her.

It seemed, however, that Peter had other things on his mind. For several minutes they exchanged some rather desultory small talk, then he suddenly said, "I shall be leaving soon. Everything's been arranged."

She looked at him blankly. "Leaving?"

"For the Americas, Claire." He pouted. "I told you about it when we were in the country."

"Oh yes." She had only a vague memory of some dinner conversation they'd had. It was about some plan of his to set out in search of his own fortune. Since it had seemed that her own was assured at the time, she had paid little attention to his conversation.

"They say it's all right there," he continued with enthusiasm. "A bit savage in spots, and not half-civilized. They say too that a man's judged there for what he does, not for his titles or his connections. A lot of younger sons have gone off there and done all right for themselves."

"How fortunate for them," she said.

"I've heard tell of places where precious gems lie about on the ground, just waiting to be picked up, and entire cities made out of gold. It staggers the imagination, though some swear that it's true. They say a man can make himself rich if he half tries."

He paused expectantly, as if awaiting some significant reply from her. When it was plainly not forthcoming, he said, "My brother's fixed a trust for me, so that I can depend on an income, though it's modest. And I've already arranged for the purchase of a house."

"Why are you telling me all this?" she asked abruptly.

He stared down at his hat, turning it around in his hands. "I have prayed, I have fallen on my knees before the Almighty, I've vowed my life to his glorious service—"

"Peter, I—"

"—I want you to come with me. To America."

She was struck dumb by the suggestion. She stared at him.

"As my wife, I mean," he added.

"Why, I—I've never dreamed of such a thing."

He stood up, so suddenly that he nearly toppled the tea table at his side. "There's nothing to keep you here now. Not since your engagement's broken."

"But this is my home, how could I leave it?"

"You had a home once with your father, but you left it to come here." He argued with the fervor of a man who has thought in advance of every objection. "And had you married my brother, you would have left here to go to Everly Hall."

"That's hardly the same thing, is it?" she replied, though by now she had gotten over the worst of the shock. "I mean, the Americas are halfway around the world."

"They speak the same language, so it wouldn't be exactly like going to a foreign land."

"I—I don't know what to say."

"I pray I haven't offended you," he said.

"With your proposal? No, but it's so unexpected. You must give me time to think."

He cleared his throat. "I'm to leave in a fortnight," he said.

He looked so anxious that she could not help smiling, for the first time in several days. "Then I promise I shall think about it at once," she said.

She had gotten up as she spoke, and now Peter dropped to his knees before her, clasping her hand and bringing it to his lips.

He was silent, and she suddenly realized that he was praying. She found the scene a trifle awkward, but she could hardly snatch her hand away in midprayer. There was nothing she could do but wait patiently until he had finished.

It seemed an interminable time later when he finally rose, smiling at her. But the time had not been wasted, true to her promise, she had already begun to think about what he proposed.

They were wed a week later, in the chapel at Everly Hall. The Earl himself, still convalescing, was unable to attend.

A week after that she found herself on a sailing ship, in the middle of a seemingly endless ocean. She was on her way to a place called Virginia.

PART I

The Cities of Gold

1

By the time they reached Virginia Claire
had realized that she had made a mistake. It
was several months, however, before the big
blowup came.

She and Peter simply had nothing in
common. She had, in fact, come to the tardy
realization that she had not known Peter at all
when she had agreed to become his bride,
and, increasingly, what she learned she did
not like.

Even his religiosity, which she had been
aware of before, had proven far more excessive than she had suspected. It seemed that
he was forever in prayer, forever beseeching
his God's forgiveness for some failing or another.

Not that she was antireligious. She had

her own ideas and beliefs, but she had not prayed, nor entered a church, since the day of her father's death. To her mind, Peter's constant knee bending profited no one except perhaps his breeches maker.

She had supposed that with all the fire he channeled into his religion, Peter would be an indifferent lover, but that had been far from the truth. He was as passionate in making love to her as he was in his prayers.

She might have found that acceptable—she had discovered that the physical aspect of a marriage was not as unpleasant as she had been led to believe—only she had gradually discovered that Peter's ardor included a cruel streak that grew more pronounced as their married life lengthened. Whereas in the beginning he had treated her respectfully, even gingerly, he quickly became more lascivious and less thoughtful of her.

He was more concerned with taking pleasure rather than giving it, and it seemed that a great deal of his pleasure came from inflicting pain. In the height of his passion he might suddenly sink his teeth into the tender flesh of her shoulder, or tear at her with such fury that his nails drew blood. Once, in the midst of a quarrel as they were dressing for dinner, he suddenly seized her and began to beat her with his belt, ending by flinging her to the floor and assaulting her cruelly.

By the time they had arrived in Virginia, it had become commonplace for her to rise from their bed bruised and bleeding, though afterward Peter was invariably filled with contrition, alternating between begging her forgiveness and praying to his God—until the next time his lust was aroused.

Under other circumstances, she might have found a certain charm in her new home. Virginia was a beautiful land of green fields and rolling hills, not unlike England's own farmlands. As it was, however, her disillusionment with her married state translated itself into a resentment of the home to which her husband had brought her, with the result that she found nothing about it she liked.

Their house was small and, compared with what she was accustomed to, cramped. It was nearly a two-hour drive to the home of their nearest neighbors, the Hensheys, Virginia planters who were crude and boisterous compared to the gentlefolk of London. She could not raise any enthusiasm for their talk of tobacco and politics and slavery, and accordingly lived in an isolation partly of her own making. This only served to intensify the differences between herself and Peter.

Unable to defend herself against her husband's physical attacks, she took to launching her own verbal attacks, lashing out with her tongue as cruelly as he with his violence. She ridiculed him for the meanness of their existence after the glitter of her London social life. She laughed at his religious ardor, inciting him to almost murderous fury.

Most of all she mocked him for the dreams of wealth and success that had brought him to America. "You and your precious gems," she said in a voice dripping with scorn. "Your cities of gold! We haven't even the land to raise tobacco like your fellow bumpkins, and must live on your brother's meager charity."

"There are fortunes to be made here." Peter defended himself, though with less conviction than before. "I've heard of gold—"

"There's your gold," Claire said, slapping at a bare arm. "The color of mosquitoes—the only gold you'll ever lay your hands on."

Yet it was not only Peter who spoke of such fantastic treasures, for whenever the Virginia planters gathered for amusement there was always a certain amount of talk of the vast wilderness that lay to the west, and always the tales included descriptions of great wealth and undreamed-of treasures. A ship's captain, the brother of one of the local women, stopped on his way back to Boston, having rounded the Horn and actually traded in the Spanish colony of California.

"They took me to see one of their farms," he said while his listeners sat spellbound. "They call them ranchos, and a single one of them might be as large as an entire state, with great herds of cattle, stretching farther than the eye can see."

"But the gold," someone asked. "What of the gold?"

"It's there," the captain assured them. "They're canny not to show it, but it's there."

"I'll wager there's no more gold there

than there is in Virginia," one of the men said.

The captain, warming to his tale, and not eager to lose his audience, gave rein to his imagination. "You're a fool to say so. I myself saw an Indian so laden down with it that he couldn't walk at all, and had to be carried by a team of warriors."

Less than a month after the captain another visitor, this one a cousin of their neighbors, the Hensheys, arrived. He had been west, to a city called Memphis, and even farther, to an outpost known as St. Louis, frequented by trappers, adventurers, and others who had actually ranged into the uncharted lands that lay beyond the cities of America. He too had stories to tell, and to add believability, he had one of the gems of which he spoke—a large milky-blue stone known as a turquoise—mounted in a disc of beaten silver.

"I traded a fortune for it," he explained, while the stone was circulated among them. "It's said to have come from a tribe of Indians who live far to the west. Their streets are lined with it, and their houses made of silver."

Claire regarded this story, as she had the others, as nothing more than a fairytale, and while the others listened in rapt attention, she initiated instead a mild flirtation with the eldest Henshey son, a sallow-faced gadabout whom she wouldn't have looked at twice in London.

In their carriage on the way home, Peter

was still agog over the stories of turquoise fortunes. "A man could return from a journey like that a millionaire," he said, speaking more to himself than to Claire.

"From what the gentleman said, I gather a number have tried, without returning," Claire said.

"Still, if a man went with God on his side..."

Claire laughed derisively. "Oh, Peter, really." She mocked him, despite the dangerous glint in his eyes. "Do you honestly think God's got nothing better to do than to traipse around with you looking for a turquoise mine? Don't you suppose all the others said their prayers? And it didn't stop them from being eaten, or whatever happened to them."

He lashed out at her, the force of the blow knocking her head back against the side wall of the carriage, bringing blood to her lips.

"Bitch," he spat at her, seizing her throat in one hand. "You have the nerve to ridicule me, after spending the night making eyes at that Henshey lout?"

"He may be a lout, but at least he works at something," she replied. "Even if it's only a tobacco farm. As for you, you're a nothing, a poor relation who hasn't the gumption to do anything for himself. You'll never find that fortune you're always prattling about because you aren't man enough to go out and find it."

"Damn you," he muttered, his fingers tightening on her throat until she thought he

really meant to strangle her. Suddenly the
hand was gone, tearing instead at the bodice
of her dress, baring her breasts to the pale
moonlight.

She struggled against him. "For God's
sake," she gasped, hoarse from the grip of his
hand at her throat, "not in the carriage, the
driver—"

"To hell with the driver," he muttered.
He forced a knee between hers, prying her
legs apart, and in a moment more he was
upon and within her. She ceased to resist,
lying limp and passive beneath him until the
quick rigidity of his body told her he had
reached his peak and was finished.

After a long period of silence he said,
"I'm sorry."

"You're a worthless fool," she told him,
trying to set her clothes right again.

It was the morning after this incident
that Peter made his announcement.

"I'm going to go," he told her, coming
into their bedroom. She was still abed, but he
had not slept all night.

"Go? Go where?" she asked sleepily.

He gestured with one hand. "Out there.
West," he said.

She sat up, no longer sleepy. "You're
mad," she told him. "You know there's hardly
a grain of truth to any of those tales, and
besides, you've heard what they've had to say
about the dangers."

"If the stories of treasure are false, then the dangers must be too."

"And they might not be," she argued, scrambling out of bed and slipping into a dressing gown. "You should be more realistic. What do you know about dealing with Indians, or—or any of the other problems? You're not an explorer, you're not even a very brave man. You've lived your entire life in ease provided by your brother's fortune."

"That's exactly the point. I came to this country to make my fortune and to escape my brother's domination. I wanted to prove—to you, if you must know—that I could stand on my own two feet, make it on my own. So far all I've managed to put between my brother and myself is distance, but at the same time, I've stretched his purse strings to cover that distance. I might as well have stayed in London. Perhaps you've been right to ridicule me."

She had a sudden sense of what she had driven him to, and crossing to where he still stood, just inside the door, she laid a hand on his arm. "Peter, I—we've neither of us been happy here, but perhaps the fault is our own. Perhaps if we tried to change—"

Peter shook his head, smiling ruefully. "No, it isn't only the treasure I'm after, I want to find something else, as well."

"What do you want to find? Your head on a platter?"

"I want to find God." He looked at her, seeing her surprise. "Oh, I know, I've talked about him, and prayed to him till I'm blue in the face, but for all that, Claire, he's eluded me. I've never felt that he was actually there, in person with me, if you understand what I mean. Perhaps out west, away from everything that I've known, I'll find him, and myself, in a sense. I've never known myself at all, except in terms of other people. I'm my father's second son, Richard's brother, your husband. I think that when I've struck out at you I was trying to shatter that particular mask and in that way get at myself. I don't suppose this makes much sense to you. I'm not even sure it does to me."

"When—when will you be back?" she asked.

"When I've found my fortune. When I'm fit to be your husband."

"But you might be gone years."

"Perhaps." He smiled. "Or perhaps I'll prove more of a man than you thought, and be back soon."

2

At first Peter's letters arrived with surprising regularity, considering the distances and the primitive areas through which he traveled. He wrote from Kentucky, and from a town called Cincinnati, and finally from St. Louis itself.

It was there, after six months, that the letters stopped.

It was a terrible time for Claire. Over and over she berated herself for her selfishness and her cruelty. It seemed to her that she had ruined not only her own life but those of everyone with whom she came into close contact. She could not forget how deeply she had hurt Richard in breaking her engagement to him. Afterward, merely to escape the scene of her selfishness, she had married Peter, only to drive him to his own destruction.

In her isolation, and the inactivity of her life, she found no escape from her own harsh judgment of herself. She spent her days pacing the small rooms of her home like a caged animal, or sitting on her verandah, staring off into the west.

The Henshey boy, hearing she was alone, came to see her, smiling smugly, but he soon left with a dour and disappointed expression. Her neighbors, though they considered her snobbish and were not overly fond of her, continued for a time to send her invitations. But when it became apparent that she meant neither to accept nor even acknowledge them, they eventually ceased.

If only she knew where Peter was! Was he alive, dead, perhaps the captive of some savage tribe? Or had he simply found a new life for himself, more to his liking? She had to smile when she imagined Peter living in sin with another woman, perhaps in some frontier log hut, but her smile was one of bitter irony.

Hearing that a traveler had arrived from the west, she went uninvited to the Hensheys one evening and questioned the man at some length, but he had no news of her husband. The Hensheys, seeing her agitation, concluded that they had misjudged the couple on their previous visits, and that they were more in love than one would have guessed, but

Claire welcomed their sympathy no more than their friendship.

The weeks stretched into months, each more unendurable than the last, and just when it seemed to Claire that she could endure no more, an unexpected visitor arrived with startling news.

It was evening. The soft Virginia dusk had settled over the house and its lawns. Claire, desperate to help the time pass, had taken up embroidery, with thus far disastrous results.

The sound of a horseman riding up the lane surprised her so that she pricked her finger with the needle. She sat sucking at the wound and glowering in the direction of the front hall. Doreen, the little maid she had been trying to train as a proper house servant, went to the door; Claire could hear her in conversation with a gentleman, his low voice indistinguishable at the distance, yet oddly familiar.

Doreen came into the parlor a moment later to announce that a gentleman wished to see her. Claire, thinking that the Henshey boy had again come courting, said, "Tell the gentleman that I have retired, and if he would care to leave his name, perhaps he could return at a more convenient time."

Before Doreen could deliver this message, however, there was a clatter of boots and walking stick from the hallway, and Richard pushed his way into the room.

"My dear Claire," her former fiancé greeted her, making a half-bow from the waist, "this time is as convenient as any for a man who's come as far as I have."

"Richard—whatever on earth are you doing here?" Claire asked, rising to her feet.

"I came to see my brother—will you offer me a glass of that port, I've worked up a bit of a thirst," he said, indicating a bottle and some glasses on a tray.

"Of course, please, help yourself. Peter isn't here."

"So I heard. He's gone west." Richard crossed to the tray and poured himself a glass of the wine. It gave her an opportunity to study him.

She could see that his legs had healed better than the doctors had hoped; one foot was splayed outward at a peculiar angle, causing a limp and necessitating the use of a cane, but his mobility was not greatly hindered.

The scars that had disfigured his face were, if anything, even more grisly looking, perhaps because they bore the unmistakable stamp of permanence.

She had occasionally given herself to wonder, since her arrival on these shores, if she might not have done better to marry Richard, scars and all. Now, in his presence after so long a while, she knew that that was only another of her foolish notions.

It was not merely the scars or the limp. She had begun to understand that outward trappings were not so important as she had once thought. Richard's appeal for her had been his money and his title, just as Peter's had been his good looks and what she had mistakenly thought was the freedom he would provide her. She had been wrong in both cases, and she could see now she would have been no more suited to marriage with Richard than she had been with Peter. Perhaps, she thought soberly, she was not suited to marriage at all.

"Well," Richard said, toasting her with his glass, "have I passed inspection?"

"I'm sorry, was I staring? It's just that it's been so long and—and you have recovered remarkably since then."

"Still not a pretty sight, eh?" He chuckled at her embarrassment.

She forced herself to look directly at him, at the livid scars, at the twisted mouth and pitiful remnant of one ear.

"At least you are alive," she said matter of factly. "That is something to be grateful for."

"Yes, but not to your husband," he said, emptying his glass and pouring another. "Did he tell you it was he tried to kill me?"

"Peter? Why, that's impossible, he would never—" She paused, remembering back to the night of Richard's accident. Peter, riding after her, asking "...if there weren't Richard..."

Richard, watching her, grinned. "I always told you your face is as easy as a book to read," he said.

She took a step backward to sit down in

the chair she had just vacated. "I can't believe it," she said.

"In your heart you must have known. He was mad to have you."

"Yes, but it was a riding accident, wasn't it?" she asked.

"It was no accident," Richard said. "I had a great many weeks to brood about it, to wonder how it had happened. Luckily they'd taken the saddle back to Everly Hall. When I was able to get about, I had a look at it myself, and saw that it had been tampered with. My groom swore it was all right when he saddled my horse for me, and only one person got close to it between then and when I mounted: my brother, in the stables mounting his own horse to set out after you."

"He came by the road."

"Exactly. Put him far away from the scene of the crime. He knew that countryside better than anyone, better than I did, at least. He knew I'd have a lot of jumps, that sooner or later the girth would give. Unfortunately for him, I didn't die as he'd planned, though he managed to get you anyway. And got out of England before anyone got on to him."

She suddenly stiffened her back. "Did you come here for revenge?" she asked.

Richard laughed again and helped himself to more of the port. "Oh yes, you're entirely right, I came here with the idea of breaking my brother's neck, like he tried to break mine."

"Then you've wasted a long journey," she

said coldly. "As I've already told you, Peter is gone."

"Yes, as I said, I knew that. I've been asking about since I arrived. Some of these people are old friends of mine, you understand. I've had some interesting conversations. I already knew Peter had gotten soured on your fair company."

"There's no need to be insulting. If you've asked about, you know Peter went west because he wanted to seek a fortune. There's all sorts of wild stories about treasures—cities of gold—that sort of folderol. Peter has dreams of grandeur."

"Driven to it by you, wasn't he?"

"That's a lie," she said hotly, angered that his remark had hit so exactly on the point over which she had been fretting for weeks.

"That's what they're saying," Richard told her. "They're saying he hasn't got a chance where he went, that he'll never come back from there alive, and they're saying that you drove him to it."

She got to her feet again. "I don't care to listen to any more of this," she said. "Will you please go now?"

Richard made no move to go, but only shook his head sadly. "My dear Claire," he said. "My dear, beautiful witch, Claire."

"How dare you!" she cried.

"It's you who's responsible for all this," he murmured. "If you hadn't flirted with Peter, made it clear to him that you'd be available if I were out of the way, he'd never have lost his head enough to do what he did."

"That's not true," she said, but without the ring of conviction. Was it true? It had always been her nature to flirt; it was almost unconscious with her. Had she led Peter on, given him the encouragement he needed to attempt to take his own brother's life?

"And then when he turned out to be less a bargain than you thought, you managed to drive him away, to his certain doom. I came here with the idea of vengeance. I wanted to punish Peter for what he did to me, but now I think that Peter's already been punished enough, by marrying you."

"If you don't leave—"

"Oh, I'm going, spare me your threats." He laughed, putting his glass down with such violence that the stem shattered, cutting his hand. The sight of the blood it brought made her feel ill.

He strode to the door, holding his hand up to prevent the blood from staining her carpet. At the door he paused to look back at her.

"It's ironic, isn't it?" He laughed again. "To think that you should have been the instrument of my vengeance."

"Get out!" she screamed.

She heard his cane on the tiles of the entryway and after a moment the door slammed loudly after him. She clapped her hands to her face and began to cry. Since Peter's departure she had tried not to face the truth about herself, and now Richard had held a mirror up before her and forced her to look. It was she who was to blame, she who had driven poor, foolish Peter to do the things he had done. Her hands were as stained with blood as Richard's had been a moment before—Richard's blood, and perhaps Peter's as well.

She thought of all she'd heard of that savage, primitive land to which he'd journeyed. Peter might die—might already be dead—and she might never know. She could spend years, the rest of her life, trapped in this house, waiting, wondering, blaming herself.

"No, I can't!" she cried aloud to the empty room. "I'll go mad."

She crossed to the bottle of wine and filled a glass with port. She drank deeply, and as she did so the wind rose, blowing through the open windows at the west end of the room and fluttering the curtain inward.

She turned in the direction of the billowing lace and in an instant she knew what the answer must be. She knew what she must do.

3

"There's a woman to see you."

Camden Summers was in the act of shaving with the blade of his hunting knife. He had, by watching his watery reflection in a polished piece of tin, managed to remove a few patches of beard and quite a bit of skin.

"Not that Frenchwoman again?" he asked. "I made a mistake giving that one a gold piece the last time; now she's got a notion I'm made of them."

"This one's an Englishwoman," the Indian said from the doorway.

Summers frowned. "I heard there was one working over at Miz Letitia's," he said, "a redhead."

"Never saw this one before. She don't look the type nohow."

Summers splashed some water from the basin over his face, washing off most, but not all, of the blood. "They're all the type, depending on circumstances," he said. "Well, I guess I'd better put a shirt on, those Englishwomen are funny ones."

He was, even half-shaved and with a shirt on, a fierce-looking sight—an immensely tall and rangy half-breed, with jet-black hair that hung to his shoulders and, in startling juxtaposition to his swarthy skin, eyes that seemed carved of blue crystal. He had spent most of his life wandering across the wilderness that had come to be known as the far west, and there was scarcely one of its dangers that he hadn't confronted. His father had been an Englishman, a murderer who had fled into the plains to escape punishment for his crimes, his mother a Quapaw squaw. He spoke a dozen or more Indian dialects, could shoot the feather from an Indian headband at a hundred yards, and had once killed a puma with nothing but his hunting knife, though that encounter had left him with a vivid scar that ran from his left cheekbone nearly to the jawline, and that turned crimson when he was angry.

Though men invariably kept their distance, women reacted to him in different ways. Some of them were frightened by his grisly appearance while others were fascinated. He regarded them alike as flesh to satisfy his desires, and otherwise dispensable.

He regarded the Englishwoman whom

the Indian ushered into his room with curiosity, but little interest. She was not the sort to arouse his desires. He liked them overflowing with flesh and femininity, and preferably a bit ripened. This one was still green, little more than a girl she looked, and so fragile she'd surely shatter under his mounting.

Only her eyes made him uncomfortable, for one seemed to see through them into the very essence of her—feelings and fears and needs made naked, as if she'd suddenly opened her bodice to reveal glimpses of her breasts, closing it again before the details had quite impressed themselves upon the mind.

"You're Mister Summers?" she asked in a cool English voice that stirred subconscious memories of his father.

"That I am, won't you sit down, Miss—?"

"Mrs. Denon." She glanced around. The only chair, a piece of hide stretched over a wooden frame, was occupied by a great frowsy-haired tomcat.

Summers gave the chair a violent shake, sending the angry cat out an open window. She sat down, unmindful of the residue of hair that littered the seat.

"Now what can I do for you, Miss—Mrs. Denon?" he asked.

"I'm told that you're the best guide St. Louis has to offer," she said.

He grinned. "Well, I've never entered any competitions. Where is it you wanted to go?"

She looked surprised by the question, as

if he ought to have known the answer himself. "West," she replied.

"There's a lot of that, Mrs. Denon," he said.

"I don't know where, exactly," she said. "You see, my husband came here a little more than five months ago from Virginia. He was on his way west. I haven't heard from him since."

"He may still be here in town. There's lots going on here in St. Louis."

"No, I've asked about, and besides, in his last letter he indicated he was about to set out with some other men, some trappers."

"For where?"

"He—he didn't say, exactly, just west. I'd like to try to find him, Mister Summers, and I'll need a guide. Of course I'm willing to pay, though I should warn you that I'm not a wealthy woman."

Summers studied her for a moment. A great many of the men who came here headed west, left their wives behind. Most, experience had taught him, had had good reason.

"I'm afraid I can't help you," he said aloud.

"Why is that?"

"Well, I could tell you it's because I don't like getting mixed up in domestic matters, which is the truth. But more important, I'd never take a woman out there. Nobody who knows the west would. It's too dangerous. And too strenuous a trip for a delicate lady."

"I can ride very well," she said, her wide, solemn eyes regarding him steadily.

"It's mostly walking."

"I can do that, too. And I can shoot, not one of those revolvers of yours, but a rifle—what are you laughing at?"

"You," he said, making no effort to hide his amusement. "You talk like we were going after a stag on some English lord's estate. You don't know what's out there. There's deserts that would make hell seem a paradise, and mountains it'd take an angel's wings to get across, not to mention Indians and snakes, and for all I know, fire-breathing dragons. A man's got all he can do to hang on to his skin, without having to look after a woman."

"I'm prepared to pay a thousand dollars," she said, her voice frostier than ever.

"That's a lot of money. I'm sorry that it's out of the question. Now, if you'll excuse me—"

"Mister Summers—"

"Mrs. Denon," he said, emphasizing each syllable, "there's a new woman working one of the local whorehouses, and I mean to look her over before she gets too shopworn. So, since our discussion is over—"

She came from the chair as if stung by a bee, her fair skin coloring brilliantly. "Mister Summers, I came to you because I was told your abilities were considerable."

"As they are." He grinned. "As I intend to demonstrate to the new woman soon, if I can terminate this interview."

She did it to him then, the trick with the eyes, the swift and sudden parting of curtains. It made his smile vanish, and if she'd pursued the advantage, she might have made some change in his feelings.

But as quickly as it had happened, it was gone, and she was moving toward the door, looking more angry than hurt, and angry women were an old story for him.

"Mrs. Denon," he said in a not ungentle tone, "a happy man doesn't leave a loving wife," there was only the briefest of pauses, "for any longer than he has to. My advice to you is to go back to Virginia, to your home, and wait until you hear from him."

"And if I don't hear from him, Mister Summers? What am I to do then, since you're offering advice?"

"This is a young country, and there are never enough pretty women, especially true ladies, to go around. When it comes to it, you won't have any trouble finding a second husband."

"That may be," she said. "At the moment, however, my concern is with finding my first husband, regardless of the trouble involved, and with or without your help. Good night, Mister Summers."

It was peculiar, but he was more aware of her scent after she'd gone than when she'd been in the room; it seemed to grow on the night air, as lilacs will in full bloom.

He made ready to go out, and as he did so he found himself wondering about her husband. He wondered if he'd met him while he was here in town, and what had become of him. Had he died, as most of them did, within a hundred miles of civilization? The plains were cruel and unforgiving of any mistake, and of those who'd gone farther, hardly any had returned to tell the tale.

The Indian came in, the tomcat sidling through the door in his wake. "Remember an Englishman?" Summers asked him. "From Virginia. Would have come through about five months ago, set out with trappers, she says."

The Indian shook his head, his single braid swaying in the lamplight. "I can ask around," he said.

"Do that," Summers said, adding after a moment, "just to satisfy my curiosity."

4

Claire was roused from her sleep by a thunderous knocking at the door of her hotel room. She was so startled that at first she did not answer, but merely sat in bed with a comforter clutched about her, staring in the direction of the sound. When the pounding came again, she clambered from the bed and ran to the door.

"Who is it?" she asked, pressing her cheek against the rough wood; she could think of no one who might be calling upon her in the middle of the night in St. Louis, unless—

"Summers," a muffled voice replied.

"Who?" The name eluded her momentarily.

"Summers," the reply came again, louder and a bit exasperated.

Then she remembered the extremely rude half-savage brute who had been recommended to her as a guide. She must remember to properly thank the person who'd recommended him.

"Mister Summers," she spoke through the door, "it's the middle of the night."

To her annoyance he pounded on the door again, virtually in her ear. Irked, she threw the bolt back and swung the door open. Summers stood there with hand upraised, about to knock yet again. He was dressed in a shirt and trousers of deerskin that had obviously seen seasons of wear untouched by cleaning. She had forgotten, after their brief meeting, how tall he was, so that at close range she had to crane her neck to look up at him.

"Mister Summers," she said indignantly, trying to look down her nose at him while simultaneously looking upward, "it is the middle of the night, and this is my bedroom. I really must insist—"

"It's eleven o'clock, m'am, or thereabouts," he said, obviously unmoved by her annoyance, "and I came cause I found someone you ought to talk to. Get your clothes on."

She remembered for the first time that she was wearing only her nightdress and quickly crossed her hands over her bosom. "How dare you?" she cried, retreating a step. To her horror, he followed her, striding boldly past her into the room. A match flared as he lit the kerosene lamp on the dresser.

"Mister Summers, if you do not leave at once, I shall call for the management and have you thrown out of here bodily."

At her threat he turned and crossed the room to her in two long strides. Ignoring her commands, he seized her with both hands in a grip so rough it was certain to leave bruises on her trembling shoulders. His ice blue eyes caught and held hers like a pin through a butterfly's heart.

"I don't know what kind of schooling you had back in England," he said, speaking in a low, unfeeling voice, "but you are a pitifully ignorant woman. In the first place, they ain't enough men in this hotel to throw me out of here, and about the same number with the courage to try, especially if they know me. In the second place, I didn't come here to see you with your titties half covered nor to try to get your pantaloons off of you. There's plenty of pantaloons to be gotten off in this town just for my asking it, and a lot better filled out than yours is anyway. No, what I came here for was to tell you I think I found the men that took your husband west."

"You—you did?" she asked in a tiny, cowed voice. Never in her entire life had anyone, man or woman, dared to speak to her in such a manner. She had never felt so completely at a loss.

"They're over to Miz Letitia's now, playing cards and drinking. I came to fetch you, figuring you'd want to talk to them, but you're gonna have to get your butt moving else they'll be too drunk to tell you anything. Now start with this."

He let her go and snatched up her chemise from the chair on which she'd draped it earlier.

"Mister Summers!" she cried, blushing and snatching it from his hand.

"Miss English lady," he said, smiling, which only infuriated her further, "I have seen every piece of lady's apparel there is, on, off, and in the process. Why don't you just get dressed and quit fussing so?"

"I will get dressed," she said, with what little dignity she could muster. "Please be so good as to wait outside."

He looked her up and down with so penetrating a gaze that she half-believed he was seeing right through the fabric of her nightdress. Then he smiled again and shrugged. "Suit yourself," he drawled. "Make it quick, though."

He went into the hall again. She closed the door quickly after him, sliding the bolt into place. For a moment she leaned against the door, feeling strangely out of breath. Then remembering the purpose of his visit, and his last words, she began to dress hurriedly. She had no doubt that Mister Summers was the sort to leave if he got tired of waiting, and the full import of his message was just now coming clear to her: the men who had taken Peter west. They would know where he was, and how he was as well.

Summers had scarcely a glance for her when she emerged from her room a few minutes later. "Let's go," he said brusquely, starting along the corridor with a stride so brisk that she had to run to catch up to him.

"This place we're going," she asked breathlessly, "This Miss...?"

"Miz Letitia's," he supplied.

"What sort of place is it? Is it a boardinghouse?"

He laughed aloud. "Not exactly," he said. "Miz Letitia's is a whorehouse—best one in town."

"A...but I can't go into a—one of those," she said.

He shook his head, still smiling. "If you don't beat all. You're all ready to set out across the prairie to look for your husband, but you're afraid to set foot in a whorehouse."

She came to an abrupt halt at the top of the stairs. To her surprise, Summers stopped too. "But people will think—"

"Have you ever given a damn what people thought?" he asked, interrupting her.

For a long moment the two of them regarded one another steadily. For the first time since he'd met her, a ghost of a smile played across her mouth. It transformed her, even in its limited and brief form, making an otherwise unremarkable face seem suddenly to glow from within.

"Now that I think about it, I suppose not," she admitted.

"First time I saw you I thought, there's a

girl's been spoiled all her life. Let's go, before those trappers get bored with drinking and playing cards, and disappear upstairs with some of Miz Letitia's girls. I never interrupt a man when he's in the saddle, not if I can help it. There's some things ought to be sacred."

The smile vanished with the rebuke. She would have made a sharp reply, but before she could think of the appropriate one, Summers was already halfway down the stairs to the street, leaving her no choice but to race after him. She was grateful for one thing, however—that Mister Summers had declined her request to guide her westward. The mere thought of spending several weeks in his company had since proved unendurable.

From down the street, Miz Letitia's looked like an ordinary house, except that it sat on a dirt track, back from the street and well apart from its neighbors. It was set apart too by the number of lighted windows on all three floors, and by the dissonant rattle of a piano, played with more force than skill.

Instinctively Claire slowed her steps as they approached the front porch. Preoccupied as she was with her own thoughts and fears, she was not even aware of the much gentler tone in which Summers spoke to her.

"There's nothing much downstairs except the saloon and some card tables," he said. "The other business goes on upstairs. No need for you even to think about that."

He opened the big front door, nodding to an enormous hulk of a man who sat just inside to observe newcomers, and led the way along the short corridor to the parlor.

At first she had difficulty seeing through the clouds of tobacco smoke that hung thick and stagnant in the air of the noisy and crowded room. The women—and there were more of them than she would have anticipated—were of a recognizable sort, buxom, voluble, overpainted. The men were more varied: young, old, boisterous, and quiet; but all of them were fierce and hardened. They were the sort of men who had abandoned city ways and city manners, had braved hardship and dangers to live here on the isolated fringe of civilization. For the first time she saw their crude, brash manner, which had so dismayed and offended her since her arrival in this outpost, for what it was—the first necessity for survival in such a place as this.

And for the first time too she realized how completely out of her element she was. She glanced around at the other women in the room—as hard and ferocious in their own way as the men—and her courage faltered.

As if sensing something of what she was feeling, Summers put a hand on her arm. "Over this way," he said, piloting her deftly through the crowd. One overeager trapper, his eyes glazed with drink, made a grab for her skirt, but Summers somehow managed to be in the way, and the hand was hastily snatched back.

Three men were playing cards at a table against the far wall. Summers paused beside one of these and asked, "Your name Morton?"

Without looking from the cards he was shuffling, the man replied, "Depends on who's wanting to know."

"I've got a lady here, wants to talk to you," Summers said.

Morton paused to glance briefly in Claire's direction. She smiled nervously, until he turned his head slightly and spat a stream of brown tobacco juice in the direction of the cuspidor, missing it and her skirt by inches.

"Already made me plans with that colored gal over at Annie's," Morton said, returning his attention to the cards. "Why don't you see if you can catch me next time, honey. And leave your business manager home. We can do without him. Never could abide them fellows anyhow."

Summers' voice when he spoke again was low, even, and icy cold. "The lady," he said, emphasizing the latter word, "wants to talk to you."

"Some other time," Morton said, laying the deck of cards in the center of the table. "Cut?"

Summers' hand moved so swiftly that Claire had not even seen the hunting knife appear in it until it had sliced through the cards, its tip plunged into the wood surface of the table.

"Now," Summers said.

The other two players, taking another

look at the newcomer, began to edge their chairs back from the table. In a moment they were gone, vanishing into the crowds and the smoke.

Morton cocked his head and glanced sideways up at the standing man. Though Summers was clearly the taller of the two, Morton was far from a small man. He was built like an ox, with massive and powerful-looking shoulders, and a thick sturdy torso set on short squat legs. His eyes, little and dark, peered out from above a tangled black beard. He wore a torn and shapeless hat that almost concealed a premature bald spot on the crown of his head.

Summers, ignoring the scrutiny, pulled one of the now empty chairs around for Claire to sit. She did so a bit shakily. The hunting knife in front of her still vibrated from the force with which Summers had imbedded it.

"What's this all about?" Morton asked, pouring a shot of whisky from the bottle on the table without offering them any.

"You took an Englishman west with you, about five months ago," Summers said.

"What if I did, whose business is that?" Morton asked in a surly tone. He reached for the hunting knife and tugged it free, studying its sharply honed blade and testing its balance in the palm of his hand.

"Mister Morton," Claire said, "I believe that man may have been my husband. Denon, Peter Denon—was that his name?"

Morton was silent for a moment. "Sounds right," he said finally.

"But—can't you be sure?" she asked.

He gave her a scornful look, as though she should have known better than to ask such a question. "Out there," he nodded his head in what she presumed was the westerly direction, "names don't matter so much. When there ain't but you and one or two others for five, six hundred miles, you can pretty well follow who's saying what to who."

Claire gave a sigh and tossed her head. "Then there's no way of knowing it was him?" she said.

"Puny-looking fellow, curly headed?" Morton asked. "Spends most of his time praying?"

Claire's flagging spirits lifted. "Yes, yes," she said eagerly, "that must have been him. Then you know! Where is he now? Is he all right?"

"I couldn't say."

"But..."

"He was, the last I saw him," Morton added. "We left him out there." Again that unconscious nod toward the west.

"Where'd you leave him?" Summers asked.

Morton regarded him steadily across the table. "We went up the Missouri, my partner and me, and the Englishman. He paid us to take him as far as we was going. Followed the Platte. You know it?"

"Some."

"Left him about where the South Platte

branches off. Told him he was a damn fool not to head back with us. It was already winter and the river threatening to freeze up on us, but he said he was going to keep on west."

The three of them were silent for a moment, exchanging glances. Summers, looking at the girl, saw that her eyes were feverish with excitement. It made him uneasy, knowing what was coming next. Hardly realizing that he did so, he gave his head a warning shake, but she ignored it, or didn't notice, he couldn't tell which.

"Could you find that spot again?"

"Nothing to it."

"Mister Morton," she asked, leaning across the table toward him, "could you take me there?"

Morton almost choked on the whisky he was drinking. "Beg pardon, m'am?" he said.

"I said, could you take me there?"

Morton laughed, shaking his head. "No, m'am, I sure couldn't take a woman out there. With the Indians, and the storms and such, and the animals, a woman wouldn't last three weeks out there."

"But you mentioned Indians," she said cooly. "I presume they must reproduce in the normal manner?"

"Huh?" Morton said.

"She's talking about squaws," Summers said.

Morton looked relieved by the information. "Oh, sure, squaws. But that ain't the same as a real woman. Couldn't take a real woman out there."

"Mister Morton, I can ride, and walk," she added with a quick glance toward Summers. "And shoot a gun, better than my husband could, I assure you. And I have the same limbs and acoutrements as an Indian woman."

"I don't know about your coot, coot—"

"And I will pay a thousand dollars," she finished.

That silenced him in midword. He stared openmouthed at her for a long moment. Summers, watching the trapper's face, followed his changing thoughts like a map: the quick flare of greed, the speculative interest in Claire Denon's bosom, weighing all the possible rewards.

"That's five hundred for you, and five for me," Summers said aloud. He ignored her startled glance, concentrating on Morton.

"How'd you get into this?" Morton asked, eyes narrowing.

"She'll need someone to take over once you've shown her the spot."

"I got me a partner," Morton said. "Four each for us, the rest for you."

"Three for me, you split the rest."

Morton was silent for a moment, his lips moving as he did the necessary mathematics. He seemed satisfied finally. "When do we start?" he asked.

"The sooner the better," Summers said.

"Ten days?" Morton nodded. Summers looked at Claire Denon for the first time since he'd volunteered the information that he was going.

It was her turn to be silently thoughtful. She was not fond of Mister Summers, and his change of heart had caught her a bit off balance, but his quick explanation that she would need someone as a guide once she'd been shown the spot where Peter had been left was certainly true. True, too, was the fact that, however despicable Summers might be as a man, he came highly recommended as a guide to the west.

Moreover, she was no fool. She too had seen Mister Morton's quick glance down the front of her dress. How long alone with him and his partner before she was forced to defend herself? At least Summers had made clear his lack of interest in her as a woman, and though hardly flattering, it was a comfort.

"The sooner the better," she agreed aloud.

Summers was silent on the walk back to her hotel. He seemed almost to be angry with her, which made her uncomfortable. She took refuge in a stream of small talk: an inventory of items she would pick up for their journey, a dry comment on Mister Morton's intelligence, a reference to the fireflies blinking on and off in the darkness as they passed. She was completely unprepared when Summers stopped and, taking her shoulders in his hands as he had earlier, but much more gently this time, he turned her about to face him.

"Look, you don't know what you're getting into," he said, his expression suddenly intense. "I know the part of the country we're heading for, there's nothing there but mud flats and hills. And that prairie, stretching west farther than the eye can see. The Indians say it goes on forever, without end. You don't want to die out there."

"I'm following my husband, Mister Summers. If need be, I too will go on forever."

"Why? Because you love him? Or because you feel guilty about something that happened in the past?"

"My motives are no concern of yours."

"Oh, but they are. We'll be together for months, maybe even longer than you lived with your husband."

"The solution is very simple. If you are uncomfortable with my actions or their motives, you needn't accompany me." Her eyes narrowed suspiciously. "Why did you change your mind, anyway?"

He stared down at her. He had been questioning his own motives since they'd left Letitia's, and cursing himself for a fool. Of course, he knew Morton well enough—or the type anyway—to know what Morton had been thinking when he looked her over. He'd been thinking that once they were away from the city he'd take whatever he wanted. Not just the thousand, but whatever else she had on her, and her as well. And if he came back two, three months later without her, who was to question his story of an Indian attack or an overturned canoe? Such things happened to *men* who set out with trappers and guides into the west, where the only law was survival. Most likely it had been her husband's fate, and her prospects of a better one were slim indeed. Though why he should care was entirely beyond him.

"I lost a lot of money at cards this week," he said aloud. "Running short. Yours is the best offer that's come along. You're overpaying, you know."

"I'd have paid twice that much."

And so much for trying to warn you, he thought. All Morton needed was to know the thousand was only half of what she'd got on her. She wouldn't have lasted a hundred miles out of the town.

"You'd best leave most of that money stashed here in town," he said. "You won't need it where you're going."

"What I don't need is your telling me what to do," she told him. "I will remind you, Mister Summers, that I have hired you for a job. I am your employer, and you are my hired help. In the future, you will do what I say, not the other way round."

To her surprise he only grinned at that. "You try pulling strings to make me dance, lady, and I'll leave you to your *Mister* Morton. And the only kind of dance he's got in mind is one you do laying down."

"How dare you?" She lifted a hand to

slap him, but he was quicker, snatching her wrist in a cruelly tight grip.

They were standing before a darkened house with a neat picket fence and a curving walk that led to front steps. Somewhere nearby at an open window a girl began to croon a lullaby, perhaps, or some wordless ballad.

He was suddenly aware of her perfume. Or was it only the flowers along the fence, hollyhock and sweet pea, and distant roses?

"Maybe that's what you want," he said in a lower voice, deliberately cruel because he was angry with her high-falutin' ways, angry with himself for having gotten involved when he hadn't intended to at all. "Maybe your husband's been gone too long. Or maybe that's why he left in the first place?"

He pulled her closer, lowering his face until it was only inches from hers, his eyes searching the depths of hers.

"Let me go," she said in little more than a whisper.

A buggy rounded the corner behind them and came briskly along the street. It seemed to break the trance into which he'd fallen. His fingers unclenched her wrist. She rubbed it gingerly with her other hand, her eyes flashing angrily back at his for a moment before she stepped past him and hurried on down the street, walking so fast she was nearly running.

Summers watched her go, thinking he ought not leave her alone. St. Louis was only slightly more civilized than the land to the west.

As if summoned by his thoughts, a stranger stepped out of the alley she had just gone by, falling into step behind her, but so stealthily that there was little doubt in Summers' mind what the man intended.

The Englishwoman rounded a corner. Before the stranger could reach it and round it after her, Summers had caught up with him, his long legs covering the distance with easy speed as silently as a wraith. One moment the stranger had thought himself alone on the dark street with the blonde girl, and the next someone had seized his collar roughly and, spinning him around, shoved him hard against a brick wall.

"What the hell . . . ?"

"Leave her alone."

"Who are you—what business is it of yours anyway?"

A cloud that had enwebbed the moon tired of its quarry and moved on. In the silver light that cascaded from above the stranger saw the knife in the other man's hand held level with his belly, its point barely touching his shirtfront.

"I was just walking," he said quickly. "Just getting some air."

"You'll breathe it better down that way," Summers said, pointing.

He let go his hold and watched the stranger run until he had disappeared in the direction pointed. Then, staying well behind and in the shadows, he followed Claire Denon until he had seen her enter her hotel and the light come on in the window of her room.

Without knowing quite why, he stood on the porch of a dry goods store across the street, watching and waiting until, some minutes later, the light went out again, and he knew she'd gone to bed. Finally he set out for his own home, wishing, after all, that he'd stayed around Letitia's, and yet not sufficiently of a mind to go back.

5

They set out ten days later in a pair of birch-bark canoes. Morton and his partner, a wiry little French Canadian named Leblanc, led the way, with Claire and Summers in the rear.

Though she disliked the look and smell of the well-worn hide outfits Summers and Morton both wore, she had been persuaded that this was the most practical apparel for the sort of journey they were to make. Accordingly she had purchased the necessary hides and after considerable searching found an Indian woman, mistress to an absent trapper, who had made her a rather unorthodox costume: a fringe-trimmed shirt not unlike Summers' own, and a wide, flaring deerskin skirt breaking at midcalf. A pair of high leather boots took care of concealing her legs, though the skirt's short length earned her some critical stares from the ladies and a few guffaws from the local men. For protection from the sun she found a flat-brimmed hat, and at Summers' suggestion she'd tied a long scarf about her neck. "You'll need it to keep the sweat out of your eyes," he'd told her a bit inelegantly. "And to swat away the flies."

Summers sat to the rear of the canoe to paddle, placing her in the bow to watch for sandbars.

"I could paddle too, you know," she argued. "I didn't intend to remain useless."

"Nothing useless about watching for sandbars," he told her. "The bottom of these rivers changes daily, hourly even. The last thing we want is a hole in the bottom."

By the time they'd traveled an hour or so, she was having misgivings about her costume; she found it quite uncomfortable, the material stiff and scratchy and unpleasantly warm in the later summer sunshine.

"It's got to be lived in," Summers explained when she complained. "The sweat and the heat will soften it up, and it stretches to mold itself to your body like it was your own skin. You'll see. Six weeks from now you wouldn't want to trade it for anything else."

"Except perhaps a bath and a clean dress," was her reply. She looked back over her shoulder at him, watching the ease and grace with which he handled the long paddle.

"Better watch where we're going," he warned.

"It's all clear ahead," she said.

A moment later the canoe buried its nose in one of the river's shifting sandbars. Summers let fly with a string of curses and attempted to use his paddle to push them free, to no avail.

"What'll we do now?" she asked.

"We'll have to get out and free it," he said. Suiting action to words, he removed the powder horn tied to his waist, and laying that and his gun in the bottom of the canoe, he scrambled over the side into the swiftly moving muddy water.

She sat where she was until he turned ice blue eyes on her. "Well?" he said.

"But I can't swim," she stammered, genuinely frightened of the treacherous-looking water sweeping about the boat. "Suppose I lose my balance?"

"Then you can remind yourself while you're floating downstream to watch out for sandbars. Now get out and give me a hand with this before it starts breaking up and we both end up floating downstream."

His look and his tone made it clear that he was deadly serious. She took another anxious look at the water and then, following his example, clambered a bit ungracefully into the water.

It was not particularly cold, but it was waist deep and the current was every bit as swift and dangerous as it had looked. She clung to the side of the canoe, trying to get her balance on the muddy bottom.

"Pull!" Summers shouted, tugging the canoe back from the sandbar. She attempted to pull with him, lost her footing, and sank beneath the water's brown surface.

He pulled her up gasping and retching, holding to the canoe with his free hand.

"Damnation," he swore. "Can't you do anything right?"

The leather outfit, thoroughly soaked now with water, felt as if it weighed a ton; she could barely manage to stand up in it, and the slightest shift in the current would have toppled her again, had he not been supporting her.

"I'm—not—used to—pushing canoes—about in rivers," she managed to reply between gasps for breath.

"If you'd been watching where we were going," he sneered.

"I didn't see it," she said, and to her dismay as well as his she began to cry. She was soaked and chilled, and her limbs had begun to ache with the struggle to keep herself upright in the water. To make matters worse, she was quite aware that their present predicament was her fault.

"Damnation," he said again, and a moment later, "Stop that infernal bawling. Here, just hang on to the canoe here, and brace yourself against the current, so's when I get it free it won't go flying downriver without us."

He left her by the stern and went to the bow to attempt to pry it free from the sand. Claire was so wet and miserable that she concentrated her energy on clinging to the canoe for safety, forgetting the rest of his instructions.

The results were inevitable. Moving directly in front of the canoe, Summers braced his feet against the river bottom, put both hands at the canoe's nose, and shoved with all his considerable strength. The canoe bobbed down and then up, swung its tail about in a graceful arc, and broke free of the clinging sand—and, with Claire still clinging to its tail, swung into the current and shot downstream.

She let out a squeal of fright and kicked out frantically with her feet, trying to get a toehold, but the muddy bottom eluded her.

"Hey!" Summers shouted. Then, seeing she was in danger of being swept away, he cupped his hands about his mouth and cried, "Let go!"

She looked back in time to see him churning the water, swimming frantically after her. For a moment more she held to the canoe, then, fearful of being carried beyond his reach, she did as ordered and let go, sinking once more beneath the brown-green surface of the water, swallowing it in desperate mouthfuls.

She struggled to reach the light and air,

but the leather skirt was a great, ponderous weight pulling her downward, where her feet slipped and churned the shifting mud.

Fool, she thought, fool, to die ignominiously in this filthy river, in this God-forgotten land. She closed her eyes, only to see poor, pathetic Peter, and Richard, carrying scars that ran clear through the fiber and being of him.

She coughed and gasped and swallowed air this time. There was Summers, and framing his face like a cerulean halo, the sky, the wonderful sky.

"Mis—Mister . . ."

"Don't talk, I've got you," he said, not even short of breath from his swim, his arm fast about her. "It's all right. I can stand down on the bottom here, see? Just hold tight to me."

The river bottom that had eluded her was an easy reach for his long, muscular legs. He held her without effort while the river swept relentlessly by them.

"The canoe—?"

"It'll run ashore, 'bout a half-mile past that bend. I know this water," he said.

"Wh—what'll we do?" she asked.

"Stand right here, and hope those trappers look behind them before they reach the north woods. When they see we're not following them, they'll turn back to look for us," he said, adding on a slightly less confident note, "I hope."

He was proven right on both counts.

They had waited only a few minutes when they heard "Hallo!" and saw Morton and Leblanc paddling swiftly downriver toward them.

"What happened?" Morton asked when he had brought the canoe alongside them.

"Miz Denon decided to go for a swim," Summers said, boosting her into the canoe with his hands on her rump. He gave her such a shove that she toppled head first into the bottom of the canoe. Morton helped her up, the back of his hand just brushing the tips of her breasts, seemingly by chance.

Summers swung himself into the canoe with the ease of long practice, and they continued back in the direction of St. Louis until they'd rounded the next bend and found the canoe swept into a tiny inlet by the current exactly as Summers had predicted.

Wet and bedraggled, and more than a bit despondent, Claire again took up her place in the front of the canoe to watch for sandbars— this time with considerably more diligence. Though the men had been remarkably restrained in their comments on the incident, she was as well aware as they that it had not been an auspicious beginning to what would be a long and arduous journey.

They traveled for five weeks before they reached the spot where the Platte River joined with the Missouri and started up the former. The Platte was an ugly, uninspiring river, shallow and pockmarked with islands and sand-bars. Now, with the summer season running riot, the water was so low they found themselves more often than not pushing and pulling their canoes upstream. Here began the real work of the trip, and for days Claire's body thrummed with pain and fatigue, though the men were sparing her as much as possible.

She began to wonder about the wisdom of this journey. Since they had left St. Louis she had seen no one but the three men with whom she traveled, nor the faintest trace of civilization. To her untrained eye it appeared certain that no one had traveled this way before them. She found it necessary to remind herself that Morton and Leblanc were retracing a previous journey.

"How much farther?" she asked at the end of the sixth week. They had made camp for the night on the marshy bank of the Platte. The fire that Summers had built was little more than a heap of embers. "Pawnee country," he'd explained. "No need to announce our presence if they aren't already aware of it."

"To the South Platte?" he asked in reply to her question. "A couple of weeks, I'd guess."

Morton, on his way into the woods, snorted disdainfully. "A month at least," he said. "With the water this low, we'll be lucky we don't have to wade the whole way."

He disappeared into the trees. After a moment they heard him relieving himself noisily. It was the sort of thing that had caused her considerable embarrassment at first, but she had since gotten used to it. It had proven necessary to surrender a great many sensibilities to the practicalities of their circumstances. She had laughed often to herself to think how shocked Aunt Tess would be to hear the details of day-to-day living in the wilderness.

If, she had reminded herself on one occasion, there ever was an opportunity to tell Aunt Tess. Though she tried not to think of that possibility, there was always a chance that she might not return from this trip. Others had set out and not come back. Contrary to the opinion that Mister Summers still held of her, she was not entirely a fool, and she had set out with some appreciation of the risks involved.

"Do you think he's right in his estimate?" she asked Summers. He was seated staring thoughtfully into the fire. Leblanc was already wrapped up in his bedding, apparently asleep. The Frenchman spoke only a few words of English and was scarcely more talkative in his native tongue. Indeed, in the weeks that they had been traveling together, conversation had been at a minimum. Occasionally as he paddled the birch canoe, Summers would point out something to her, naming the trees aspen, birch, and cottonwood. Once a shadow had sped across the canoe and with a whoop of exultation he had pointed the paddle skyward at a great, glorious soaring thing: "Eagle!" he'd cried, and she was as moved by the sheer awe of his expression as by the wonder of the bird.

But he was not a man for small talk, or any talk, apparently, and she had grown accustomed to the long days of silence and her own thoughts.

"He knows this territory better than I do," Summers replied to her question. "Trappers live on their rivers; they get to know them."

"I haven't said this before, but I am grateful that you decided to accompany us. I don't think I'd have liked being alone with Mister Morton and his friend," she confided, giving voice to something she'd been thinking for several days.

Summers' lips curled in a faint grin. "Beginning to look a little harder at you, is he?" he asked.

"Then you've noticed it too?"

He shook his head. "Don't have to see it to know," he said.

"I don't understand."

The wind fanned the embers, making them suddenly glow with a false promise of renewed life. He was so long in taking up the conversation that she decided he meant to let it end.

"A man spends a long time away from women, off to himself, or with another man, he gets to missing 'em," he began. "Only it don't do to let himself start thinking about that sort of thing. Out here a man needs his wits about him, all of them, if he's to survive. He starts daydreaming, thinking about his wife or his sweetheart, things he's left behind, he gets careless. Next thing you know, he's parted company with his scalp, or become dinner for a mountain lion. So the frontiersman, the trapper—least, the ones who live to keep on doing it—they learn not to think about those things; they shut their minds to them."

He paused and turned his head to look at her; his face was in shadow now, impossible to read, but the timbre of his voice had changed.

"'Cept, when there's a woman around," he said. "It kinda makes you think, even when you don't want to. You start remembering the way a woman feels, and the way she smells, and the taste of her. You get to thinking about the last one you laid atop of, and how you buried your face in her long hair, and—"

Morton, coming out of the trees, belched loudly. "Wish there's some more noise in these woods," he said, squatting across the fire from them. "Makes me nervous, the woods being too quiet. Makes me wonder who's out there scaring off the animals."

He glanced across the fire to find Summers and the woman staring at one another, funny like, he thought. Now what do you figure?

"You'd better go to bed," Summers said, addressing the woman.

It was a moment before she moved, as if stirring herself from sleep.

"Yes," was all she said. She got up and crossed to where her bedroll was lying.

6

Morton's estimation of their traveling time proved accurate. They had reached the Platte the end of July, and August was nearly over by the time they reached the South Platte, having waded a great deal of the way.

"This is the spot," Morton announced near the end of one day, pointing along the low river bank with its cottonwoods. "Last we saw of him he was camped right over there, between the two branches of the river. Said he was heading for some place called California."

California. Claire's gaze went from the desolate campsite to the western horizon, where the sun was drifting earthward. Since she'd first arrived in Virginia, she'd heard talk of this California. This was the land of fortune and precious gems; where the cities were made of gold. She remembered the ship's captain who'd visited in Virginia, and who had actually been to California. He'd spoken of vast farms and Indians so laden with gold they were unable to walk. Yes, that was where Peter would have gone.

She turned to Summers. "Can we go there? To California, I mean?" she said.

"California? That's clear to the other end of the land," he said, astonished by the request. "Impossible to reach, far as I know."

"But people have reached it," she argued. "I've talked to them myself."

"They got there by ship. Or up land from Mexico. It's a Mexican colony. But I never heard of anybody going there overland from the States."

"But they could have," she said. "Who would have heard, if they didn't come back?"

"If they didn't come back it's because they never made it," he said. "No one could. It's another thousand miles, maybe two thousand from here, and most of it mountains or desert. I've been in those mountains, and I've seen the deserts. It's impossible."

"We could follow Peter's trail."

"If there is a trail, if he actually set out for California. For all we know he changed his mind after Morton left him. If, I say, then his bones are probably bleaching in the sun somewhere between here and there."

"Then let us find his bones," she said.

"You're talking about a needle in a haystack. Look," he began, making a gesture that took in the vast expanse of land lying open before them, uncluttered by signs of man's habitation, "Look, you think we can find one man in that?"

"I'm going to try," she said with an air of finality.

Morton and Leblanc had already begun to set up camp. She left Summers and went to help them, collecting driftwood along the bank for a fire.

It was not until later, when they were eating fresh-caught fish before the fire, that Summers spoke to Morton of their plan.

"We'll be leaving you here too," he said, not looking at Claire. "Miz Denon and I are going to travel west for a ways, see if we can pick up her husband's trail."

"You walking?" Morton asked.

"Maybe," Summers replied. "Unless I can swap for some horses with them Pawnee that's been following us the last couple of days."

Morton chuckled and said, "I wondered if I was the only one noticed that."

Claire, who had noticed nothing untoward, gave the two men a sharp glance and instinctively looked over her shoulder at the dark lines of trees and shrubs behind them.

"Are they dangerous?" she asked, lowering her voice, though the men were speaking normally.

"Pawnee are treacherous," Summers said, helping himself to another fish from the still sizzling skillet. "If it'd been one man or even two they'd probably have made a move before

95

this. But four of us? They've been taking their time, sizing us up."

"We traded with a village not far from here," Morton said. "Collected some good beaver skins, traded them beads and blankets."

"Think they'll trade with you again?" Summers asked.

Morton and Leblanc conferred briefly in French, Morton's frequently punctuated by entire phrases in English, which the little French Canadian took in stride.

"They named us their brothers," Morton said to the others. "Said we was to feel welcome to their village any time. Course, with Pawnee, that could mean they was waiting to skin us."

Summers nodded grimly. "Let's find their village tomorrow and see," he said.

The Pawnee village at which Morton and Leblanc had previously traded lay a bit less than three miles up the north branch of the Platte. The foursome approached it on foot, having hidden their canoes and most of their supplies among the cottonwoods by the river. They carried with them little more than their guns and the items they'd brought for trading: more beads, blankets, some trivial pieces of silver from Germany.

They traveled single file, Morton leading the way followed by his partner, and then Claire and Summers bringing up the rear.

Though he considered they were in little danger of ambush, since they were so obviously on their way to the village, Summers nevertheless kept a sharp eye out as they went.

At the same time he was mulling over a brief conversation he'd had with Morton shortly before, while they'd been engaged in storing their belongings.

"I want you to bargain with those Indians for three horses instead of two," Morton had said unexpectedly.

"What for?" was Summers' surprised reply.

"Leblanc and I been talking. He's fixing to travel a bit farther up the river, find himself a place to camp until winter. Beaver furs no good in the summer, you gotta take them in the winter."

"What about you?"

Morton gave what was intended as a disarmingly friendly grin, revealing the considerable spaces between his few teeth. "I figured maybe I'd head west with you and the lady," he said.

Summers remained unimpressed by the grin. "Why?" he asked bluntly.

Morton's glance flicked like a whip in the direction of Claire Denon and as quickly back again. "Never saw that part of the country, figured this'd be a good chance to size it up. 'Sides, can't say I'm much of a mind to sit around a camp waiting for winter. I'd as leave head back down to St. Louis."

"Maybe that's what you ought to do."

Morton ignored the suggestion. "So I thought about it, figured there's no telling what you might be getting into, but three people ought to be lots safer than two, specially when one of them two's a woman."

Summers, busy tying together the branches of two small shrubs to better conceal their packs, made no reply, and after a moment Morton had gone about his own business.

The conversation had lingered in Summers' mind, however. A decision would have to be reached before he began bargaining with the Pawnee. He did not question the trapper's capabilities; there had been ample opportunities thus far on the trip for the man to demonstrate those. And Morton had made a telling point: they were setting out into uncharted and undeniably dangerous territory, he and a woman. Claire Denon had proven herself surprisingly competent, far tougher than her frail appearance had at first suggested. There had been none of the complaining and helplessness he'd expected; indeed, he'd traveled with men less valiant than she.

Morton was right. It would be a good thing to have another man along, particularly one who was strong and capable, and accustomed to living in the wilderness.

The trouble was he didn't trust the man. Even without that glance in Claire's direction, he'd be a fool not to know that Morton was interested in her.

Well, and what of it? he asked himself

irritably. The Englishwoman had set out on this trip of her own free choice. She had been warned it was dangerous. Surely she ought to figure out for herself that not the least of her worries was being ravaged by men. Who was to say she wouldn't get exactly what she asked for? And for all he knew, maybe she was hoping something like that would happen.

No. That thought had no sooner crossed his mind than he rejected it. She was, if nothing else, a lady. It didn't take any special insight to see that. Besides, he had the impression she was afraid of Morton. It was, he thought, the only reason she'd been friendly toward himself, sort of keeping him between herself and the trapper, rightly figuring that he had no interest in her.

But it wasn't only on her behalf that Summers distrusted the trapper. Summers, the solitary plainsman, trusted few men. Some he trusted even less than others. Morton belonged to this latter group. The man would scalp them quicker than any Indian if he thought it would be to his profit. They could count on him just as far as it was to his advantage to be an ally, and not a step further.

It was always like that when he let himself get involved with other people, he told himself grimly. He had no particular grudge against his fellow man, but experience had taught him to rely on himself and not on others. He was most comfortable with his own company. When he grew low on supplies, or began to itch for the relief a woman could provide, he headed for St. Louis or one of the other outposts, but he could not help seeing the stains that the white man left on the wilderness as he settled westward. It bothered him in a way he had never tried to articulate and soon, in a week or a month perhaps, he was ready to go again. Had the Englishwoman not come along when she did with her preposterous request, he would soon have set out anyway for somewhere, it hardly mattered where, so long as it was west. For he understood, as few men who used the term did, that "the west" was not merely a direction. It was a world, a life apart from that other, "civilized" life.

He liked to ride or walk across that great open plain that lay like a woman's belly between the far mountains and the fertile rivers of the east. He liked to strip naked, to feel the caresses of the sun, that most ardent of all lovers, on his flesh; to bathe in the cold clear waters of mountain streams; to lie on his back at night and contemplate the unfathomable stars of the western night.

He was not a philosophical nor religious man, but like the Indians, whose blood shared his veins with that of an Englishman, he sensed a something, call it a Presence, that was everywhere in nature—in the tree, in the mountain, in the hawk and the deer. A harmony that rang like a tolling bell in his soul when he breathed the free untainted air of the great west.

Long ago he had dreamed of finding someone who felt as he did, someone to whom he could voice these crazy feelings. He had since then come to the conclusion that there was no one who shared his viewpoints, and he had become even more of a solitary man.

Something moved in the brush just to their right. It was a Pawnee, he was sure of it. His long rifle was cocked, held before him so that he could swing it up in an instant and fire, but he was sure the Pawnees would let them enter the village, if only out of curiosity. This would no doubt be the first time they had seen a white woman. White men were few enough in these parts, but the yellow-haired Englishwoman must be causing quite a stir.

He watched Claire Denon traversing the path in front of him. She had acquired a nice stride since they'd set out on this journey, long, graceful, easy of the hip. She'd thinned down a bit, but contrarily it made her look less fragile.

He was suddenly surprised with himself to discover that he was thinking of her sexually, imagining her moving her tail that way under a man.

He laughed at himself and thrust the thought aside. She would make a nice piece for some man, but not for him. Now if she were only fleshed out a bit more generously and weren't so much of a bitch...

The three Indian braves appeared in their path so abruptly that Morton nearly collided with the closest of them. Summers just had time to realize he had broken his own rule against daydreaming when he ought to have been paying full attention before the three others had stepped onto the path behind him, and he saw that they were surrounded.

7

"Stay calm," Morton said. "If they'd meant to kill us they wouldn't have introduced themselves first."

One of the braves approached Claire. Summers moved faster. Striding to her and putting one arm about her, he pulled her against him in an unmistakable gesture of possession.

The Indian paused, looking from one to the other. Then he reached with one hand for her golden hair.

"Let him touch it," Summers told her in a low voice.

She resisted the impulse to draw away from the outstretched hand. He touched her hair lightly, stroking it with the mere tips of his fingers. Grinning, he looked over his shoulder and said something to his companions. One of them came to join him, and he too had to touch her hair. Summers said something sharply in an Indian dialect, and the Indians' grins vanished. They began a dialogue with him, speaking in short, guttural barks.

The news last night that Indians were watching them, had in fact been following them for days, had cost Claire a bad night. She had lain awake for hours, imagining them on the verge of attack, though the men had apparently had no such concern.

Now for the first time she had the opportunity of observing these "savages" she had heard so much about. They were certainly savage looking, with fierce dark eyes and long black hair. They wore elkskin trousers and were naked from the waist up, though two of them somewhat incongruously wore strands of cheap glass beads about their necks.

Of course there was no denying they were dangerous. Only one of them carried a gun, but the others were armed with bows and arrows at the ready. Still there had been something rather disarming in the childlike awe with which they had wanted to touch her hair. It hadn't occurred to her until now how rare a sight blonde hair must be.

Morton had now come back to join in the conversation. Something, it seemed, was being agreed upon, because everyone had begun to nod their heads, and the Indian who had first approached her had begun to grin again.

"They're going to take us to their village," Summers said to her. When she started to move ahead of him, he caught hold of her hand and held her at his side. "I'm afraid you'll have to be my woman for the time being."

"And whose benefit was that for," she asked, lifting an eyebrow, "yours or theirs?"

"Don't be an ass," he said simply. When she tried angrily to pull her hand away he held it fast, forcing her to fall into step beside him, though it meant walking to the side of the path and tripping over tree roots. Silently she cursed Summers for an arrogant fool.

The path followed a bend in the river around a stand of trees, where it widened. In the clearing ahead she saw the Indian village. It consisted of a collection of the tipis she'd heard of, cone-shaped structures of animal skins stretched over long poles. These were scattered in a seemingly random pattern about a central clearing in the center of which a large fire was burning. The smell of roasting meat wafted to her.

The entire village had turned out for their arrival, including dogs and children. These last two groups ran about them making a considerable uproar. The women, Claire saw, remained well back behind the braves, though they looked no less curious. She could see that she herself, particularly her hair, was the main attraction, and though mostly the Indians seemed excited about it, her gaze fell on one squaw who glowered at her sullenly.

Their eyes met and to her surprise Claire recognized a familiar emotion: pure jealousy. Perhaps the squaw's own sweetheart had made too much of the visitor's blonde hair?

The extent of the squaw's jealousy was made clear to her a moment later. No sooner had Claire looked away than the Indian brought up her hand and hurled the stone she'd had clenched in it. It struck Claire a glancing blow on the forehead, hardly bruising her though she cried out in fright.

The entire procession stopped and one of the braves, the one who had first approached Claire, strode quickly through the parting throng. To Claire's horror, he knocked the squaw to the ground, giving her a hard kick in the rump when she tried to crawl away.

"Oh, stop him," Claire begged, tugging at Summer's hand.

"And get us all killed?" Morton said. "That's the chief's son, and how he punishes his wife is nobody's business but his."

"Can't we do anything?" Claire asked.

"Yes," Summers said, "you can act like she half-killed you with that rock. It puts them in our debt, sort of. Go on, put your hand over it and act like you're suffering some."

She shot him an angry look, but she did as he instructed, pressing one hand over the barely painful spot where the stone had hit her. The squaw, she saw, had managed to scramble to her feet and run off among the tipis. The chief's son, shouting something after her, came back to the column, and they resumed their procession.

They were heading toward a particular tipi, larger and more imposing than the others. From this stepped a tall, dignified-looking man that she took to be the chief, flanked by two others nearly as somber. Morton, leaving the group, approached this trio and addressed the chief, who seemed to recognize him. When the two men actually embraced one another, Claire began to breathe more easily.

For a few moments everyone—Indians, Morton, Summers, even Leblanc—seemed to be speaking at once, sorting out some detail or another. Finally the Indians gestured for them to enter the chief's tipi.

There was one difficult moment when Claire went to precede the men inside. One of the Indians said something angrily.

"They don't like women in their councils," Morton said.

"She stays with us," Summers replied. He said something short and sharp to the chief. There was another moment of heated debate, which Summers apparently won.

"After you," he said, ushering her into the low, squat structure.

It took several moments for her eyes to adjust to the gloomy interior. A hole had been left open in the roof for the smoke from the central fire to escape, but the air within was smoke filled nonetheless, making it difficult to breathe and darkening things considerably.

They sat on the ground in a circle about the fire. Two women came in bearing carved wooden bowls that were handed first to the chief, then passed about the circle in either direction, each person using his fingers to eat a little of the contents.

"What is it?" Claire asked as Summers handed her the bowl.

"Eat it," he said.

She thrust a tentative finger into the gooey-looking substance in the bowl and her eyes widened. "It's moving," she gasped, whispering, though it was unlikely anyone could decipher her words. She was uncomfortably aware that all eyes had turned toward her.

"Eat it," Summers said tersely out of the side of his mouth.

"I can't." She stared at the mass in the bowl. She recognized nuts, berries, and worms. She did not dare to try to guess the rest of the ingredients.

"They're liable to be eating *us* for their next meal if you don't," he said. "To decline their hospitality is a grave insult, and I for one don't intend to fight these boys just to defend your delicate sensitivities. Now eat it, before I stuff it down your lily-white throat."

He reached toward the bowl with his hand as if he meant to do exactly as he'd threatened. "Damn you all to hell," she snapped, but the anger helped to overcome her squeamishness, and she managed to get a small and hopefully wormless dab between her fingers and lift it to her mouth. Her stomach gave a warning turn. Holding her breath and focusing her eyes on the veins in her wrist, she stuffed it into her mouth and swallowed hard, hastily passing the bowl on.

"Kind of tasty once you get used to it," Summers said, clearly enjoying her discomfort.

"Shut up, or you'll get mine back."

After the food had gone round—she was thankful it only went round once—they passed about a pipe, from which everyone was expected to smoke. By this time, with the heat and the close air, not to mention a tipi filled with unwashed bodies, she had begun to feel more than a little ill. She fought against the threatening nausea and dizziness and tried to concentrate on what was going on. Serious parlay had begun, but as it was conducted in the Indians' language, in which all three of her companions seemed conversant, she could tell little of how the talks were progressing. It seemed to her that they'd been sitting there in what was proving to be an increasingly uncomfortable position for hours when Summers, speaking in a loud angry voice, started to get to his feet. The others, in tones ranging from placating to equally angry, managed to coax him back down.

"Let me handle this," Morton said.

"He knows my terms," Summers replied. The Indians began discussing something heatedly among themselves.

"What was that all about?" Claire asked.

"The chief just made us an offer to give

us all the horses we need," Summers replied.

"Well, isn't that what we came here for?" she asked, letting her exasperation show. "Really, Mister Summers, it's quite one thing for you to be rude to me, as you so often are, but I must object to letting your temper hinder our current negotiations."

"I didn't like his terms."

"Oh for God's sake, give him whatever he's asking for. What does it matter, so long as we can get out of this abominable place with our skins intact?"

"You really mean that?" he asked, turning to look down at her.

"Of course. Why?" she asked.

"He wants to trade us the horses for you," was the reply, delivered with a perfectly straight face.

After that she made no further attempt to interfere in the negotiating process, though she kept a sharp eye on the various facial expressions about the circle.

Finally Summers opened his pack and began to remove the trading goods he'd brought along. He laid a blanket on the ground before him and several cards of beads atop that. The Indians looked scornfully at the pile.

He brought out a silver bracelet, weighing it in his hand while he gave Claire a long, measuring look, before adding it to the pile.

At last, with the addition of several more silver trinkets and another blanket, the Indians were satisfied, and once again the pipe was passed around. As this was so preferable to the prospect of the wooden bowls, Claire puffed at it almost gratefully, and the negotiations were concluded.

It was nearly sundown when they started back to their own camp, each of the men having embraced the chief, who bowed his head gravely before Claire. They brought with them the skins and poles for two tipis, which Summers had insisted they would need as the weather turned cold, and four horses. Summers had decided that the benefits of having Morton accompany them at least marginally outweighed the risks. Sometime or other Morton was sure to become a problem, but he would handle that one when he got to it.

Claire, who was still feeling sickish, was not cheered by the news that Morton would be joining them, but at the moment nothing seemed quite so important to her as getting on their way. Before the Indians had a chance to change their minds, and reopen negotiations, she found herself thinking.

"How soon can we leave?" she asked when they'd reached the bank between the two branches of the Platte.

"Late tonight," Summers said. "Let's get this camp set up quick."

"But if we'll be leaving tonight, why bother setting up camp?"

"Cause we want to be ready when those

Indians come to get their horses back," he informed her. "We don't want them to know we suspect anything."

"But I thought everything was settled," she said. "They were so friendly when we left."

"Why shouldn't they be? They had all day to size us up, see what kind of goods we had with us. They'll wait till we're asleep, then they'll sneak in here, lift our scalps, take our goods, and get their horses back. Least, that's what they've got planned."

"But if that's the case, shouldn't we just ride out of here now?" she asked.

"They'll be ready for that," Morton said. "They'd cut us down before we got half a mile. No, our best bet's to do what he says, catch them off guard same as they were trying to do to us."

"We learned one piece of news, though," Summers said, setting up camp as if there were nothing out of the ordinary. "Your husband was here, stayed for a week in their village."

"Peter? Are you sure?" Claire asked, momentarily forgetting the danger they were in.

"Said he was the one came with these two the last time, left after they did and headed west."

"Do you believe them? Perhaps they murdered him," she said. She glanced around, shuddering. Perhaps his very grave was right here.

"They say not," Summers said, seeing

her fright and speaking more gently. "They say he headed west. Apparently he impressed them with a lot of religious mumbo-jumbo. They seemed to think he was a holy man. Look, why don't you start looking for some firewood. Oh, you'd better take this."

He handed her one of his revolvers. She stared at it for a moment before thrusting it into the belt of her skirt. Then she set out to look for wood.

8

It was an eerie feeling to watch the sun set and know that she might never see it rise again.

"You stay over here," Summers was saying, loading the rifle for her. "It's far enough from the fire they won't be able to tell much about you. Once it's good and dark, you take your blanket and move around there, between those two big rocks. No one can sneak up on you over there." He hesitated. "If things don't go our way, you should be able to slip off into the bushes and hide out of sight."

"But I can shoot," Claire argued. "You'll need every gun."

"The guns won't do us as much good as the surprise will," he replied. "I reckon they think they've got us fooled. The thing is, you're not to shoot unless you've just got to. We don't want to attract their attention to you if we can possibly help it."

He left her in the shadow of the large boulders, and went back to consult with the other two men.

Their plan was simple. The fire they'd built was small and would soon burn low. The three men had spread their blankets farther from the fire than usual, and under cover of darkness Leblanc, the smallest of the three, would crawl out of his to the shelter of some brush near the river bank. The other two would remain, feigning sleep. This was by far the most dangerous choice of positions. An arrow fired from the woods might kill either of them before an alarm could be raised. Both were dependent upon Leblanc's keen senses.

The horses had been tied to a solitary tree near the river, ready to ride. Three of them were saddled; the fourth would carry their gear, including the two tipis. They were fine, strong-looking animals, two big red geldings, a bay mare for portage, and a spirited pinto mare, which Claire would ride. The Pawnee, expecting to get the horses back, had been generous in giving their best beasts.

She could not remember a night so long. Under cover of darkness she had wrapped herself in her blanket and crawled as Summers had directed between two oversized rocks, where she would be well shielded, not only from sight but from stray bullets and arrows.

There she waited, her rifle propped across her knees, through the seemingly endless hours of the night.

She must have finally dozed, for when the trouble came it startled her awake. One moment there was a deep stillness, with seemingly nothing moving, then Leblanc's long rifle exploded and from the edge of the woods came a death cry.

All hell broke loose for the next several minutes. The Indians had waited for the moon to rise, and in its ghostly light she saw a swirl of half-naked savages racing into the clearing. Morton, flinging aside his blankets, had thrown himself sideways to the shelter of a tree, but Summers crouched where he was, firing at the attacking Indians first with his rifle, then with his revolver.

Summers' exposed position in the open clearing left him vulnerable to attack. While the three men were firing in the direction of the woods from which the Indians had originally attacked, Claire heard a pebble rattle across one of the boulders. Realizing at once that someone was climbing over the rocks, and that it could be no one but the Pawnee, she flattened herself against the larger of the two rocks as far back into the shadows as she could shrink, not even daring to breathe. A moment later a shadow flitted across the ground before her as first one of the Indians and then the other leaped the short distance between the two rocks.

For a moment they were invisible to her.

Then one of them dropped to the ground at the edge of the clearing. As she watched, he crouched and began to steal toward Summers, whose back was to the brave.

Her heart pounded. The other Indian was still somewhere above her on the rock. If she cried out to warn Summers, she would reveal her presence to the man above.

The opening between the rocks gave her a clear view of both Summers and the man edging ever closer to him. She waited, praying that either Morton or Leblanc, or Summers himself, would discover the Pawnee.

No one did. The Indian was no more than ten feet from the still unsuspecting Summers. He lifted the ugly tomahawk in his hand, preparing to rush forward and bury it in Summers' skull.

At that moment Summers fired the last shot in his revolver. He breached the gun, preparing to load it again, and as he did so he glanced back and saw the Pawnee. The Pawnee gave a yell and rushed toward the defenseless man.

At the same time Claire took a deep breath and stepped from between the boulders. Lifting the rifle to her shoulder, she fired.

The Pawnee arched violently, staggered a few more steps, and fell, practically in Summers' arms. Claire remembered the man above her just as the Indian jumped to the ground before her. The rifle was yanked violently from her hands and flung aside, and she found herself face to face with the fiercely grinning savage, the moonlight gleaming off the blade of the knife in his hand. With a cry of triumph he seized her with one hand, the other lifting the knife to plunge it into her breast.

There was no time for Summers to reload his gun, and the shots and cries had gone unremarked by the other two men in the general melee. On the ground before him was the tomahawk the Pawnee had dropped. Seizing it, Summers stood and hurled the weapon with an expertise the Pawnee would have envied straight, for the skull of the Indian struggling with Claire.

It happened so quickly that it was some minutes before she had fully comprehended what had happened. She was struggling with the Indian, her face only inches from his, so that she could see the veins standing out at his temples and the little rivulets of sweat that ran down his brow. Then his head seemed to explode in two, splattering her with a shower of blood and shattered bone and cartilege. The man fell forward into her arms, dragging her to the ground with him as he fell.

The unexpected and fierce defense threw the remaining Indians into confusion, and with a few last, wild shots they fled into the forest.

Claire struggled to free herself from beneath the dead Pawnee. Suddenly Summers was there, helping her to her feet and grinning with boyish enthusiasm. In a flash of insight she realized that notwithstanding the danger they had been in Summers was enjoying himself.

"That was pretty good shooting," he said.

"Is it over?" She looked around. The clearing was strewn with fallen bodies. Morton and Leblanc were just emerging from cover.

"Just round one," Summers said, taking her arm and hurrying her toward the river. "We'd better skedaddle, before they get up the nerve to come back."

Leblanc, the only one who was not going west with them, would take one of the canoes and continue upriver, to look for a place to camp until winter set in. The other canoe would be left as a peace offering to the Pawnee.

"But won't they kill him when he comes back downriver?" Claire asked.

"Not likely," Summers said. "They'll probably greet him as an old friend and pretend they know nothing about this. Or chalk it up to renegades."

They helped Leblanc get his canoe safely into the shallow water. When he had begun to paddle upstream, the others mounted their horses and headed south and west, following the course of the South Platte.

They had ridden only a short distance when they heard an uproar behind them as the Pawnee discovered the empty camp.

Summers, glancing over his shoulder, frowned. "Not like them to come back so soon," he said. "They must have been pretty sore."

They urged their horses on, fearful that the Indians might attempt pursuit. It was nearly dawn when Summers suggested they stop for a rest. While Morton and Claire set up camp, Summers climbed an outcropping of rock to peer in the direction from which they had come. There was no sign they were being followed. He put his ear to the ground as the Indians did. On the hard, flat surface of the plains, a single horse's hooves could reverberate for miles.

Finally satisfied, he joined the others. After a hastily contrived meal, they took to their blankets and slept.

The sky was already grey with the approaching day when Claire was awakened by the thud of something being thrown into the middle of their camp. A moment later there was an abrupt clattering of hooves, swiftly diminishing into the distance.

She bolted upright, instinctively reaching for the gun Summers had insisted she keep by her bed. He was already up, gun in hand. He ran at a crouch in the direction of the rock outcropping, from beyond which came the fading sound of riders.

"Pawnee," he said, staring after them. "Hightailing it out of here."

"Here's why," Morton quietly added. He had the object that had been thrown into the camp and held it aloft. It appeared to Claire to be no more than a handful of hair tied to a rock.

"What is it?" she asked.

"It *was* Leblanc's scalp," Morton said. With a gesture of disgust he threw it aside. Claire, horrified, buried her face in her hands.

"It's unlike the Pawnee to be so vengeful," Summers said. "They must have been plenty angry over that trap we sprang on them."

"Then why didn't they attack and kill us?" Claire asked. "If they'd gone to the trouble to follow us this far?"

"Probably afraid of another surprise like the last one. And it's getting light. We're lucky they didn't take our horses too."

"Will they be back?" she asked, trying to avoid looking in the direction of the Pawnee's grisly trophy.

"I doubt it," Summers said, "but I don't think we ought to hang around, just in case."

It was a subdued trio who pushed on to the west a short time later. They had been uncertain what to do with Leblanc's scalp. Claire felt that out of decency they ought to bury it, but Summers pointed out that it was a man's body that got buried. In the end Morton decided the matter by announcing that he would carry the scalp with him. Wrapping it in a piece of burlap, he added it to his back.

"He had a wife somewhere up in Canada," he explained. "And this is the only proof the man's dead."

A day passed, then another, and they concluded that they were no longer in any danger of pursuit by the Pawnee.

"This is Cheyenne country now," Summers said, "and they're no friends of the Pawnee."

They had a new concern now, though. Having left behind the flat banks of the Platte River, they had been climbing steadily. Mountains had begun to appear on the horizon, and here and there were low mesas and buttes. It was now September, and in the mountains it was already autumn. Though the days had remained balmy, the nights were turning noticeably cool.

"We'll never get over them mountains in the winter," Morton said, eyeing the jagged peaks no bigger than anthills on the horizon.

"I've heard there's no end to them," Summers said. "And they get worse the farther you go."

"Can't we go around them?" Claire asked.

Summers shrugged. "Near as I've found out, they reach all the way to Mexico. Like a wall, protecting the far west from outsiders."

"But if we can't get over them, and we can't get around them, what are we going to do?" Claire asked. "We can't just sit around and wait for spring."

"No, but we can go looking for it," Summers said. They gave him uncomprehending looks. "Look," he explained, taking up a stick and beginning to scratch in the dust, "if these are the mountains I think they are, they cut about straight south and north. Like I said, a wall, damn near impossible to get across in the winter. But there is a place where winter doesn't get." He marked an X with the stick. "Somewhere down here is another river, the Colorado. Cuts right through these mountains, down to the south, which is where California is, best I can tell."

"But won't this river be frozen by the time we reach it?" Claire asked.

"It would, only there's a canyon, a canyon the likes of which man never dreamed of. The walls must be a mile, maybe two miles deep."

"I never heard of such a place." Morton scoffed.

"I saw it. It plain takes a man's breath away. It's like someone had painted those walls, all red and blue and brown. And there's rocks like cathedrals."

"Okay," Morton said, still sounding unconvinced, "let's say it exists. Let's even say we could find it, which I'm not convinced of, in those mountains. What then? You going to tell me that it's a magical river, stays summer all year round, something like that?"

"Exactly," Summers said, grinning.

"Ah, now just a minute." Morton looked disgusted.

"Look. Here, past the mountains, that's the great desert I talked about before, with the mountains sitting on top of it." He went back to the canyon he'd sketched alongside his river. "But here, the river's cut right down through the mountains, right down to the desert below. So even when it's winter up here, it's still summer down there, on the desert floor. If we can find this river, and you're right, that's a damned big if, all we got to do is follow it through this canyon, right on out to the desert, and California."

The last word seemed to cast a spell. The three sat in silence for a long moment, each staring wistfully into the fire.

"Do you suppose there's really cities of gold there?" Morton asked, breaking the spell.

"Peter thought so," Claire said. "I thought he was a fool, but now . . ." She shrugged.

"Don't tell me you're starting to believe it too?" Summers asked.

"I didn't, but it's easier to be a skeptic back there." She nodded her head in the general direction of the States. "Out here, well, I don't know. There's something so unreal, so mystical, about this land. The plains, the rivers, those mountains; it is like another world. We haven't seen another white man in months, not even an Indian since we left the Pawnee. Not a house, not a carriage—one could almost believe that all that had vanished, like a dream with the dawn. Perhaps there *are* cities of gold in California."

Summers smiled and shook his head. "My guess is there's just more towns and houses and people. Maybe a fresh cooked meal . . ."

"I'll settle for that." Morton chuckled. "And lots of them *señoritas*. And music! Old Leblanc dearly loved it when I used to play the harmonica."

The mention of the French Canadian cast a shadow over their mood. Each was reminded of the tenuousness of their present position.

Claire found herself thinking of what she had left behind. Not so much, really. Aunt Tess in England, but they'd hardly been the close-knit sort of family that would cry her homeward. England, of course. There was much to miss of England itself, though truth to tell she'd spent most of her life being bored and restless. Richard hated her. Peter was gone. Virginia had never been home to her.

In a flash of rare insight she saw for the first time in her life that all she really had, all she could lay claim to, was *now*. Not the past or the future, but this present moment, here on a high plateau somewhere in the land known as the American west.

"Won't you play for us, Mister Morton?" she asked on impulse.

He looked flustered but pleased. With loud disclaimers regarding his ability, he fetched the harmonica from his pack, and placing it to his lips, began to play. If it was not fine music, nor particularly sure of pitch, it was nonetheless welcome in the vast darkness of the night, and after a tentative line or two of melody, he began to play a jig, accompanying himself as he danced clumsily but spiritedly about the fire.

It was such a spontaneous expression of good cheer that Claire laughed with delight and began to clap her hands in time to his dancing. Even Summers managed a smile for the trapper's antics.

Suddenly Morton stopped before her, and making a little bow from the waist, said, "I'd be honored if you'd go around this one with me, Miss English lady."

"I'd be delighted," she said. She rose and Morton crooked an elbow through hers and began to dance her around, gracelessly but energetically. He caught her about the waist, swinging her so hard that her feet left the ground and she had to cling to his burly shoulders for support. She had recently begun to let her hair hang loose and now it swung gleaming and golden in the firelight, framing her face and making her look girlish and innocent.

She was only gradually aware of the change of atmosphere, of the way his arm had tightened about her waist, and the new light that had begun to glint in Morton's eyes.

Gasping for breath, she put a steadying hand against his chest. "You've stopped playing," she said, trying to keep the tone light.

He leaned his face close to hers. "There's more than one way of making music," he said in a coarse whisper.

"Please," she gasped, trying to free herself from his embrace.

"Mind if I cut in?" Summers asked. He had been so silent, had risen so quietly, that both Claire and Morton were surprised to discover him there at their elbows.

"The lady and I are talking," Morton said in a chilling voice.

"I expect the lady'd rather dance than talk," Summers said.

"Yes," Claire said too quickly, "yes, I would rather."

There was an ugly pause in which the two men stared at one another. Morton's eyes flashed angrily; Summers' were calm and cold.

Morton gave way first, thrusting Claire roughly away from him. "To hell with it," he said. He spat noisily on the ground and strode off into the darkness.

"I'm afraid we've made Mister Morton angry," she said, glancing after him.

"He'll get over it."

She looked up into Summers' face and for the first time saw it in a new light. There was still the long jagged scar from cheekbone to chin, the swarthy complexion, and the cruelly sensual cut of his mouth, but Claire now saw Summers as strong and rugged, even handsome, although certainly not handsome as Peter had been. It was like the difference between a beautiful piece of architecture—ordered, balanced, perfect, and those mountains toward which they rode each day—raw, imperfect, yet thrilling in a way that stirred something deep within.

"You yourself reminded me, he's a dangerous man," she said aloud, partly to mask the confusion of her inner thoughts.

"Not as dangerous as I am. I thought we were supposed to be dancing."

She was surprised, having thought his interruption was only an excuse to rescue her from Morton.

"If you like," she said.

He took her into his arms, not roughly as Morton had done, but easily, naturally, and began to waltz her around the campsite. To her surprise he was very good.

"You waltz very well," she said, not even concealing her amazement.

"My father taught me. Said a man who wasn't light enough on his feet to dance a waltz would never last in Indian territory. Can't you sing something? We could use a little music."

She thought for a moment, then began one of the tunes that had been popular in London, making *la-la-la* do for the words. Together they swayed and circled about the fire, his hand firm in hers, his step sure and light. She closed her eyes, tilting her head back, letting the song trail away. They didn't need it. Their music was the rustle of the trees in the night wind, a distant murmur of water, a sudden brief call of a coyote somewhere far in the distance.

Summers stared down at the upturned face, realizing for the first time how pretty she really was and realizing too, in a flash of insight, something else. Perhaps it was her hair; he liked the way she'd taken to letting it hang loose. Or it may have been the way she rode, straight and confident in the saddle, never lagging behind, never complaining of the long hours or the distance covered. Partly it was that easy, ground-covering stride she'd developed when they'd been hiking. Partly the way she'd learned and remembered the things he told her. She'd always remember the name of a bird the second time, or know its call once he'd identified it for her. It was the way her once ivory skin had reddened under the sun to turn golden tawny.

Maybe most of all it was the way she could waltz around a mountain campfire in boots and an elkskin skirt, as if she hadn't even noticed the orchestra was missing. She was a woman born to this land, to the west, to the mountains and the freedom and the sweet, unsullied air.

The insight scared the dickens out of him. He realized that he'd been looking for her all his life.

He stopped dancing so suddenly that she tripped over one of his feet and nearly fell. "Time to turn in," he said, and with that he turned and strode away from her, leaving her to stare in astonishment after him.

9

There was now snow on the high peaks of the mountains, warning them of what lay in store. They traveled steadily south and west, staying close to the low fringes of the mountains to be less conspicuous.

"No telling just what Indians we might meet up with," Summers warned, "Arapahoe, Ute, and I've heard of Apaches traveling this far north, though it isn't their usual terrain."

"You seem to know so much," Claire said, curious about this man with whom she'd lived for several months. "Have you traveled this entire land?"

Summers chuckled. "No man could travel this entire land, not in a dozen lifetimes. But I've seen my fair share of it, bad and good."

"It's a beautiful place," Claire said, "so unspoiled."

"Unspoiled for now, maybe," Summers said. "An Indian friend of mine used to sing one of their songs:

> 'When the eagle is gone,
> Who then will we see soar
> From high mountain aeries,
> Over the blue sky?
> When the eagle is gone,
> Who will climb the skies?' "

"It's very sad," Claire said. "But why should the eagle go at all?"

"He'll go," Morton said and for once the two men were in agreement.

"As the men come, the eagle goes." Summers nodded.

"But what men would come here to this wilderness?" Claire asked.

"Men following other men, just as we're doing. Men following us. Same as they've pushed their way across the old west. Ohio, Kentucky, the Limberlost—they were empty and unspoiled once too, and the men came, looking, always looking, if not for cities of gold, then for other treasures, land, for one. Sometimes just looking for the very thing their presence destroys—unspoiled beauty."

"But if only a few came," she said, "if they treasured what they found, if they left it untouched..."

"Can they?" he asked. "Wherever we've gone we've left our mark of dead men and dead animals, cut trees and trampled flowers. And we are only three."

"Watch it," Morton said unexpectedly, reining in his horse. Claire's mount had flared her nostrils uneasily, warning of some approaching danger. From the underbrush along the trail came a crashing sound. A moment later an immense bear waddled into the path several yards ahead of them followed closely by two cubs.

The bear turned toward them, snorting threateningly. She rose up on her hind legs, towering eight feet in the air.

"She's only protecting her young," Summers said, calming his frightened horse. "Just let them get past. Jesus! Don't!"

Morton had raised his gun to aim at the grizzly in the path. Summers leaned out from his saddle, attempting to deflect the other man's shot. Morton fired just as his aim was knocked awry; the bear gave a startled grunt as the bullet struck her shoulder. Then with a terrifying roar, the bear charged straight at them, her cubs disappearing into the thickets.

There was no time for Morton to load and fire again. He attempted to wheel his mount out of the way of the charging beast, but the bear came with a speed that belied her massive size.

The horse reared, terrified, to kick out with its front hooves, but the bear charged straight in, catching its underbelly. With a rippling slash of one giant paw it sent the horse toppling to the ground.

There was no doubt that the horse saved Morton's life, for the bear went for the helpless animal first, ignoring the trapper scrambling to free himself from beneath his fallen mount. It was only a matter of seconds before the powerful paws would have torn him open as well, but those seconds gave Summers the time to steady his own horse and, bringing his rifle up, fire almost point blank into the brain of the enraged grizzly.

The confused beast looked backward at him, looking more frightened than angry. She attempted to wheel about, to confront this new attacker, but her legs gave out and she lumbered sideways a few steps before sinking to the ground, where she thrashed about for a moment before falling still.

"Goddamn you!" Morton shouted, managing to free the leg that had been pinned beneath his horse. He got unsteadily to his feet. "You almost got me killed. I'd have gotten her with that first shot if you hadn't interfered."

"You'd no need to kill her at all," Summers replied, equally angry. "And you've left her two younguns without any protection. I ought to have let her kill you. Serve you right."

"I ought to put the next bullet right in your head!" Morton shouted, shaking his fist.

"Please!" Claire cried, jumping from her own horse and putting herself between the two men. "Please, it's over and done. And Mister Morton's horse, it's hurt badly."

The men swallowed their anger and went to examine the horse. Its stomach and throat had both been laid open by the grizzly's deadly paws, and one leg had been broken. There was nothing to do but shoot it. Claire looked away as Summers put his revolver to the animal's head and fired.

Though both men remained bitter, their tempers had subsided enough that they were no longer threatening one another. There were sharp words when Morton insisted on cutting some of the meat from the dead bear, his stated purpose in shooting her in the first place. Summers objected, but Morton was adamant, and though Claire shared Summers' distaste for the unfeeling way in which Morton had claimed the bear's life, she sided with the trapper in agreeing that, the damage having already been done, bear steaks would make a welcome change from the dried meat that had been the staple of their diet.

It was already late afternoon by the time the canyon they had been following ended abruptly in a cul-de-sac. They decided to camp for the evening and look for a pass through the mountains in the morning.

On the surface the two men had gotten over their quarrel, but Morton at least made it clear that he was still deeply resentful. He refused to engage in any conversation with Summers, or even eat with the others.

Claire made an attempt to coax the trapper out of his mood, pointing out that Summers had only been trying to spare unneces-

sary bloodshed. Morton's answer to this was,
"He wanted me to get killed."

"But that's preposterous," Claire replied.
"Why should he want that?"

Morton's eyes narrowed coldly. "So's he
could have a free hand with you, that's why."
He spat on the ground. "He's afraid you
might take a shine to me over him."

"But that's ridiculous."

"Is it? You notice how he comes running
every time he sees you and me together? Like
right now. Look."

As if to prove his point, Summers did
approach them at just that moment. "I found
this in the woods just over there," he said,
showing them a broken arrow with a flint
head. "It's Ute. Looks like it's been there a
while, but it'd be a good idea if everyone kept
their eyes open just the same. Oh, and I
found a stream too, nice clear water. Good
place to fill canteens."

"I'll find my own water," Morton said.
"And I don't need anyone to warn me about
Indians." He turned his back on them, but
not before he'd given Claire a look as if to say,
"See?"

"I could use some fresh water," Claire
said.

Following Summers through the woods,
she thought of Morton's suggestion that Summers might be jealous. It was preposterous,
of course. If anything, Summers had been
more distant than ever with her since that
evening they had danced together.

She studied the tall, lean form ahead of her on the trail. The truth was she was rather sorry that he was so standoffish. Her feelings toward Mister Summers had changed considerably since they had left St. Louis. Summers did not show to his best advantage in the city. He was too coarse and too primitive for polite society. But in the wilderness the very qualities that served him so poorly in St. Louis became assets. He fitted into his surroundings, seeming as right and as natural as the aspen or the eagle. The scar that was so frightening to see in town seemed a symbol of his ability to survive out here. He was strong, fearless, self-reliant, a creature of animal instincts.

And animal passions? The thought crept unbidden into her mind, and she scoffed at herself for even thinking of such a thing, particularly where such a man was concerned.

And yet... She watched the hide costume alternately stretch and relax over the muscles of his wide shoulders and his lean, firm buttocks. He moved with the unconscious grace of a racing stallion. Yes, he would make love with an animal's passion—lustily, without inhibition or reservation; cruelly even, but with the cruelty of heat and urgency, not the calculated perversity to which her husband had submitted her.

They emerged from the forest at the edge of a fast-running stream that sparkled and danced through a narrow rocky channel and then widened into a sunlit pool a few yards below.

She was unaware that she was staring at Summers until he asked, "Is something wrong?"

She started guiltily, as if her wicked thoughts had been etched on her face for him to read. "No," she said, blushing and turning away to hide her confusion. "I—I was just admiring the scene. It's quite lovely, isn't it? And just look at that pool. I can't tell you how I'd like a proper bath."

"Go ahead," he said, grinning mischievously. "I'll keep an eye out."

She gave him a haughty look, taking her embarrassment out on him. "I'm sure you would," she said. "But I'm not accustomed to bathing before an audience."

"There's a lot of things out here you weren't accustomed to, but that hasn't stopped you from diving right in. And I'll tell you the truth, you're a hell of a lot better woman for it, too."

"Thank you. If I ever find that I need testimonials, I'll be sure to call on you." She knelt, filling her canteen with the clear, cool water. When she had thought about his remark, though, she found herself smiling; coming from Mister Close-Mouth Summers, that had been high praise indeed.

10

She woke late, to find Morton in the process of taking down the tent in which he and Summers had slept, and Summers nowhere in sight.

"He went off on foot," Morton explained in a surly voice. "Looking for a pass through the hills."

Since the evening before she had been thinking of the pool nearby and the prospect of a real bath. It seemed the ideal opportunity and, taking with her the small sliver of soap she had been hoarding for weeks, she announced her intentions to Morton.

"I could come along and help with your back," he said, leering.

"I'll thank you to stay right here. And if I so much as hear a footstep in the woods, I'll shoot," she added, indicating the revolver she had tucked into her belt.

"I ain't the type to go sneaking around after something if I want it," he said furiously. "If I wanted you bad enough, I'd take you right here and now, Miss High and Mighty."

He took a step toward her as if he meant to do just that. For an answer, she drew the revolver. He stopped, his eyes going from her face to the gun, and back to her face again.

"It's him, ain't it?" he demanded, his lips curling in a sneer. "You're wanting him as bad as he's wanting you."

"Don't be a fool," she said, angry that the charge had turned her cheeks red.

"You're the one's being a fool." His voice became low and ominous. "You picked the wrong man. When he's rotting at the bottom of some canyon, then you'll be stuck with me or no one. And I'm telling you now, I don't take to being second choice."

"Then I can assure you, you won't be. Not second, not third, not ever."

For a moment she thought she might really have to shoot. He looked as if he would like nothing so much as to spring upon her, though his look was more murderous than desirous.

At length he turned his back on her with a muttered oath and went back to his work, dismissing her. She glanced over her shoulder once or twice as she started for the woods, but he seemed to have forgotten her.

She found her way to the stream with no

difficulty. She waited a few minutes, standing in the shadow of a tree in case Morton really did try to follow her, but the woods remained empty and silent and after a time she concluded that she was truly alone. She shed her clothes quickly, eager to make the most of the privacy, and plunged into the icy water.

Summers himself had paused to bathe in the same stream, though considerably downstream. Now, carrying his shirt in his hand so that the morning sun could dry his back, he made his way to the camp. He had found the pass he had been seeking, and as soon as they broke camp they could be on their way. In addition he'd found some ripe berries, which were now tied neatly in a bundle in his neckerchief. They'd make a nice addition to breakfast.

It was not breakfast, however, nor the mountain pass that was occupying his thoughts. It was the girl. He wanted her. He wanted her bad.

Of course he was no fool, and he knew that months of doing without could make any woman more attractive. He was no stranger to abstinence, however, and he was fully aware that this was something more.

The very depth of his desire for her frightened him. He had lived too long free and untrammeled. Worse, he had seen what happened to other frontiersmen who thought they had found the right woman and gotten married. It never worked. There were just certain men, and he was one of them, who couldn't get themselves roped in that way. A man was never free after that, never able to call his life and his time his own. They stopped rambling, those married men, or when they went it was with a heart heavy with guilt, or with no heart at all. A heart couldn't be two places at once, no matter how you tried.

Now his heart belonged to the west, to these mountains and plains, and even that damned desert lying somewhere ahead of them, waiting to scorch the meat off their bones. How could he give it to a woman? Where was a woman worth all that?

Not even the Englishwoman. He'd just have to put her out of his mind, stop thinking the way he'd been thinking lately. No good could come of it; and worst of all, it made a man careless. And that, to a man who lived as he did, was an even worse sin than marriage.

Yet for all his efforts to put her out of his mind, he knew instinctively when he came into the camp that she wasn't there. At once he was alarmed.

"Where's the girl?" he demanded.

Morton jerked his head in the direction of the woods.

"You damned fool," Summers swore. "I told you this was Ute territory. You shouldn't have let her go off by herself."

"She didn't exactly ask my permission," Morton snapped. "And who the hell are you to tell people what to do anyway?"

Summers was already gone, running lightly and noiselessly through the woods. He had remembered her remark yesterday about a proper bath. Though he had teased her about watching, that was the furthest thought from his mind just now. Even after all this time traveling, she was ill prepared to be off in the woods by herself. An Indian would be upon her before she had any warning, not to mention a mountain lion.

He slowed his pace as he neared the stream. There was a sound of splashing from the pool. Plenty of noise to attract anybody or anything that happened to be in the area, he thought disgustedly.

He paused on the fringe of the woods, first looking around to see if the noise had indeed attracted danger, but everything seemed safe.

Finally he turned toward the pool, opening his mouth to call to her, but the sound died in his throat.

She had climbed onto a rock to lather her body with the soap. The sun glinted on her naked flesh, on the upturned breasts with their roseate tips, on the tiny waist and the flaring curves of her hips. By God, she was beautiful. How had he ever thought her figure spare?

He stood transfixed, watching her lower herself into the water again and splash around, rinsing off the soap. She swam back to the shore and climbed out, shivering in the cool morning air.

Her clothes had been folded neatly and left on a rock, her gun atop the pile. He watched her move toward them, his eyes drawn to the fringe of golden hair that marked the V of her thighs.

He was so entranced by her naked beauty that he almost didn't see the danger threatening. But some instinct, born of years in the wilds, noted the tiny flicker of movement on the rock by her clothes, and all thoughts of desire and beauty left him, replaced by a cold chill.

"Don't move," he said sharply, stepping into the sunlight.

She stopped short, mouth forming a surprised oval. "Mister Summers!" she cried indignantly, trying unsuccessfully to cover her more intimate parts. "How dare—"

"Goddamn it, I said don't move!" he roared. The tone of his voice halted even her protestations and she stood frozen in place, staring wide eyed at him.

"There's a rattler not more than a foot away from your hand," he said, watching the snake and not her as he drew his gun. "He'd have got you for sure when you reached for your clothes."

She let out a long, shuddering "Oohhhh," and tried to stop the trembling that had set in. She watched Summers, too frightened to turn her head and look for the snake. But she could hear it now, the rattling sound, the warning that he was about to strike.

The gun roared; she screamed and stumbled backward, throwing her hands over her face, beginning to cry. It seemed only a second later that he was there holding her to him, comforting her. She opened her eyes and saw that there was blood on one arm.

"Bullet kicked up a piece of stone that nicked you," he said, seeing her eyes go to the blood. "Just a scratch. I'll wash it out for you."

She saw the snake lying dead on the rock, or rather, the snake's body, as its head was gone. She shuddered again and buried her face against his bare chest.

Only gradually did she become aware of the feel of him, of his bare, hard chest with its faint cover of dark hair, of his arms, strong and warm, about her, of his thighs, pressed against her, and the unmistakable swelling there. She stirred in his arms, trying not to feel the heat that was spreading from her sensitive nipples as they brushed against his chest.

"I must dress," she said, trying to free herself from his embrace.

He made no reply. For a moment he continued to hold her tightly against him. Then swiftly and easily he bent and swept her up into his arms.

"What are you doing?" she asked weakly as he carried her along the stream's bank. "I—please," she stammered, putting a resisting hand against his chest.

"You knew this would happen sooner or later," he said. "I just decided on sooner."

He put her down gently on a bed of pine needles, warmed by the morning sun. She felt dazed and frightened, yet strangely exhilarated. She watched him shed his trousers and his boots.

How magnificent he is, she thought, with the sun behind him and the blue sky framing his naked body. There was his powerful chest, the muscles rippling like a washboard over his flat belly, and the line of dark hair that led downward to the long, thick column that stood out before him as if leading him to her.

He paused, about to toss his trousers aside, and said, "You ain't going to scream or fight me or anything, are you?"

She let her eyes move slowly upward until they had met his, and her lips parted in a tremulous smile. "No," she said in little more than a whisper, "I'm not going to fight you."

He was at once urgent and searching and yet, as she had somehow known he would be, gentle. He explored and ravished with his mouth, his tongue, his hands. Finally she felt the insistent probing between her thighs, and then the sweet warmth seemed to engulf her.

She lifted her arms about him, running her hands over the smooth hard surface of his back. "I don't even know your name," she said.

"It's Camden," he said, kissing her ear.

"Camden," she breathed, "Camden," saying it over and over like a song on a gently rising note, until it had become more a moan than a name.

11

Winter came, cold and white, and she was grateful for Summers' body, warm against hers in the tent they now shared. She was grateful too for the way he had skillfully awakened her body to the full pleasure of sex. She had always thought that it could be enjoyable with the right man, but with Peter it had quickly deteriorated into a test of her endurance. With Summers, no matter how long it lasted, it seemed always to end too soon.

She tried not to think too often of the husband she was cuckolding. Perhaps in London or Virginia, or even St. Louis, she might have been consumed with guilt for what she was doing. Though her marriage to Peter had not been a happy one, and though she had flirted with other men—as much to annoy him as to flatter herself—she had never seriously considered being unfaithful to him.

Here things took on a different perspective. Perhaps it was the towering mountains glittering under their snow wraps, or the tall, majestic pines, or timeless sea of stars in the night sky that dwarfed man's petty problems. Peter might be a thousand miles or more in any direction, or just a few feet below where the horses' hooves sank into the snow. It was impossible to guess if he were alive or dead, and if alive, whether she would ever again see his face. She had begun to perceive that a journey such as this one might be forever, even if one reached the mystical land of gold. If Peter had reached it, it was unlikely he would have set out again to return to her.

But Summers was here. His warm, strong body covered hers at night, and by day he led the way through the winter-treacherous mountains. Summers knew which nuts to gather before the snows had caught them. Summers killed deer and dried the meat to replenish their meager supplies. Summers had even made a poncho for her from deer hide. It was most welcome as the temperatures dropped lower and lower.

They spoke rarely of their relationship. She supposed he was no more in love with her than she was with him, though she loved much about him. She was, for want of a better term, "at peace" in his company. He

was as rugged and spectacular as the land-
scape through which they rode, and it seemed
entirely right, at least here in this wilderness,
to have become his mistress.

Morton accepted the change in their relationship with quiet resentment. He no longer
made direct overtures to her, but once or
twice she had a peculiar feeling, as if she had
been suddenly stripped naked in the cold.
She would turn to find Morton's eyes on her,
burning with a deep, almost feverish light.
Afterward she would cling to Summers in the
darkness of their tent with a passion kindled
by fear, until his skilled ministrations had
released the tension built up within her.

The two men were coolly reserved toward
one another. Both were too acquainted with
the dangers of the wilderness to risk expending
their energies on their animosity. There was
no telling when one's survival might depend
upon the other, but they made no pretense of
friendship and spoke to one another only
when the trek necessitated it.

They had been traveling better than four
months, and with each passing day their progress grew slower. At first the snow that fell
was light and often followed by rain that
turned the snow hard and made it easy to
ride over, but gradually the snow became dry
and powdery and ceased to melt away between snowfalls. It lay a yard deep and more
on the trail, and there were drifts higher than
a man's head.

Still the snow fell. They had been riding

gradually upward into the mountains, following where the easiest trail took them so long as it was south and west. Now, faced with what was taking on the appearance of a blizzard, they worked their way downhill to the lower slopes of the mountains, but to little avail. They could no longer see more than a few feet in any direction. The snow became so deep that to move forward the horses had to rear on their hind legs and then leap forward to breast the snow, disappearing into the white powder up to their heads.

Tragedy was inevitable. It would have been difficult terrain in the best of weather; in the violent storm now raging about them, it was impossible. The pinto mare on which Claire was riding was having a hard time keeping up with the two bigger, stronger horses. It lost its footing, and Claire was thrown into the snow.

Summers was there in a moment, dragging her to her feet, but the horse had broken a leg. Claire's tears froze to her cheeks as Summers shot the unfortunate beast.

"We'll have to find some shelter!" he shouted over the howling wind.

"Better if we all walk," Morton said.

They set out on foot, leading the two remaining horses. By this time the snow was neck deep on the men. Summers led the way with Morton bringing up the rear and Claire between them, following as best she could the opening made in the snow by Summers and the horse he was leading.

For the first time she understood why the two men had regarded the mountains as impassable. There was nothing but a nightmare patch of white through which she struggled, trying not to lose sight of the shadowy forms before her. Once she lost her footing and plunged for a second time into the powdery snow. So poor was the visibility that neither of the men saw her fall. She was saved by Morton's tripping over her as he struggled blindly forward. How easily she might have been lost to the others; and once out of sight, impossible for them to find until the storm had ended, when it would have been too late.

Half-frozen, she trudged forward, more careful than ever now to keep Summers in sight. He was faring little better. Twice he had walked into obstacles, and once he took a fall in a snow-filled gully. He had hoped to find some sort of shelter, perhaps a cave in the hillsides, but now he faced the hard fact that they might pass within a few feet of a cave and not be able to see it.

He saw a dead pine that had broken off halfway up its considerable length. It lay at a sharp angle in the snow. He got the pine, which was filled with pitch, burning, and the three of them and the two remaining horses huddled gratefully about its warmth.

It was twilight, and despite her insistence to the contrary, Claire was clearly too exhausted to push on. They ate gathered about the fire. It was impossible to set up the tipis in the storm, but they could cover themselves with the skins, which would keep them dry, and by the time these had in turn been covered with an insulating blanket of snow, they were surprisingly warm.

Numb with fatigue, Claire slept while the two men, their animosity laid aside temporarily, sat and discussed their best hope for survival in the unexpectedly bitter storm.

Summers offered to walk and let the other two ride the remaining animals, but Morton, who had had some experience with bad winters, pointed out that the horses were now burdened with the supplies that had been strapped to the sides of Claire's pony. They'd all have to walk.

Summers would like to have argued, at least insofar as Claire was concerned, but he knew that Morton was right. They had come to a point when it was no longer a question of comfort, but survival.

Summers had slept no more than an hour when he woke to a sense of danger. The snow had turned to sleet, with the result that the fire they had left burning had been all but extinguished. As Claire slept soundly at his side, Summers turned his head to and fro, his senses straining at the darkness about them. He had earlier heard a distant chorus of wolves. Had they picked up the human scent?

The snow muffled any sounds of approach. He peered into the darkness and saw something dart through the shadows beyond the glowing embers of the fire. Cautiously he slid from beneath the blanket and began to load his rifle. Nearby Morton said in a hoarse whisper, "It's wolves, must be eight, nine of them out there."

Summers got to his feet and went to the fire, gathering up two or three branches that had fallen aside and tossing them onto the fire. They hissed and crackled, and after a moment began to burn.

"Cover me," he said to the other man as he walked beyond the fire toward the encircling darkness.

It was so good to feel warm, after the long trek through the falling snow. For a long time Claire fought against the threatening wakefulness, but an instinctive voice kept nagging at her, urging her back from the deep sleep into which she had fallen.

She turned and reached for the warmth of Summers' body beside hers and was instantly awake. Summers was gone. Even in sleep she had known when he had come to lie beside her earlier. Without thinking she reached for the revolver beside her. Her fingers curling around it, she turned her head to the side and saw Morton, out of his bed, crouched on one knee with his rifle to his shoulder.

She moved just her eyes, following the direction of his rifle barrel; and saw Summers standing just beyond the barely burning fire.

Morton was going to kill him! Fear shot

like an arrow through her heart. As slowly as she dared, she inched the revolver free of the blankets until it was aimed at Morton. She sighted along its barrel, then, squeezing the trigger ever so carefully, she fired.

The cold and exhaustion had dulled Summers' senses. He stood for a long moment staring into the darkness, seeing nothing. He had just turned, meaning to return to the fire, when he caught a flurry of movement out of the corner of his eye and whirled in time to see three low grey shapes dart from the shelter of the trees and race toward him. The wolves ran low to the ground, their fangs dripping, their eyes gleaming yellow in the reflected glow of the fire.

No time to aim. He lifted the rifle and fired point blank, hearing Morton's gun explode behind him and, inexplicably, a revolver fire at almost exactly the same moment.

He hit one of them, the animal flip-flopping into the air to fall thrashing on the snow. Morton's bullet must have caught a second one in the shoulder, because it fell snout first; but the third, snarling, leapt for his throat. Eighty pounds of flying muscle caught Summers in midchest, knocking him backward to the ground. As he fell he saw two more of the beasts dashing forward to join the fray.

Claire's attention had been on Morton. Not until her bullet had felled him did she hear the ugly snarls and turn to see Summers set upon by wolves. She saw him go down and screamed, but it was impossible to shoot at this distance without risking hitting him.

She jumped up, running forward and cursing herself for a fool. She had killed Morton at the very time when they needed him most. She snatched up a piece of burning wood from the fire and ran to where Summers was slashing with his knife at the wolf atop him. His knife sliced open the wolf's belly, steam rising as the blood spilled onto the icy snow, but the other two were upon him now.

Claire struck out at them with the burning torch, the smell of burning hair and scorched skin filling her nostrils. The beasts retreated from the dread flames. One of them crouched a yard or two away to spring at her, but she fired the revolver, catching it between the eyes.

There were others out there. She could hear them crashing through the snow.

"The rifle," Summers gasped, holding one torn and bleeding wrist in his good hand. "Reload the rifle, quick."

She had just gotten the rifle loaded again when she heard another of those hideous snarls and looked to see a grey shape charging toward her. The wolf leapt as she fired. She felt claws tearing at her as the beast's weight crushed her back into the snow. As she waited for the fangs to tear open her throat, she realized that the animal had been dead when it had hit her.

She struggled free of the lifeless weight, shuddering at the sight of the horrible fangs that by now might have been ripping open her throat or feasting on her flesh.

They had killed four of the wolves. The others had retreated, disappearing into the darkness from which they had come.

"They're gone now," Summers said, getting to his knees. "You all right?"

"Yes, I—I've killed Morton."

His eyes widened with shock. "Why?"

"I thought he was going to kill you," she said.

He started to rise, then sank to his knees again. "You're going to have to help me," he said. "I've lost a lot of blood."

"My God," she said, getting a good look at him for the first time since the attack. His left forearm had been mangled by the wolves' fangs, and one shoulder had been laid open as well. His normally swarthy skin had taken on a pale, yellowish pallor.

With her help he was able to get to his feet and make it back to the fire, but the last few steps she was all but carrying him, staggering under his considerable weight. He sank to the ground, tried to say something, and passed out.

She knelt over him, staring in horror at his mutilated arm and shoulder and the feeble rising and falling of his chest.

God in Heaven, what have I done, she thought in rising panic. Morton was dead by her hand, and Summers seemed to be no more than a heartbeat or two away from death. Something snapped behind her and she screamed aloud in terror, but it was only the fire, burning low.

12

Summers stirred on the ground, reminding her that she could not afford to sit wringing her hands. She began melting snow to wash out the ugly wounds, tearing up one of her undergarments to make a bandage.

He regained consciousness while she was working over him, wincing with pain as she probed the torn flesh. "Whisky," he muttered in a hoarse voice. "Morton carries some in his pack. Pour it on the wounds. But give me a shot of it first."

She rummaged through Morton's things and found the whisky, bringing it back to where Summers was sitting. At his direction she held the bottle to his lips and he drank deeply. Then he nodded for her to take care of the wounds. She saw his body go rigid as she poured the raw whisky on the open wounds, but his face, though pale, was composed.

When she had bandaged him as well as possible, she began looking about for more wood to add to the nearly dead fire, but Summers forestalled her.

"No good," he said. "Too much blood, it'll bring the wolves back, or worse. We'll have to find some place to hole up."

"But you can't travel like that!" she cried.

"Have to. What about him?" He jerked his head in Morton's direction.

"I think I killed him."

"Let's see."

With her help he managed to make it across the campsite to the figure sprawled in the snow. He knelt over him, putting an ear to his chest and prying open an eyelid. Finally he tore open the other man's shirt and examined a dark wound in his back.

"He's alive, but just barely. The bullet went through his back muscles to lodge in his chest," he said finally. "We'll have to tie him on one of the horses."

They had been too exhausted when they'd camped to unpack most of their gear so that breaking camp was relatively simple. Even so, it took an hour or more to get their bedding stowed on the horses, and that long again, pausing often to rest, before the two of them together were able to hoist Morton's bulky body over the back of the larger horse.

In the grey light of dawn they set out again. The snow was still falling, but more gently now so that they could at least manage to see where they were going.

It soon became clear, however, that for all his determination, Summers was in no condition to travel on foot. When he stumbled and sank to his knees in the snow for the second time, Claire insisted that he mount the second horse.

"Can't ride and leave you to walk," he murmured, struggling for breath.

"Please," she begged. "I don't want to be left out in these woods with two corpses."

He tried to laugh but he was too weak even for that. She was right, he knew, and though it galled him to do so, he let her help him onto the mare's back. Claire took the animal's reins and trudged forward in the snow, the horse bearing Morton's unconscious form trailing after them.

It seemed an eternity later when Summers called her name and she looked back to see him pointing up a hillside. At first she saw nothing, but as the snow thinned for a moment she made out the opening of a cave.

Though the opening was small, the cavern itself proved to be roomy and surprisingly warm. A fissure in the ceiling let in a trickle of snow but served as well for the smoke from the fire that she built first thing.

Despite their newfound shelter, she was frightened for Summers' sake. He looked ghastly, but despite her insistence, he would not rest until he had again examined Morton's wound.

"That bullet's lodged against one of his ribs," he said, grim faced. "It's going to have to come out of there."

"But how?"

"You'll have to cut it out," he said.

"Me?" She was horrified. "But I—I can't, I'm not a surgeon. I'd kill him."

"He's just about dead anyway. Will be for sure if we don't get that bullet out. And I can't." He held up his mutilated hand.

"But I wouldn't even know what to do!" she cried.

"I'll help you. Take my knife and lay it on the fire, get the blade good and hot."

He spoke matter of factly, as if the decision had already been made. And no doubt, she thought, moving finally to do as he instructed, it had. Having brought about Morton's condition, she could hardly fail to do everything in her power to attempt to save him.

"Get the whisky and the bandages," Summers said, tearing off Morton's shirt to bare his upper torso. "That knife ought to be purified by now."

The leather-wrapped handle protected her hand, but she could see that the knife blade was nearly red hot. "Won't it burn him badly?" she asked.

"Help to sterilize the wound. Bring it here," he said. "Now it's a pretty neat hole, bullet went straight in, lodged down here. All you got to do is cut straight down and pry it out with the tip."

"That's all?" she said dryly.

"Only be careful not to go too far, that's his heart just the other side of that rib."

She had been about to put the tip of the knife against the wound, but at this remark her hand jerked back and began to tremble.

"I—I can't!" she cried, turning her face away from the sight of the dark hole in his chest.

"You got to."

"Please, no..."

"Damnit, that's what's wrong with a woman, they always fall apart just when you need them the most," he snapped, snatching the knife out of her hand. Grimacing with pain, he pulled himself up to a kneeling position over Morton.

It was obvious, though, that with one wounded shoulder and the other arm and hand swathed in bandages he would be lucky not to cut the man's heart out entire. Claire watched him try to get a firm grip on the knife and knew that it would be impossible for him to do what had to be done.

"No, I'll do it," she said, holding out her hand for the knife.

He breathed a sigh of relief and managed a faint grin. "Just take it easy," he said. "It's the only metal in there, ought to be easy to find."

Her own hands were trembling. She tried to will them to be steady, with only slight success. At first the flesh seemed to resist the blade, but it was only because in her fear she was putting no pressure on the knife.

"You got to cut," Summers said. "Just push it in, slow now."

The flesh parted before the blade. For a horrible moment she thought she was going to be ill and had to look away.

"For Christ's sake, watch what you're doing."

She forced her eyes back to the knife. She remembered something she'd heard once about students fainting in medical school at their first incision. She well believed it, for she felt as if she might faint any moment. The cave seemed to tilt and sway about her, and there was the taste of bile in her mouth.

"That's it, straight down toward the bone." Summers encouraged her.

She bit down hard on her lip, drawing blood, and, holding the knife in both hands, cut down into Morton's chest. The unconscious man, perhaps reacting to the heat of the knife or its advance into his body, suddenly gave a loud gasp. She nearly dropped the knife. Summers put a firm hand on her shoulder.

"Steady. You're doing great," he said. "You ought to just about be there."

The tip of the knife scraped something hard. She jerked it back, widening the wound she had laid open. "I—I hit something," she said. Her face had gone a sickly yellow-white.

"Bone or steel?"

"Bone, I think." She probed tentatively along one rib. "Yes, bone." After a moment she glanced in wide-eyed fear at Summers. "I can't find it," she said, her voice revealing a rising panic.

"Goddamn! It's got to be there, right along the rib."

"It isn't! Oh, Jesus..." Tears were forming in her eyes, threatening to blind her. She knew she could not go on; her hands had begun to shake like leaves.

Something shifted before the knife's tip. She caught her breath, holding it even after her lungs began to ache, and felt tentatively along the bone. There, just below the rib— metal on metal...

"I've got it," she whispered, beginning to cry without even knowing it. "I've found it."

"Good girl. Get it out of there."

That, as it turned out, was easier to say than to do. Two times she lost the bullet in the shifting mass that was a man's flesh. The third time, she felt gingerly around in the gash she had cut with the knife, searching, and all at once it was there, at the surface. She plucked it out with the knife, letting it roll down Morton's back until it fell to the cave floor. She let the knife slip from her hands to the ground and sat back wearily on her haunches.

Summers held her comfortingly in his good arm. "You were wonderful."

"I've never done anything like that." She was still trembling.

"I never have either," he said.

She sat back, staring at him. "But, you said . . ."

"I know. It had to be done. You'd never have done it if you thought I didn't know anything either."

For a moment she was furious at his deception. Then unexpectedly she began to laugh, half with relief and half with real humor. At first Summers stared, as if afraid she was losing her mind, but then he too began to laugh.

They were there three weeks while the storm raged. For a time it seemed as if Claire's surgery had been unsuccessful after all. Morton contracted a fever and for a week lay in a delirium. Summers cauterized the wound once again with a red hot knife blade, filling the cave with the stench of burning flesh. The infection checked, the fever began to subside.

For the most part their haven was a comfortable one. It was not necessary to go far outside to find wood for the fire that they kept going around the clock. The first day, when he had rested, Summers went out during a break in the snowfall to return pulling a sling he had filled with fresh meat cut from the body of Claire's little pinto.

"Something had gotten part of it already,"

he said. "But there was still plenty of meat left, and the snow kept it good and fresh."

Claire, remembering the beautiful and spirited animal, crinkled her nose in disgust and turned away. "I couldn't eat it," she said.

"Suit yourself." He shrugged. "We might be here a while."

He roasted a piece for himself and ate it with obvious relish, while she made do with some jerky. By the next day, however, she had overcome her squeamishness. The meat, hung well back in the cave where it was cool and dry, lasted almost the entire time they were there.

By the end of the second week Morton was able to sit up and eat with them. A few days after that the snow stopped falling and the sky broke clear and blue overhead. It was time to push on. Though both men were still weak, they were also hardened by long years in the wilderness. Summers was now able to use his hands.

Morton said little about what had occurred. Once, on the day they were preparing to leave and press southward, Claire found herself alone with him in the cave while Summers cared for the horses.

"He says you took that bullet out of me," Morton said without preamble.

"That's right," Claire replied, surprised at how proud she felt of the fact.

"Well, it was you that put it there," he said, and carried some of the gear outside, ending the conversation, once and for all.

13

For six weeks the trio trudged southwest, enduring the most hellish weather Claire had ever seen. She had known occasional snow and cold weather in England, but nothing like the storms that swept suddenly down upon them from the mountain peaks. They hunted continuously and with reasonable success, so though her diet of beaver and deer and mountain sheep was quite unlike anything she was used to, at least they were in little danger of starvation.

Summers led them up, attempting to find a pass through the mountains before the snow sealed off all chances until spring. The air was so thin and cold that it burned the lungs, forcing them to wear their kerchiefs over their faces. They all walked now, leading the two horses packed with their gear. They had cleared the snow from a meadow before they started upward and cut the grasses underneath, tying them in little bales to carry along. Once in the high range there would be nothing for the horses to eat. Even so, at the height of the pass, the patient beasts plodded through the snow for two days with nothing on which to feed.

They traveled deep into the heart of the mountains, each fearing what he dared not voice aloud to the others. A man might wander forever in such mountains without ever finding his way out again.

Claire had become so accustomed to the high mountain world of rocks and snow that it was a shock to mount a ridge one afternoon and suddenly find herself looking down upon a broad, rolling plain. It was punctuated here and there with huge outcroppings of rock, and even occasional patches of green and brown among the more thinly scattered snow.

Morton, coming up behind, gave a grunt of satisfaction, but Summers was quick to warn them that their hardships were not over.

"This is just the first range of the mountains," he explained. "There's more of them, as bad or worse, between us and California. But if we can find that Colorado River, we'll take it through."

As if to bear out his warnings, they had been only a day on the plain, thinking themselves at last out of the worst of the snow, when another storm struck. This one was the worst of all, for there was nothing here for protection. They took the full brunt of the wind and snow in their faces, and they lost another of the horses.

Perilously low on supplies, they pushed on. With each step the possible alternatives had narrowed until they were now faced with only two: go on or perish. And the two might well be one.

Gradually, though, the land was descending. The mountain plateau became the high desert, and in less than two days they had walked out of the snow. To their right the mountains rose ice capped and forbidding; to the south, at their left, lay a vast desert. It was a desert unlike those Claire had ever imagined. Instead of the rolling dunes of sand that she expected, there were rock formations in brilliant colors of red, purple, green, and brown. Even the land itself seemed to have been painted by some giant hand.

She paused to stare southward at this splendidly colored scene. "It's magnificent."

"We're not far from the river now." Summers urged them on. "And down that, the great canyon."

It took them three days of steady travel to reach the walls of the canyon through which the river ran, and another to climb down to the river itself. Summers warned them that these rocky bluffs were mere hillsides compared to the canyon through which they must travel.

At last they reached the Colorado, so

called, Summers said, for the reddish color of its dirty waters. Now they faced a new question—how to travel down its length. Morton was for hiking along its banks, rather than building a raft as Summers proposed.

"Water's too low and too rocky," Morton pointed out. "There's bound to be rapids."

"That there are," Summers agreed. "But there's places where it's impossible to get through the canyon except in the water, as the walls come straight down to the river. And if we're going to build a raft, better to do it here where there's plenty of wood."

In the end Morton reluctantly yielded. They set about gathering the wood necessary to construct the raft. They used their ropes and the last of their hides, cut into strips, to tie the logs together.

"Might as well use the bridle and reins too," Summers said, indicating the harness that was on the last of their horses. "We'll be lucky to get a raft to carry the three of us down this river."

"But couldn't we let him swim after the raft?" Claire asked.

"He'd never make it. Anyway, we're low on food."

Claire had, of necessity, long since overcome her scruples regarding horse flesh. But in the past the horses had been lost by mischance or wounded, so that taking their lives had been as much an act of mercy for the horse as well as for themselves. To cold-bloodedly slaughter an animal that had served

them so faithfully and so well was to her one
of the saddest decisions they had yet had to
make.

Out of consideration for her, Summers
led the horse some distance away, beyond a
huge boulder. Even so, tears stung her eyes
when the pistol shot ricocheted among the
walls of the canyon.

They were a week beside the river, building their raft and drying the meat that would
be the staple of their diet over the next several weeks.

After the rigors of the mountain snow-
storms their stay by the river was almost idyllic. The temperatures were warm and it was a
relief to sleep at night without the wind howling about them. The river water was dirty but
drinkable.

It was almost with reluctance that they
moved on when the raft was ready. The
thought that they might be on the last leg of
their journey, and that California lay somewhere beyond the river's bend, quickened
their efforts toward the end.

The raft had been built under Morton's
instructions, for the trapper was an experienced riverman. It was a crude, even clumsy-
looking affair, an eight-foot-square bed of logs
lashed together with another at each side to
form a low wall. The bulk of their provisions
were lashed to these side walls, with the rest
divided into packs, which each of them carried.

It was hardly the most confidence-inspiring

craft she had ever seen. When Morton climbed aboard after her, it threatened to capsize completely. Still, when Summers had waded into the water to shove it off from shore and clambered aboard, dripping, the raft righted itself safely. It turned about twice in the swift current, then began to rush downstream.

The two men had provided themselves with long poles to steer the raft. In truth, once the swift current had taken them, there was little they could do but cling to the rough sidewalls and try from time to time to shove the craft out of the way of the rocks that thrust up from the river's surface.

It was frightening and yet undeniably exhilarating. Claire stared upward at the canyon walls, which grew taller and steeper with each twist in the river's course. There were dragonflies skimming low over the roiling surface of the water, and overhead she caught sight of a blue heron, flying downriver slightly ahead of them as if guiding them on their way.

Only gradually did she become aware of a distant rumbling sound. When she first became conscious of it, she mistook it for thunder and thought another storm was upon them. Then she realized that the sound was too constant. She started to ask, but the men were already exchanging worried glances.

"Rapids," Summers said curtly. "Hold on tight."

She followed his advice so wholeheartedly that her hands began to ache before they had even reached the rapids themselves. Suddenly, staring anxiously ahead, she saw the river vanish from sight, and she realized that they were approaching a falls.

The distant rumble had become an ear-splitting roar drowning out all other sounds. The two men were shouting at one another, but even as close as she was she could not make out their words. Apparently Morton thought they should take the craft ashore, and they began earnestly plying their poles, but it was too late. They were in the grip of the rapids now and their efforts were futile.

The raft lurched and bobbed as the river's shrieks echoed from the sheer walls of shale and sandstone on either side of the canyon. Claire was as drenched as if she had been swimming in the red brown water, which was white now, a sea of foam.

The raft turned this way and that, so violently that the two men no longer tried to control it, but like Claire held tightly to the sides as they were swept forward. Before them lay the falls, a drop of thirteen feet. For a second they seemed to hang suspended over the edge of the water; then they were plunging downward nose first, the roar of the water drowning out Claire's instinctive scream.

The front of the raft struck deep into the water. In a twinkling they had turned over. Somehow Claire managed to keep her grip on the raft and when it came to the surface she was still clinging to its side. Morton clung to the other side, with Summers a few feet away in the water. The raft spun around as if going out of its way to meet Summers, swimming after it. For a few minutes they rode downstream hanging on to the sides, till the white water had subsided somewhat and the water had gotten shallower, allowing the men to push the raft to the shore.

Wet, weary, and bedraggled, the three stumbled onto the river bank. Yet for all their exhaustion, there was a sort of exhilaration too. Their makeshift riverboat had passed a critical test. They had survived their first rapids.

They rested for the day and set out again early the following morning. They had learned from their first encounter. When they approached their second rapids, Summers moved to the rear of the raft with Claire. The added weight to the rear made a difference, and though this rapids had an even greater drop, they managed to stay afloat.

Claire could now give some attention to the land through which they were traveling. This was indeed Summers' "great canyon," with walls that towered at least a mile above them. Sometimes the walls were miles apart, and sometimes they crowded in upon the river so that there was no shore at all, only sharp rock ledges hanging out over the water.

It was even more colorful than the painted desert they had seen a few days before. Every color of the rainbow was represented, not only in the canyon walls but in huge agate boulders—reds and blues, lavenders and bright green. And everything was on a scale so grand that she felt lilliputian.

Their third day was largely uneventful, through small rapids that may have concerned her earlier but were now too tame to warrant real concern after what they had been through. The canyon opened into a wide valley with trees and prickly cactus.

Late in the afternoon they found a place to beach the raft, a narrow strip of sand and rock surrounded by towering cliffs. Somewhere ahead they could hear the now familiar rumble of rapids, which they decided to attempt fresh the following morning.

Summers found a path that led part way up one of the cliffs before coming to an abrupt end. It provided, however, a fine view of what lay beyond the river's bend.

Ahead of them lay rapids worse than any they had traveled thus far, stretching on for a considerable distance and disappearing out of sight without a break in the white water. There was a drop perhaps twice as deep as the worst they had yet encountered, with a rock island in the center as an added danger.

"The raft'll never make it," Morton declared flatly. "Some of those ropes are giving out already from the strain."

"There's no other way," Summers said. With the exception of isolated sand bars, the river ahead cut straight through the sheer walls of the canyon. It would be impossible to walk around the rapids without climbing to the top of the canyon, which was equally impossible. "We can't go back, we can't go up, we can't go around. We've got no choice but to go through."

This grim knowledge made for a restless night's sleep, and by the first light of dawn all three of the travelers were ready to go. The raft itself seemed to shudder as they pushed off into the water. Summers moved to the rear beside Claire and to her surprise put one arm about her.

"Will we make it?" she tried to ask over the noise of the water. He shook his head grimly, but whether this was an answer to her question or whether he had even heard her she could not say.

The next moment they were caught in the rapids. The raft was jerked violently to and fro as if on strings manipulated by some giant hand. It thudded into a huge boulder and for several seconds sat motionless, until the current wrenched it from the place and sent it hurtling forward. The raft was shaken and battered so badly that Claire wondered if they would even last to the falls. Then they were hanging suspended in space, staring down into a veritable abyss—thirty feet or more straight down, with the shining island of black rock in the center. The raft creaked and groaned beneath them, and in a flash Claire knew as they began to plunge downward that the raft would never survive.

They hit with a monstrous crash, sending

broken logs and passengers flying in all directions.

Claire thrashed about helplessly in the churning water. She broke the surface, gasping for air, and at once vanished beneath the water again.

Something caught at her skirt. For a second she imagined some horrible water creature but this was a human hand.

Summers! She stretched, reaching, her fingers closing in the others, the two of them fighting the water together. The water, violent, rushed onward, turning and flinging them about till her lungs were burning with the need for air.

"Hang on!"

Not Summers' voice, but Morton's.

"Summers!" She tried to call his name but the sound ended in a gurgle of water. Morton, his face contorted with the effort of trying to keep them both afloat, was pulling her against the current, swimming with her.

In a moment he had grabbed hold of a log, one from their own raft, and was shoving her against it. "Hold on to it!" he shouted.

She held on as well as she was able, though the river fought her, trying to pry her from the log. Morton was clinging to the other end, shouting something at her, but she could not hear him over the dull and angry roar of the river. From time to time the log would roll, and she would slip beneath the water, only to come up again.

It was a nightmare struggle. She could

feel her strength draining from her and knew she could not hold out much longer. All the while she was thinking of Summers, who had vanished with the raft.

Morton was shouting again. She tried to catch the words over the din: "...for shore," was all she made out.

She looked and saw that the river had carried them a considerable distance down the rapids. They were past the area where the cliffs cut straight downward into the water, and now she could make out a sandy shoreline at the river's edge.

She was no longer sure that she had the strength to swim so far. It looked horribly distant. She tried to shake her head, but just then Morton let go of the log and it spun round violently, dragging her under the water.

This time she might really have drowned, but somehow Morton got to her. She felt his strong arm about her, under her arms, holding her up.

"I—I can't," she managed to gasp, but he either did not hear her or chose to ignore her.

"Swim," he said, giving her a shove.

She swam, helped along by Morton. Her heart pounded and it was difficult to get her breath. She felt frightfully weak. The bank looked so far away, and all the while the water beat in her face.

Her arms were leaden; she could scarcely lift them over the water. She was done for.

She could feel herself being pulled along by the current. It was so much easier to drift, little caring now, too exhausted for fear.

Morton was dragging her, stumbling and falling every step or two. It took her a moment to comprehend. He was walking on the bottom, or crawling at least, trying to drag the two of them ashore. She tried to help, putting her feet down and feeling sand beneath them.

They floundered on, Morton doing most of the work, she scrambling along the sand as well as she could. There was the bank itself, wet sand at which she clawed with her hands. At last they scrambled out, free of the water's pull. She sank into a clump of grass, so weak she could not move at all. For a brief time she sank into a stupor barely removed from unconsciousness. She had but a dim awareness some time later, it might have been minutes or hours, of Morton stirring, getting shakily to his feet.

Morton. Morton who had saved her, but not Summers.

That thought brought her awake. Summers was gone, lost in the river. She opened her eyes, staring for a moment at the damp sand. Finally she struggled to get to her knees.

"Summers?" she asked, though she knew the answer already.

Morton was kneeling by the water a few yards downstream. She saw that one of their packs had been washed ashore, some of the contents spilling on the bank. He was examining things now, laying aside what could be dried out and salvaged, tossing the rest back into the river.

"He's dead," Morton said without looking at her. "I saw him washed downstream. One of the logs had cracked his head open, and his foot had gotten tangled in some of the ropes. You can forget about him."

She got shakily to her feet and staggered to the river's edge, staring downstream, but there was nothing to be seen, only the red-brown water, rushing to disappear down the canyon and around the next bend.

Summers was gone. It was like the wound of an arrow through her heart, a high, piercing pain that shot through her all at once, leaving a great open ache behind.

She was left with Morton. As if reading her thoughts, he turned to stare at her then. For a long moment she met his gaze, trying to look unafraid. He outlasted her. She turned away finally and began to walk along the bank, searching as he had done for anything that might have been washed ashore.

Beneath the rapids the canyon opened into a wide, almost tropical valley. Here the water grew calmer, and here too they found several of the logs that had made up their raft, along with the main pack of their provisions, wet but most still usable. The dried horsemeat had gotten soaked and had to be dried again before it spoiled, but their salt and flour, wrapped in packets of oilskin, had come through safely. Summers had taken the precaution of wrapping their guns in oilskin as well, and these too had been washed ashore, so that they were neither without food nor without weapon.

Nonetheless, the incident could be called nothing less than disastrous. A great many of their provisions, already getting perilously low, had been lost. The raft was gone, and they had many more miles of canyon river to navigate. They were without horses, only vaguely aware of where they were, with only the sketchiest idea of where California lay to their west.

Worst of all, Summers was gone, the one man familiar with the west, the one she had depended on to get her to California. The one, too, she disliked reminding herself, who had stood protectively between herself and Morton.

By evening they had set up a crude camp and were able to have a meal of flour cakes and muddy-tasting coffee made with river water. Neither had spoken much, absorbed in their own private thoughts, and both were still exhausted from their ordeal.

They had lost much of their bedding, and even in the warm climate of the canyon nights were cool. She took one of the blankets and carried it to the far side of the fire from where Morton sat, spreading it on the ground for a bed. Morton, however, got up and came around to her.

"Not enough blankets for two beds," he said. "You'll sleep over here with me."

"I'll be all right," she said, trying to sound more unconcerned than she felt.

"Well now, I say you won't be," he said stubbornly. "I say you sleep over here with me."

She glanced past him. He had oiled the guns lest they rust from the dampness. They were sitting out on a rock near the fire. She tried to calculate how quickly she could get to them.

"Mister Morton," she said, getting to her feet, "I realize I am indebted to you for saving my life and I assure you, when we get to California, I will make every attempt to repay you, but..."

"You repay me here," he said. "Like you been repaying him. It's my turn now."

He put out a hand for her. She tried to dodge it, making a dash for the guns, but for all his size Morton could move quickly. In an instant she was in his arms.

"Let me go!" she cried, struggling against him. He held her arms pinned at her sides. She tried to kick him, but lost her footing on the loose sand and fell against him.

"I listened to you," he said, breathing heavily as he tried to find her mouth with his, "all them nights, listening to the two of you, thumping and moaning, and I thought, all right, I'm going to get my turn, some of these days, old Summers is going to make a mistake, getting all bright eyed over a woman like that, makes a man careless. Just you be patient, I told myself, you'll get her 'fore it's over. And I have."

She twisted her head to and fro, trying to avoid his kiss, but at last he buried her mouth under his, his breath foul, his beard coarse and scratching against her tender skin.

She fought him, but her puny efforts were as nothing to the powerful trapper. He threw her to the ground with such violence that she was stunned for a moment. Before she could recover, he was upon her, pawing at her clothes, forcing her knees apart.

He bit at her throat. She sank her teeth into his ear, trying to bite it off. He gave a yelp of pain, and lifting himself over her, struck her across the face with the back of his hand, so hard that it gave her a nosebleed.

"Bitch!" he snarled, yanking his trousers down and falling upon her. Dazed and helpless, she felt a shockwave of pain as he entered her brutally.

She lay sickened and bruised, her thighs still sticky with his spending. She could not bear to look at him, at the thick hairy body, at the fleshy mouth with the missing teeth and the unkempt beard.

Morton grabbed one of her breasts in a huge paw of a hand, squeezing until she whimpered from the pain. "You thinking I ain't as nice as your mountain man, with his sweet talking and his fancy dancing, ain't that right?"

She turned her face then to look up at him, revulsion rising within her as she did so. "What a loathsome animal you are," she said flatly.

For a moment he glowered down at her. Then, to her surprise, he laughed softly. "Loathsome," he said, repeating the word as if feeling it out. "Loathsome? And an animal to boot." He laughed again, then his smile faded. "Well, I suppose I am, but you listen to me just the same, and you listen good. Summers is gone, dead. They ain't nobody but you and me in this goddamn canyon that he led us into. Now I'm going to try to get us out of here if I can, but I ain't going to have you shooting me in the back, and I ain't going to have you giving me no trouble while I'm doing it. You are going to do what I say, and you're going to give me what I want, when I want it, or I am going to leave you sitting on your pretty pink ass all by yourself here, till the Indians find you or the goddamn coyotes eat the tits off your corpse. It's all the same to me. Are you listening to me?"

"I despise you," she said, her voice dripping venom. She hated him all the more because she knew the truth of what he was saying. Without him she would perish. He was her only hope now of reaching California alive. And she was only too painfully aware of the price she must pay.

"Yeah, I know," he said, grinning unconcernedly. "And I'm loathsome on top of it. All the same, you mind what I say and we'll get along well enough, and I just might get us out of here with our skins on."

He got up and, without bothering to find a discreet spot or to conceal himself, relieved himself on the ground. She turned away in disgust.

He brought the rest of the bedding and lay down beside her, curling his body against hers, burying his face in her hair. She lay numb and exhausted, sure she would be unable to sleep as they were, but fatigue had its way, and she was asleep before he was.

14

She was surprised by the intensity with which she missed Summers. It was not only that she was now at the mercy of Morton, though that certainly was a part of it; but she missed the man himself, not merely his protection.

As she hiked along the canyon river with Morton, she came to realize that she had loved Summers without ever having known it. She could not think when it had happened, for it had been subtle, a process of growing together. Now he was gone. She watched the river eagerly, looking for any sign of him. Occasionally they found some piece of gear, or a scrap of their raft, washed ashore well downriver; but of Summers' body they saw nothing.

At night Morton invariably assaulted her. She could think of no more fitting term for the forced and violent use he made of her body. She had learned not to resist him, but neither did she participate, merely lying passively beneath him until he had relieved himself.

"Damned cold, ain't you," he grumbled, plainly dissatisfied with her performance and unable to improve upon it.

It was hard not to compare this brutish act with what she had known with her former lover. She regretted now the frictions and ethics that had kept them apart for so long; she would rather have lain with him a hundred nights, a thousand, than the few she had known.

Summers, though, was gone, as Morton was fond of pointing out. They were the living, faced with the task of remaining so. However she felt about his nightly assault on her, Morton was competent at survival. She found herself torn between despising him at night and being grateful for him by day. With him, her situation was precarious; without him, it would be hopeless. She did not, therefore, attempt to shoot him, as he had warned, or to run away from him when she had the opportunities. Where, after all, could she run?

Daily they marched westward along the river. When they reached another of those stretches where the canyon walls came straight down to the water and walking was impossible, it was Morton who insisted they swim.

"We'll hold on to a log," he said. "Let the river take us past this."

"But we might drown," Claire argued.

"We might, but we didn't before, not in this river's worst rapids."

In the end she had no choice but to enter the water with him, clinging anxiously to a driftwood log while the water, whose dangers had been all too forcibly impressed upon her, carried them swiftly along.

In this way—walking when they could, swimming when they must—they traveled for a week through Summers' great canyon, until at last the walls began to shrink and the valley to widen. Finally they emerged into a great, broad plain, its horizon marked by low, rock-carved mountains.

"It's a desert," Morton said, staring westward toward the end of a day. The river, having carried them generally westward through the canyon, here turned sharply south. They had discussed this and decided jointly that their best hope lay in pressing toward the west where, from all that they had heard, lay the Mexican province of California.

Now, staring with him at the vast, barren expanse before them, Claire wondered once again if they had made the right decision. She remembered Summers' remarks on the great desert lying ahead of them. A desert that would make hell seem like paradise. How far did it reach? A day's march? Two, three days? It looked endless, unconquerable. Though Morton seemed unfazed by the hardships they had endured, she was already exhausted. For weeks they had toiled onward with only brief pauses for rest. Even rested, she would have flinched to contemplate crossing the desert before them.

At first the weather was mild, for it was winter and they were in the high desert. As they descended onto the desert floor the temperatures rose steadily. Even in winter the temperatures rose into the nineties at midday. They had rationed their water and food when they set out, but as the days passed and there was no end to the desert, they tightened their belts and reduced their rations still more, so that by the end of a week they were reduced to a mere mouthful of water twice a day, and two portions of dried meat, each portion weighing an ounce or so.

The desert went on. They followed a course at an angle southward from the route of the sun. Before them lay another mountain range, not the high, snow-covered peaks they had left behind, but low and grim looking and bare of any vegetation. At first they had thought these the foothills of a taller range, and though there was always the threat of snow and more cold weather, the thought of mountain meadows, green grass, and clear cold water had given them the impetus to push on as their physical reserves dwindled.

But when after a week of desert travel they at last crested one of the low hills, their hearts sank, for beyond they could see nothing but the desert, reaching far out of sight to the distant horizon.

"Must be a hundred miles, maybe more," Morton said grimly, staring ahead. He did not say what both knew. Even at their present parsimonious rate of consumption, food and water would be gone before they had crossed even a quarter of that distance.

Before starting out, they had lightened their packs of everything they had regarded as nonessential. Now it was time to lighten them even further. Ruthlessly they cast aside all but the barest essentials for survival.

Though time had now become their chief enemy, they spent the rest of that day camped on the mountain in the welcome shade of a great boulder. They planned to start out at night when the air was cooler, and they were less likely to sweat away their bodies' precious reserves of fluid.

With sundown they set out again; but travel by night had its drawbacks too. Nights were cool, which meant that their bodies were working harder to stay warm; the animals of the desert also prowled at night, so that they risked encounters with rattlers and fierce bobcats.

There was one thing for which Claire could be thankful. Since they had started out into the desert, Morton had foregone his nightly rituals, not out of concern for her, but rather for the sake of conserving his own energy. By this time even the rugged trapper was beginning to show the effects of a week in the desert. As for Claire, her clothes now hung loosely upon her, and her hair, bleached almost white by the sun, hung tangled and dirty to her shoulders. Her boots were worn nearly through, so that the sharp stones of the desert cut her feet as she walked. Her lips, chapped by the hot dry air, were cracked and bleeding in several places. No one seeing her now would have recognized the elegant and frail-looking English lady who had set out scarcely more than a year ago from London. Gaunt and parched as she was in her filthy and tattered dress of elkhide, she looked every bit as much a creature of the wilderness as the man trekking beside her.

They dared not stop for more than brief rests, pausing only in the worst heat of the day. They advanced into the desert, nearly out of provisions.

It was during this time that she came closest to admiring the man who was both her captor and her protector. Whatever private assessment Morton might have made of their predicament, outwardly he clung to a stubborn optimism that, if it did nothing to solve the problems facing them, at least kept her from despair. Perhaps they could survive now as they had survived the mountains. If they found water; if they found food; if there was an end to the desert soon.

But they did not find an end to the desert soon. It stretched on before them, mile after endless mile. The sun beat down upon them from above and reflected blindingly back from the desert floor.

Glancing upward, Claire was startled to see a line of hikers stumbling across the sand in single file before her. She blinked, realizing that each of them was the same, a duplicate of herself.

The mirage vanished even as she stared at it, but the hallucinations began to appear after that with frightening regularity. Once it might be Morton appearing in the distance ahead, or a cool, serene lake shimmering in the sunlight.

She stumbled and fell and would have been content to remain where she was, but Morton came to her and literally dragged her to her feet.

"Got to be water here somewhere," he muttered, half-carrying half-pulling her across the desert.

Somewhat to their south they could see another line of low mountains and on these Morton was certain he could distinguish some green. Green plants meant water and perhaps some food, so they veered in that direction, stumbling doggedly on.

Hope turned to despair, however, for when they reached the low rocky hills the green turned out to be greasewood, whose roots were able to find streams buried far beneath the earth's surface, too deep to be of use to them.

Their strength failing rapidly, they climbed feebly to the crest of the hill and looked westward—to see, after a second week of desert hardships, the unbroken desert still sprawling toward the distant horizon.

They were out of water now and had no more than a spoonful of dried meat between them. Claire, thinking of Summers, could almost envy him his watery death in the river.

They took what shade they could beneath the greasewood trees, waiting once again for the cool of the evening. For herself, Claire might have given up at this point, but Morton, his determination apparently unquenchable, would not hear of quitting. He gave her the larger share of what little food was left and insisted that she carry a small, smooth stone in her mouth.

"Keeps it from getting so dry," he explained, popping one into his own mouth as well.

Here began the most tortuous stretch of their entire journey. They abandoned their packs altogether. Claire fastened the pouch containing her money to her belt and took the revolver and its bullets. Morton carried the rifle and their empty canteens, still hoping that somewhere within reach was water.

Once more they set off across the desolate sands. Claire's mind began to wander periodically. She imagined herself back in London, at her aunt's or riding on the grounds at Everly Hall. She thought of Peter, long since dead, no doubt. And Summers: his death lay at her door as well. His ghost had no need to rail at her, she thought grimly, for surely she was to be punished. She would pay for his life with her own.

Still she plodded on, stumbling and falling and getting to her feet again, only to stumble a few yards farther on. She lost track of time. They walked and paused for rest, and walked some more. The sun rose, reaching to its burning heights, and fell, only to rise again. She was sleeping, thinking she was dead, and then somehow she was staggering onward, Morton's arm about her to support her.

It was when Morton himself dropped to his knees in the sand that she truly thought the end had been reached. She knew that it was his strength that had carried her onward for at least a day, perhaps even two or three. She could no longer lift her feet from the sand, but only managed to drag them over the surface. She was nearly blind from the sun's incessant glare, and her tongue was so swollen with thirst that she could form words only with great difficulty.

Released from Morton's supporting arm, she sank limp and immobile upon the sand. Above, the sky was an unvarying sheet of blue stone, unmarked by cloud or wing of bird.

"Pigs," Morton said beside her.

The word made no sense to her and she did not attempt a reply.

After a moment or two he said it again. "Pigs," he said. "There's been pigs here."

Thinking he had at last sacrificed his

own sanity to the sun, she turned her head to stare at him. To her surprise, to her fear even, he was grinning, his eyes gleaming with a feverish light.

"Look." He put an arm about her again and dragged her to a sitting position, pointing to the ground just before them. The sand, crusted hard on the surface, had been broken by a trail of prints leading off across a hillock beyond them. Here and there the trail was marked by animal droppings.

"I don't know a damn thing about the desert," Morton said. "But I was a boy on a farm in Kentucky, and I know pig shit when I see it. Get up, girl."

"I—I can't," she murmured, too weak and too tired to make the effort to stand.

He shook her, trying to penetrate her apathy. "Pigs," he repeated yet again. "Pigs mean food, and water, somewhere around here. Ain't no pig can live without water. Get up, damn you."

He literally dragged her to her feet. She tried to stand, but her legs simply would not support her. Morton stared at her in frustration and disgust. She knew what he must be thinking, that his best course lay in abandoning her to the desert and pushing on alone.

"Goddamn it all," he muttered. He bent and, embracing her about the hips, lifted her clumsily, throwing her over his shoulder as if she were a bag of flour. In this manner he proceeded to carry her over the sand.

Claire, her head jouncing roughly off his

broad back, stared downward at the tracks they were following. Slowly the sense of what he had been saying began to penetrate her dazed condition. She beat feebly against him.

"Wait. I'll try again," she cried in a hoarse voice.

He stumbled and lowered her roughly to the ground. Ordinarily he could have carried her for miles without strain. Now the labored state of his breathing was pitiful evidence of his own weakened condition.

For the first time since they had set out alone, she gave him a grateful smile. "Thank you," she said. "I—I think I can go on."

He did not reply. After a moment to regain his breath, he took hold of her arm to help her along, and together they set out again.

They crossed the hillock and before them lay a wash, a creek bed for the run-off when the infrequent rains soaked the desert, a dry, flat ravine elsewise. Now it was dry, but even as they stared down at it, something grunted off to their right. They saw Morton's pigs— desert peccaries, a half-dozen or more of them. The peccaries had led them to a waterhole, a muddied remnant of the last deluge that had washed through this ravine days, perhaps weeks, before.

Claire would have stumbled forward at once, but Morton held her back. She watched as he loaded his rifle and, lifting it to his shoulder, took careful aim. He fired, and one of the wild pigs leaped into the air, giving a final shriek before it died. The others scattered in every direction.

Claire and Morton ran forward, if running it could be called. They clung weakly to one another, each barely able to put one foot before the other.

She almost made it. One foot slipped on a pebble. She tried to hold on to Morton but it was no good. She went down, not just to her knees, but flat on her face.

Morton went on. She saw him fall face forward in the brackish water and she closed her eyes, trying to summon the strength to crawl on.

How long she lay there she wasn't sure. To her surprise, Morton came back. He slipped an arm under hers and tugged her up. She felt something cool and wet brush her lips.

"Here," he said. He had soaked the tail of his shirt in the water and brought it back to her. He wrung it out now, the precious drops of fluid falling upon her parched and swollen tongue.

"Easy," he said. "Got to go slow at first."

Too weak himself to lift her again, he began to scoot awkwardly across the desert floor on his bottom, tugging her along with him. She helped as best she could, crawling and scooting with him, and finally she felt her hand sink into thick, oozing mud. Another yard, another after that, and her burning skin sank beneath the surface of the water.

She would have drunk the pool dry, but

Morton jerked her head back after only a taste. "Slow," he warned again. "It'll kill you otherwise."

They sat like two scarecrows, staring at one another, each marveling that they were still alive. A desert wind rose suddenly, sweeping through the ravine. In the distance the wild pigs, apparently still frightened by the shooting of one of their number, squealed afresh.

Something rattled on a stone nearby. "Jesus," Morton swore, his eyes going wide. She looked over her shoulder and saw an Indian arrow lying a few feet from them.

They both looked in the direction from which the arrow had come. A dozen savage faces stared at them over the crest of a sand hill. One of the Indians leaped up and loosed another arrow from his bow. It stuck in the earth a few inches from Claire's foot, its shaft quivering angrily.

"Bad ones," Morton said. He brought the rifle up and fired. The Indian yelped and fell backward, but at once a shower of arrows began to rain about them.

"We're ducks in a pond here," Morton said, crawling backward away from the arrows. "We got to get up there, among them rocks."

He nodded in the direction of a pile of boulders on the opposite side of the wash. Claire stared at the rocks and then at him.

The next arrow nicked her arm, drawing blood. It gave her the impetus she needed.

Frantically sucking air into her lungs, she got to her knees. The rocks glittered in the blinding sun some twenty yards away. It looked like a thousand miles just now. Morton was mad, they could never reach that. She got to her feet. Behind her Morton was firing at the Indians, trying to give her cover, but the rocks were too far. Even without the Indians, if she had been able to husband what was left of her strength and crawl on her hands and knees, she wasn't sure she could have made it. Now it seemed impossible, trying in this pathetic desperation to run, scramble, jump, anything to propel herself along, scraping her hands on the hard rough walls of the wash, tearing the flesh. The fire of the hot desert sun was nothing to the fire blazing in her left side. She almost thought it would be easier to die than to go on like this, foot after foot, inch after inch, racing toward those distant rocks that seemed almost to recede as she ran.

Morton was running after her now, and behind them she heard a horrible shouting. She did not need to look back to know that the Indians were after them, pouring in a yelping wave over the banks of the wash.

She ran now, ran as she had never run before, and in her fear-crazed mind she thought she might already have died. It felt as if her feet weren't even touching the ground.

And still the rocks seemed far, far away.

An arrow clattered among the stones at her feet. Behind them the shouting was louder, nearer. She could hear Morton's breath rattling in his chest as he too struggled for some last measure of strength.

Ten yards now to go. She had reached the top of another hill, but her legs gave out and she pitched forward, knowing that she was falling not only down a hill, but out of life as well, plunging into death. She rolled and tumbled, striking her head on a rock, filling her mouth and her eyes with sand, until finally she rolled to a stop at the bottom of the hill. It seemed that the screaming was everywhere now, before her as well as behind.

She lay stunned and helpless, the last reserves of her strength gone. Something moved near her head and she forced her eyes open.

A pair of moccasin-clad feet. She strained her eyes upward and saw brown legs and an Indian loincloth.

Too weary now even to care, she closed her eyes again and let her face sink into the burning sand.

15

Strong arms lifted her, and she was being carried, so swiftly and lightly that she was almost convinced she was dreaming. She was dimly aware of the shouting and yelping of the Indians, growing gradually dimmer until it had faded with her consciousness.

The air, when she woke, was stale and smoky. She opened her eyes and stared upward at a leafy ceiling with an opening through which smoke was escaping. She was in a tipilike structure, but whereas those Summers had bartered from the Pawnee had been made of long poles covered with hides, the poles here seemed covered with nothing but leaves and shrubs.

Still, it provided shelter. She could see through the opening that the sky above was dark, and she had reason to know that desert nights could be cool.

She turned her head to the side. Three bare-breasted Indian women sat about the central fire. One of them saw that she had awakened and barked something in a guttural tongue to the others, the youngest of whom jumped up and ran from the hut.

The other two approached the bed. They offered her food and water from bowls that appeared to be woven baskets, drawing the vessels back when she would have taken too much. All the while they stared at her in unabashed curiosity.

"Am I a prisoner?" she asked when she had gotten a little of the food down.

The two women looked at one another and giggled, exchanging rapid phrases in a tongue unfamiliar to her, though once or twice she almost thought she recognized a Spanish word.

The third woman suddenly reappeared, followed by an Indian man. He was so tall that his head, adorned with a single feather attached to a band, threatened to brush the walls of the tipi.

He bent his head to come stand over her, studying her with open, intelligent eyes. "You are Spanish?" he asked, to her surprise speaking in that tongue.

"No, English," she replied. When that elicited no response she said, "I come from America."

Though he spoke English too, albeit halt-ingly, her attempts to explain where they had come from seemed to confuse him. He seemed to have difficulty grasping the fact that they had actually come across the great desert in which he had found them.

She learned from him that Morton was alive, but when she asked the same question she had asked of the women, "Are we prisoners?" the Indian seemed surprised.

"You are our guests," he said simply, and with that left her to the women.

For three days the women tended her in the tipi while she gradually regained her strength. The tall man with the single feather, whose name, appropriately enough, was Lone Feather, came each day to see how she was getting on.

Only one of the women, the youngest who had first gone to fetch Lone Feather, spoke any English, and that clumsily at best, but from her and from Lone Feather's brief visits, Claire gradually learned something of what had happened.

These Indians were not the same as the ones who had attacked Morton and her by the waterhole. They had, indeed, driven those others off. Having rescued the travelers, they brought them back to their camp in the nearby hills.

Exactly why they had been rescued was a bit more difficult for Claire to grasp, but as she talked with the Indians she began to understand that this desert was not their customary home.

"We are of the Malibu," Lone Feather said with noticeable pride in his voice, "on the edge of the great sea."

The great sea, Claire thought. That must mean the ocean! "Then we are in California?"

He seemed surprised that she knew the word. "California, yes," he said.

Her initial excitement paled somewhat when she learned that they were in fact many days' travel—a week at least—from the California coast. Whether this desert was actually a part of the province of California, Lone Feather could not say.

Wanderers in what was for them a foreign land, these people had had occasion themselves to quarrel with the fierce Indians who lived in this area. When they had heard a shot and, coming to investigate, had seen two whites in danger of being killed by the locals, the Indians had reacted instinctively to save them.

Though her nurses treated her kindly, Claire began to see that they were impatient for her to be up and about. This was because they feared further trouble from the local savages. Knowing this, and none too eager to wear out her welcome, Claire exerted herself to a maximum effort, so that at the end of three days she was able to stand and walk about for a short period, and on the fourth day was ready to venture out of the tipi.

What she found was a smaller camp than she had imagined. There were only half a dozen ragtag tipis such as the one in which she had convalesced, cooking fires, and here and there a makeshift bed on the desert rocks. It was vastly more primitive and squalid than the camp of the Pawnees had been, and she might have been inclined to regard these people as contemptuous had not Lone Feather explained to her with an unmistakably defensive tone that this camp was only makeshift. They had traveled long and far from their home, and were now nearing the end of their journey, homeward bound.

Morton, she found, had been up and about a day sooner than she. She found him seated before one of the cookfires, engaged in conversation with another brave and hungrily devouring the dried meat that was the staple of the tribe.

"Nice piece of luck, ain't it?" He greeted her. "Just when it looks like we're about to hand over our scalps to the Indians, and who rescues us but some more Indians, and from California at that."

"I want to thank you," she said. "It seems I once again owe my life to you."

It had been so long since he had approached her sexually that her former loathing of him had receded somewhat. She had tended to be forgiving of his faults and appreciative of his merits, so that, though she would hardly have thought of him with love or even abiding affection, there was a closeness impossible to explain to others that was not unlike a deep friendship.

It was with genuine dismay, therefore,

211

that she saw in the look he gave her the almost forgotten gleam of sexual arousal. She knew at once that he would expect her to pay for whatever he had done for her.

"I've talked to that head Indian, Lone Feather," he said, running his tongue over his fleshy lips. "He says we can have a tipi to ourselves the rest of the time we're here. Says they'll be moving out pretty soon now."

"No, please," she said, shaking her head, "I beg you I am grateful to you, but..."

He did not wait to hear her objections. He strode off to speak to Lone Feather about something.

That night the women left the tipi, leaving her alone. Though water was in short supply, they had brought her a vessel of it earlier, so that she had been able to take at least a token bath and wash some of the desert dirt from her hair. She wished for a mirror and told herself ruefully it was probably just as well that she was without one, for she could well imagine what she must look like. Her lips had begun to heal, but were still broken and occasionally bled. Her hair was now nearly waist length, matted and tangled.

She thought of the men who had plotted and flirted and, in one instance at least, attempted murder, for the sake of marrying her, and laughed to herself. Which of them, seeing her now, would burn with desire? Perhaps, she thought bitterly, Morton was the best she could hope for now.

As if in reply there was a sound outside, and Lone Feather stepped into the tipi. Oddly, he did not speak, but only stood for a long moment staring at her. She had been attempting to comb out her hair with brush of bound twigs the women had given her, and she stood with it in her hand, raised to her brow. Her hair, newly rinsed, gleamed wet and golden in the firelight.

She waited for the Indian to speak, but he only regarded her for a long moment as if weighing her in some invisible scales. Then, still without a word, he turned and left the tipi.

Morton came later. At first she pleaded with him, and even briefly tried to resist him, but the outcome was inevitable and at last, weary and dispirited, she submitted passively, grateful that his lengthy abstinence made the ordeal brief.

It was not until he was dressing the following morning that Morton said, "I'll be leaving today."

Claire, who had been lying with her back to him, sat up, forgetting for the moment that she was nude. "But I thought we would leave with the Indians."

"The Indians are heading back to their village, someplace called the Malibu. But that

Lone Feather tells me there's a white man's town, some place he calls Los Awn-hell-ace, off to the south a little ways. That's where I'm headed. Don't figure on living in no Indian village, not any longer than I have to."

"But how will we live?" she asked. "We've no food, no supplies, nothing."

He gave her a peculiar look. "The Indians have given me everything I need," he said. "And I got a petty good map from what he told me."

Irritated, she got out of bed and began dressing. "Well, you might have told me a little sooner," she said. "I could have been ready to go by now."

"You *ain't* going," he said.

She paused in the act of lacing her skirt closed and stared at him uncomprehendingly. "I don't understand."

"I said I was going to leave today. You'll be staying here."

"But I can't stay here, alone, with these Indians," she protested.

"I sold you," he said, avoiding her gaze. "To that Lone Feather. That's how he come to give me the supplies and stuff."

She took a step backward as if he had struck her a blow. "You sold me? My God, you can't mean it." She gasped, hardly able to believe her ears. "You can't be serious."

He turned from her, starting toward the opening of the tipi. "I got to go," he said. "Want to get an early start, 'fore it gets too hot out there."

A rage fanned by fear blazed up within her. She ran across the tipi and began to beat upon his back with her fists.

"You're mad!" she screamed, beginning to cry. "You can't sell me as if I were a chattel. I'm an Englishwoman, this is the nineteenth century, do you hear me, you can't do this, it's monstrous!"

For a moment he suffered her pounding. Then in a swift, cruel movement, he whirled about and struck her a blow that sent her stumbling backward and crashing to the ground. She lay helpless, beginning to sob uncontrollably. To be sold like a common slave to a savage Indian. It was inhuman.

"It's for your own good as well as mine," Morton said in a harsh, angry voice. "Them Indians know where they're going and how to get there. They know where to feed and water, and what to watch out for. At least with them you know you're safe. There's no telling what I'm going to run into, and anyway, by myself I can travel a lot faster and easier. It'd take me twice as long with you tagging along, and we might not get there with our skins on."

"I won't let you do this!" she screamed through her tears. "I won't stay, I'll leave, I'll follow you."

He gave a derisive snort. "Suit yourself. If you think you can keep up," he said. "But you'll be on your own. No food, no water, no supplies, like you said. You won't last a day."

"You're—you're . . ."

"Loathsome, that's what I am," he said. "And you're a cold-assed bitch, and I'll be glad to be rid of you, if you want the truth."

With that he went out, leaving her sobbing on the ground. She felt defeated and helpless. To have come so far, endured so much, only to become the slave of an Indian. If only Summers were alive; if only she had stayed in London, if only...but what use was that, she was here, within reach of California at last, only to have her dreams turned to disaster.

She cried until the tears would come no more; but tears would not change the facts. She had been sold. Until she could get to where there were white men, she was the property of an Indian.

Morton came back a short time later. At first she thought perhaps he had had a change of heart, but his surly manner was not likely to inspire much confidence.

"Something's come up," he said, pausing just inside the door. She did not reply, only looked back at him sullenly. After a moment he went on: "The Indian says they've found something back in the hills a ways. Near as I can tell, it sounds like a mineshaft."

"Why are you telling me this?" she asked.

"He says it's a white man's place. So, it ain't likely, but I thought there might be a chance—well, you was looking for your husband, wasn't you? And he came this way, didn't he? There's always a chance. Anyway, he says he'll take us there, if you want to have a look see. Might be you'd recognize something of his."

"I thought you were leaving."

"I can leave tomorrow just as easy," he said, adding quickly, "Don't get no ideas, though, this don't change nothing. I'm still leaving, and you're still staying. But a mineshaft now, say there was gold. Well, it wouldn't hurt to know where it was. And you just might find out what you came looking for."

It was hard now to remember that she had set out on this quest searching for Peter. So much had happened. California itself had become their goal, and finally it had been simply the will to survive that had kept them traveling westward. Was it possible that now, after so long a time, they might have found Peter's trail? Perhaps even the end of the trail?

She got up slowly from the ground, brushing the dirt from her clothing. "When can we go?" she asked, not looking directly at him anymore. She could no longer bear the sight of him, or the memory of what had passed between them.

"Now," Morton said. "Soon's you're ready."

She finished tying her shirt. "I'm ready," she said.

When she would have gone past him out the opening of the tipi, he caught her arm and held her. For a brief space in time his eyes caught hers, and she saw something in them that she had not seen before.

"If you'd been nicer to me—" he started to say.

She spit in his face. His grip tightened cruelly on her arm, and she thought he meant to strike her again, but with a violent gesture he flung her arm away and pushed out of the tipi ahead of her.

16

It was nearly a two-hour hike into the foothills. Lone Feather and one of the braves led the way with Claire following and Morton bringing up the rear. They walked in silence, speaking only when necessary.

The mine, when they came to it, appeared to be a natural cave, the opening of which someone had widened and shored up with half-rotted timbers. It was not very prepossessing, but the presence of a broken and rusted pick outside seemed to confirm Lone Feather's assessment that it was a "white man's place."

It was also none too safe looking. Standing in the opening required that everyone except Claire bend down. One could see that some of the timbers used to support the roof of the cave had already collapsed under the weight of the mountain. There were animal droppings just inside the entrance, but these were old, and there was no evidence of recent habitation, either by man or beast.

"It's hard to imagine Peter digging a mine out here," Claire said doubtfully.

"He was looking for gold, wasn't he?" Morton replied, advancing into the cave. "Maybe he learned something from the Indians. If anybody'd know where the gold was, they'd be the ones."

"They didn't seem particularly eager to share their knowledge," she said.

"He charmed the Pawnee, didn't he, and they're a lot sharper than these bastards. Excuse me, I mean the ones that like to lifted our scalps." This last was for Lone Feather's benefit, though no change of expression had indicated that he might have taken offense. "Anyways, there's no telling what might be back inside, maybe the miner himself for all we know. Me, I'm going in. Anybody coming along?"

The Indians, probably out of curiosity, decided to venture within as well, and Claire, reluctant to be left alone on the outside, swallowed her misgivings.

They wound some dried grasses about a stick to make a torch, which Morton carried in the lead. The cave led at an angle downward into the hillside. Probably it had been little more than a fissure, which the unknown miner had widened and shored up with still more of the rotting timbers. Claire found herself wondering how far afield he must have wandered to have found so much wood, for even the greasewood was sparse here. That, no doubt, explained the patchy job that he had done, and the fact that the floor was littered with rocks and debris that had fallen in from the walls and roof. They had only to bump a wall to bring down yet another shower of dirt and stones. Even the Indians had begun to look apprehensive, glancing over their shoulders toward the fading light in the opening.

They had gone thirty yards, perhaps forty, when the cave veered to the right and angled sharply downhill. Here they left behind the light altogether, depending upon the flickering torch to light their uncertain path. It penetrated the gloom poorly, making gargoyles of rocks and phantoms of every shadow.

They all but stumbled over the skeleton before they saw it, sprawled amidst a pile of debris. A cave-in had apparently caught the miner unaware, ending his search for treasure. Here too his mine ended. Beyond was a mere fissure, which he had been in the act of hacking wider with his pick.

Claire shuddered and looked away from the grisly sight. Animals, or time, had stripped the flesh from the bones but left the clothes, which hung in graceless folds over the skeleton. The fingers still curved about the pick's handle, and one hand had been lifted above his head, as if in a futile effort to ward off the falling debris.

"Pretty hard to know who it was," Morton said, stooping to examine the grim discovery more closely. "Don't recognize the clothes, do you?"

"No," Claire said, without taking another look. One glimpse had been quite enough. And still her questions remained unanswered, for Peter probably had changed wardrobes many times since leaving Virginia, just as she herself had.

"What's this?" Morton said, picking up a rock at the miner's feet. "Turquoise, ain't it?" He handed it to Claire.

She took it with reluctance. "I don't know," she said. "I've never seen one unpolished."

"Looks it to me." He chuckled and looked about, seeking another such nugget. "So that's what he was after, turquoise, not gold. Looks like he found it too, for all the good it did him."

"Or us, if the roof falls in on us the way it did for him," Claire said. "Let's get out of here." As if to punctuate her warning, a shower of dust and pebbles suddenly cascaded down upon them. Lone Feather's companion had already begun to back apprehensively the way they had come, and even Lone Feather's normally unruffled expression was slightly uneasy.

"Not so fast," Morton said, crawling

about to examine the walls of the cave. "If there is a fortune here, I want to know about it. Might make this whole trip worthwhile."

He laid the torch upon the ground. Its light sent their shadows dancing up and down the rocky walls. A fine shower of dust cascaded from the roof. A rock fell with a clatter.

She was not sure afterward. It may have been that one falling rock, making Morton start, that brought it all down. She was certain that Morton jumped back instinctively. Perhaps he had brought his hand down on a lizard, or maybe seen something in the rock that excited him.

He bumped the support holding up the roof timber. The wood, old and rotted, and no doubt weary of holding up a mountain of rock, snapped in an instant.

The fine shower of dust became a choking cloud in which larger rocks and clods of dirt began to fall.

"Christ Almighty," Morton swore. He looked, saw the roof timber begin to sag and, without pausing to think, leapt to stop it.

It was a mistake, in an instant too late to be reversed. He might have jumped free. Together they might have outrun the collapse, made the safety of the opening. As it was Morton himself, with his great broad shoulders and powerful arms and back, had taken the place of the fallen timber. It was upon him that the mountain of rock was now resting, as much of it as was not crashing down about them. There was little doubt that if he went, the cave went too.

His face, even with the strain etched upon it, showed that he too had realized his mistake. "Get out of here," he gasped.

Claire moved toward him, narrowly missing a falling rock. "Let us help," she said. "If we could get something under there—"

"Goddamn it all, lady, how long do you think I can hold this mountain up?" He looked at Lone Feather; the other brave had already fled. "Get her out of here."

She had a last glimpse of him, the veins and muscles in his arms and thick neck standing out in violent relief. Lone Feather snatched her arm and jerked her around. She let him drag her along the cave for a few yards.

"No!" she cried suddenly, forcing him to a halt.

It was too late though. With a great roar the roof where they had been standing a moment before came down. She was blinded by the dust, choking and coughing as it filled her lungs.

Lone Feather got her to the outside. By the time the cave-in ended, only the timbers at the opening remained to show that there had been a mine there at all. The rest had been filled in.

A turquoise tomb, she thought. With a sense of shock she realized she was still holding the nugget that Morton had handed her. She stared down at it, remembering the one she had seen in Virginia. It had sent Peter westward, seeking his fortune, and no doubt to his death. Morton had followed the same trail, to die in a hole in the side of a hill. She had hated him, and yet they had come together through the mountains and the snow, through the great canyon, and over the desert. He had been her last link with the civilized world.

With a rush of bitter resentment against the fate that had led them here, she hurled the stone into the dusty mouth of the cave.

She did not know at first why the Indians lingered at their camp. The water supply was dwindling, and Lone Feather himself had said the time was due for them to return to their village.

He came to her tipi that night. Though it was late, she had been too restless to sleep and had been pacing the cramped interior. He entered and without preamble attempted to embrace her. When she resisted he seemed surprised.

"He told me you were willing," he said.

"It was a lie," she said bluntly. "I had no idea."

His face remained as expressionless as usual. "I have never forced a woman," he said with such dignity that she understood that he

225

had never had to force one before. No doubt in his village, among his people, the women must regard him as a fine catch.

To her surprise, he left. She half-suspected he might return during the night and she slept restlessly, waking at every little noise, but she remained unmolested.

The following evening he brought her a gift, a long robe made of rabbit skins stitched together. She knew that he could not have found so many rabbits where they were, nor had them skinned and tanned in such a brief time. He must have gotten it from someone else in the camp, or perhaps it was his own. That it was of considerable value was beyond question. Though they were in the desert, it was winter, and their nights were genuinely cold. The robe was very welcome, and she thanked him profusely. He made no reply to this, but again left her to sleep undisturbed.

The following night he appeared again. This time he brought what proved to be a nugget of gold through which a hole had been bored and a leather string threaded.

"It was for my bride," he said, tying it about her throat. He took a strand of her hair in his fingers and held it to the nugget. "Yellow," he said, indicating the hair and the nugget together. "The same."

The third night he brought a platter made of an old piece of wood on which there was some freshly roasted meat—rabbit, she thought—and berries that he had found she couldn't guess where, along with a slab of bread that tasted nutty and sweet. By the standards of the camp it was a Lucullan feast, one surely fit for a queen.

This time she was prepared for his visit.

Over the objections of the women, she had insisted that they accompany her to the waterhole, where she had filled not one but three of the tightly woven baskets with water. They had been carried back to the tipi for her bath. The youngest of the women, grinning slyly, had brought her a little clay urn filled with a faintly perfumed oil. Claire rubbed this into the chapped skin of her lips and hands, as much for softening as for scent.

When Lone Feather came in, just after sunset as was his custom, she was waiting for him, standing off to the far side of the tipi. She was wearing the fur robe he had given her, the gold pendant, and nothing else.

She opened the robe, removing it slowly and bending to spread it over the ground as a bed for them.

He was less patient. After a frozen moment he flung the banquet he had brought onto the ground and crossed the tipi in two long strides to seize her roughly in his arms. He would have flung her to the ground as well, but she grasped his wrists in her hands and said gently but firmly, "No."

He looked startled and puzzled, but when she guided him to the ground to lie beside her on the fur robe, he came willingly, eagerly. Once again he grabbed for her in a brutish way, as Morton would have done, and again she stayed his hand. She showed him in as clear a way possible how to be gentle and coaxing, where and how to touch with hand and mouth, so that by the time he knelt over her she was ready for him.

It was necessary after all to pretend her pleasure, but she could see that the pretense pleased him. At least, for the first time since Summers' death, there was no pain in the act. In this manner she became the lover of an Indian prince and completed her journey to the fabled land of California.

PART II

The Children of Light

17

"Here they come!"

"The Coyotes are winning!"

"The Jackrabbits have fallen into the water!"

Claire laughed with the others crowding the ocean's shore. In the water three boats made of planks and darkened with some thick tarlike substance that made them waterproof struggled against the surf as they made their way toward the beach. The boats' crews, three competing teams of youths from the tribe, rowed valiantly, with the exception of the Jackrabbits, who had overturned their boat and were ignominiously pushing it to shore.

The Coyotes came in first, to a loud chorus of shouts and cheers, supporters of the losing teams joining in, as the competition had been a friendly one.

Gradually the tribe began to drift back from the beach toward their camp. Claire caught sight of a woman she knew. Recently widowed, the woman had singed the hair from her head as custom dictated and covered both the stubble and her face with the same pitch used to waterproof the boats. At first that practice, like many she had encountered since joining the tribe, had shocked and horrified Claire. In time she had grown used to much of the ritual.

Though their life was primitive, the tribe were not barbaric people. She had known far more cruelty at the hands of white men than she had witnessed since she had been here. There was some occasional friction with a neighboring tribe, the Chumash, but this rarely involved more than some shouting and fist shaking from opposing knolls, with one or two young firebrands tossing rocks back and forth. Probably the most savage event she had witnessed had been the initiation of the young men into full manhood. Much of this ceremony had been closed to her, as it was to all the women, but the entire tribe had watched while the young men were tied down upon the ground and their bodies rubbed with sweet honey. Great hordes of ants, attracted by the honey, quickly swarmed over their bodies while the tribe's shamans, or wise men, knelt beside the squirming youths and spoke to them in low voices.

"That's horrible!" she had cried, turning her face away to Lone Feather's embarrassment. She had insulted the tribe, he protested later. The rituals, he had explained, were more than a mere test of a youth's manhood. They were a means of impressing upon him the lessons of the tribe's history and culture. A young man's mind might wander from a dry lecture, but he was unlikely to forget the lore imparted to him during the time of his trial.

In other respects, though, they were a gentle and kindly people. Though the search for food occupied much of their time, they ate well on fresh fish from the ocean and small game, nuts, and berries foraged from the land.

The tribe had accepted her presence among them with a surprising lack of resentment. She found that she was less an object of curiosity here than she had been with the Pawnee. For one thing, these people were fair skinned, many of them lighter of complexion than she had been at the conclusion of her desert crossing. For another, many of the women bleached their hair with urine, giving it a reddish-yellow cast not so much darker than her own.

Her name was She-Who-Dares, and the Indians, particularly the youths, had made something of a minor legend of her crossing of the great desert beyond the mountains, a story she had to relate countless times over.

She knew that not more than a day or

two's travel to the southeast lay the Spanish settlement of Our Lady of the Angels. Morton had been intending to journey there when he had sold her to Lone Feather.

Closer still, just across the low mountains that fringed the ocean, was one of the Spanish missions, hated and feared by the Indians.

She was not, however graciously accepted, one of these people. She was an Englishwoman who had journeyed from an American colony in search of her husband. She reminded herself often that she must eventually make the journey to the pueblo, or at least to the mission. There she could not only be among her own people, but she could make inquiries regarding Peter. If he had managed to survive the journey from the States, there would surely be word of him in one or the other of these places. Settlements were hardly commonplace here, and the arrival of any stranger from the east would be well noted.

She supposed she could even make arrangements for her own return east by sailing ship, though exactly what she had to return for she couldn't say.

Yet the days had passed into weeks, the weeks into months, and still she made no move to contact either of the white outposts. For one thing, the rigors of the journey she had made had taken their toll upon her mentally as well as physically. The peaceful existence she shared with Lone Feather and his tribe had proven therapeutic. There were dangers here in the wilderness, but she lived sheltered from these by the strong and gentle man who was her adoring lover. Now there were other, more compelling reasons why she could not leave.

She entered the tipi she shared with Lone Feather. The interior was dark and still. Lone Feather was still with the tribes' elders in the temescal, the large communal building that dominated the camp. It was here the men met to make important decisions and sometimes, Claire suspected, simply to get away from their women. It served also as a sweathouse. Great fires were built until the building's interior was oppressively hot. When the braves were perspiring profusely, they would dash from within and plunge into the cold waters of the ocean. The practice was said to be health giving, though it sounded to Claire quite unattractive.

At the moment there was no smoke emerging from the top of the temescal. This was a meeting to decide some question that had come up, something requiring agreement among the tribe's leaders. Lone Feather was the son of the tribe's headman, or chief, and himself next in line for that position. That and his natural authority made him a man to whom the others frequently turned for guidance.

As a lover Lone Feather had proven both ardent and considerate. Though Claire did not love him, she was fond of him. There was much about him to admire, and though she would have preferred to dispense with their sexual relations, she understood well enough that it was for this he had purchased her and brought her with him to the California coast. Truth to tell, she had fared far worse at the hands of Morton, or even her own husband.

There was a movement outside. Lone Feather came into the tipi, grinning broadly as if he had just scored some triumph.

"Tomorrow you and I will go into the mountains," he announced.

"Why?" she asked. Since their arrival at this camp none of the tribe had ventured more than a short distance beyond its perimeters.

"Our tribe is old, far older than the Chumash," he said. "They came here from a great distance, long long ago. In the mountains is a shrine, placed there by our ancestors. It is the most sacred spot of all to our people, and it is known to no other. The elders have agreed that I may take you there."

"I'm very flattered, but what will I find there?" she asked.

He came to stand before her, reaching for the gold nugget he had given her, which she wore on its leather thong about her neck.

"This," he said, cradling the nugget in the palm of his hand.

"There," Lone Feather said, pointing. "The white man's fortune."

It was the first day of their journey, and Claire, remembering the gentle herds of cattle that dotted the English countryside, was unprepared for the sight that lay before her on the wide valley floor. It was a sea of cattle, each as fierce and untamed looking as any wild beast. There must have been thousands of them, seemingly unattended.

"Do they belong to no one?" she asked.

"From here," Lone Feather said, pointing in the direction of a peak perhaps several days' journey to the north, "to there, beyond where the eye sees," pointing southward, "was once the land of many tribes. Now it and all within it belong to one man."

"Is this a rancho?" Claire asked.

"It is a small one. There are greater ones."

It was almost more than one could comprehend. The land he had pointed out to her was as large as many an English county. What sort of land was this, where individual men lived greater than kings? Once she had scoffed at the tales of California wealth, but here, seeing for herself what a man might own, she was ready to believe any tale, however lavish. Here anything was possible, and a man was bounded only by his own imagination and his own weaknesses.

It was a journey of learning for her. They traveled generally eastward, toward a range of mountains that grew gradually larger as they neared. It was not until the third day that Lone Feather told her they were nearing one of the Spanish missions.

"Here we must go with caution, for there is more to fear here than from the lion or the snake," Lone Feather warned her.

For the better part of a day they had been traveling in relative silence. They dismounted and walked their horses, climbing a gently sloped hill that soon gave them a view of a cluster of adobe structures below.

"The mission," he said in a whisper tinged with awe and fear.

It looked peaceful and innocent. Smoke curled from a number of chimneys despite the warmth of the day. She saw that the buildings were enclosed within a high wall, and that the area between the buildings had been converted into a garden, with blooming plants and even a fountain. As they watched the bells over the chapel began to toll, great sonorous peals that rolled lazily over the valley floor. A trio of brown-robed friars passed from one of the structures to the chapel, following well-worn paths through the courtyard.

"Why do your people fear the missions so?" she asked.

Lone Feather's expression grew grim. "They come to the villages," he said, "with soldiers and guns. They take our people, and the Chumash, and the Gabrieleño and the Juaneño for converts to their god."

"But he is a good God," she said. "Your people can serve him with honor."

The look he gave her was one of withering scorn. "It is not their God our people serve. It is the brown-robed men and their greedy appetites," he said. "Look again, there, and there, and there."

She followed his pointing finger. Beyond the far wall of the mission were the fields where the food was grown. She squinted, peering into the distance at the acres of corn and other crops she couldn't identify. There were scores of workers in the fields, weeding, digging, planting, doing the hard work of feeding those who lived within the walls.

All about the mission, inside and out, could be seen the activity of daily toil. There must have been two hundred people at work, providing for the needs and comforts of the little mission colony.

"Why they're all Indians," she said, realizing at last the significance of what she saw.

"Our people are the children of light. We know ourselves from the earth we trod, from the waters in which we bathe, from the air and the high mountains with their silver crowns. All of nature reminds us of who we are.

"But then the mission men come. With their guns they bring the Indian to these places. They have our land, they have the Indian's corn, but they must have the people as well. The Indian is forced to kneel and pray to a strange new God. Our Gods are taken from us. No longer do we bathe, for water is precious and saved for the white man, who bathes seldom. No longer are our maidens pure, for the white man taints them. No longer is there time to rest, or to play, which is the soul's rest, for always there is the white man's work to be done. When we have the white man's diseases, we die. When some, longing for the life of their ancestors, longing for the free air and the song of the bird and the coyote and the waters, leave this accursed place, they follow with their guns, gathering herds of men as they gather their herds of cattle."

"You speak with the bitterness of knowledge," she said, moved by his angry words.

"It is how I speak their tongues." He nodded. "It is how I know their ways. Many times they have come, stealing our best young men and women. The one who was to be my bride is now the bride of many men there. This is how we came to find you in the desert. We were searching for a new place where we could move our people, somewhere beyond the reach of the missions. But our people could not live there. Wherever we went, it was the same. Either the land was hostile, or there were already tribes claiming the land as their own or there were more of the missions. There is no place left for our people. Soon there will be none left. Only those, the mission servants."

She stared again at the cluster of buildings, at the outlying fields and herds. She realized for the first time how similar it was to what she had found in Virginia. There was the same grand manor house where the lords lived, and the same army of slave laborers maintaining it all by the sweat of their brows.

She had found it repugnant then, but had accepted it as the way of the country. After all, at the time she herself had been something of a slave. Any woman was, who married.

Since then she had tasted freedom on the great plains, in the high mountains, and even here in California with Lone Feather and his people. Their existence was poor but free, and not without dignity.

"Let's go," she said, turning her back on the idyllic scene. She was glad now that she had not earlier sought out the missions. She was sickened by the knowledge that the very people who had sheltered and befriended her over the past few months might have been, might yet become, slaves like those toiling below, joyless, freedomless, hopeless.

They traveled for a day along a narrow canyon. No breeze reached to stir the sultry air, and deer stood fearless to watch them pass. Claire, remembering that they had come without water, began to wonder if Lone Feather had gotten lost. Then unexpectedly they came upon a small stream of clear, fresh-running water, and by it a little hut of mud and thatches.

They spent the night and traveled on the next day, wending their way slowly upward into the mountains. Now there were trees and scrub oaks, without magnificence but gnarled and deformed, as if they had battled with

great effort against the ravages of time and
nature. The walls of the cliffs were of sandstone carved by the centuries. They saw the
tracks of grizzly and lion and of the bighorn
sheep. They came to a great fissure in the
earth where layers of broken rock thrust sharply
upward. Lone Feather told her it was a crack
in the earth that ran from far to the north to
the deserts of the south.

They came at last to the high forest,
following a path that wound over the water-
worn rocks of an old creek bed. They entered
a vast horseshoe-shaped canyon that seemed
a dead end. But there was a path hidden in
the thick brush, though it forced them to
leave their horses behind. On foot they entered
what was little more than a gap in the rocks.
She followed Lone Feather, awed by their
surroundings. Suddenly they emerged into a
clearing and before her was the opening of a
cave.

"Here," Lone Feather said, "is the place
sacred to our people. Come with me."

He led the way into the cave's interior. At
first she could see nothing, but as her eyes
adjusted to the gloom she noticed a faint
glimmering. She crossed to the far wall and
found at her feet a pile of what appeared to be
small rocks. When she knelt and lifted one in
her hand she saw that they were gold nug-
gets. Near them stood a delicately shaped
urn. It was filled to the brim with gold dust.

This was the fortune that Peter had sought. Even knowing little about such things, Claire could guess that there was a fortune in this cave.

Nor was gold all that the cave contained. Now that she could see more clearly she discovered pieces of delicate and lovely broken pottery of a style she had never seen before.

"This is the history of our people," Lone Feather said, indicating the gold and the broken pottery. "This, and what we carry in our memory. It is this that we pass on to our young men while the ants crawl their bodies, for they need to know, especially when the white man comes. There will be a day, our elders have long predicted it, when the white man will rule all of the country, and every Indian will be a slave like those at the mission."

"But I don't understand. Surely with this gold you could buy the freedom of your people," Claire said.

"In our world gold was for beauty only. In the white man's world, it does not mean freedom, but slavery. We put gold upon bowls and cups, we wore it about our necks."

"But I've seen no bowls or cups."

"Long ago, in the time of our ancestors' ancestors, our people lived in a—a..." He struggled for the right word. "A pueblo, but not like those known to your people. And one time the earth began to shake. For a week it trembled, raining dust and ashes upon us, and when it was finished, our people and all they had built had vanished like grass before the fire. Some ran to the sea, where the great waves devoured them. Some perished in the great desert. Others hid in the mountains."

He paused, seeming to see beyond her into the distant past. "For us the day is almost done. We quarrel with the Chumash and hide from the white man. We were a people who once talked to the stars. The old gods weep, for they too die with us."

Claire came to him, laying a hand upon his chest. "But why do you tell me of these things?" she asked.

"You are one of us, yet not one of us," he said. "You have the willingness to learn and the wisdom of silence. Like us you are a child of the light. What I have told you, you will carry, not only here," he tapped his forehead, "but here," he thumped his chest. "Soon we must go from our camp, for it is no longer safe. We will journey to a new place, chosen by our elders. This shall be our last home, and when we have faded from the light, we will be no more. But in you the truth of our people will still burn."

She smiled fondly at him. She had waited, wanting to be sure, and wanting too the right moment. Now the time had come to tell him her secret.

"Not only in me," she said. "For I shall tell another."

Lone Feather frowned. "It is forbidden to share our knowledge with any who is not one of us. That is why I had to seek the permission of the elders to bring you here."

"The one I shall tell will be one of your people," she said. "Your son will have a right to know."

It took him a moment to comprehend. She saw the great wave of joy as the knowledge grew in his eyes.

"My son," he murmured. He took her in his arms, kissing her gently at first and then with mounting urgency.

They sank to the floor of the cave, and under the watchful eyes of the old gods they made love.

18

It was not a son after all, but a daughter whom she gave into the hands of Lone Feather.

"Are you sorry it's not a son?" she asked, knowing how badly he had wanted a boy.

He examined the squealing bundle gingerly, as if looking for flaws. "She has yellow hair," he said, "that shines like the great star to the north. I shall call her Shining Star."

He suddenly grinned at Claire. "She will be very beautiful," he said, "like her mother."

Content with that, Claire closed her eyes and slept. The child had come early, far too early, and not until she had heard the first plaintive cries had she believed it would live. Too eager, she thought dreamily, too eager to enter so harsh a world.

The white men came less than a month later, soldiers directed by the brown-robed friars of the mission. They came in the first veiled light of the dawn, catching the sleeping Indians unaware.

There was little fighting. The tribe had no weapons but clubs and rocks, and when he saw the guns and swords of the soldiers, the headman ordered his people not to resist.

Lone Feather, who had resisted bitterly until the command from his father, was among those chosen to be taken. Claire had come from their tipi with her month-old daughter in her arms. Seeing her, one of the soldiers snatched her arm and turned her about for a better look in the uncertain light.

"You don't look like no Indian to me," he said, peering closely. "You human, gal, or are you one of them?"

She glowered angrily back at him and said in the language of the tribe, "Let us alone."

For a second or two longer he stared into her face. Then with a grunt he shoved her over with the others to be taken. "Must be a half-breed," he said. "Lots of them sailors jump on squaws when they can't find a woman."

"You should have told the truth," Lone Feather said, taking her in an embrace.

"I'd rather be an Indian slave," she said angrily, "than one of them."

Besides herself, twelve of them were taken, seven strapping young braves and five squaws, of whom one was little more than a child. The mother of the girl and the wife of one of the braves followed them for some distance, sobbing and pleading to be taken as well, but they were finally driven off by the soldiers.

They traveled on foot, following much the same route that Lone Feather and Claire had followed previously. At night they camped at the bottom of a hill by the banks of a small stream. Though Lone Feather had carried Shining Star most of the way, Claire was exhausted from the strenuous pace and would have dropped off to sleep at once. Before she could do so, however, the soldier who had questioned her in camp came for her.

"You, come with me for a spell," he said, gesturing to make his meaning clear.

Lone Feather attempted to intervene. Other soldiers came running and he was beaten to the ground. The soldier who had come for her raised his gun as if he meant to shoot him, but Claire threw herself in his path.

"I'll come with you," she said.

In his anger the man did not even notice that she had spoken in English. Spitting on the ground by Lone Feather, he took Claire's arm roughly and led her to a spot a little distant from the camp. Stumbling over the rough ground beside him, she saw two other soldiers carrying the youngest girl to another location.

She was assaulted twice before she was allowed to gather up the clothes he had torn from her and return to the other Indians. Lone Feather, shamed by his inability to defend her, lay unspeaking with his back to her, his head buried in his arms. She lay behind him, resting against the broad expanse of his back, unable to give him the comfort she knew he needed.

After months in the wilderness with only savages for company, she had at last returned to her own people.

"Father?"

The padre, his brow wet with perspiration, turned from the book from which he had been lecturing the Indians, stories of the lives of the Saints.

"The Alcalde is just arriving."

Padre Barragan nodded and closed the book. To the rear of the hot, airless room a child had begun to bawl lustily. He saw the yellow-haired woman open her blouse and offer the child a breast. She saw the padre's disapproving scowl and gave her head a defiant toss.

He sighed, not for the first time. He thought they had made a mistake letting that woman keep the baby with her. It might have been better if they'd left the woman behind as well. This last band of savages had been exceedingly difficult to convert to the faith, and he placed a great part of the blame on her and the child's father. Both of them remained defiant and unbroken, despite the scoldings and the whippings.

The woman was a mystery. He would have sworn she was no Indian. Twice he had questioned her himself, but she had insisted that she was one of these people. He might have thought her demented or suffering from some loss of memory, but there was little doubt that her faculties were intact. Often when he had been lecturing the new converts he would glance up to find her eyes on him, something in their expression seeming to mock him. She was intelligent, that much he was certain of, intelligent and stubborn.

For the moment, though, he must dismiss the problem from his thoughts and deal instead with the Alcalde's arrival. He wondered what the King's representative from the pueblo of Los Angeles wanted this time. Probably only all their food and their wine as well, to be paid for with another of those worthless royal drafts. While the mission fathers and the Spanish government fought separately to conquer this wilderness, they fought another war with one another, to see whose power would reign. In that war Padre Barragan was a seasoned veteran.

"Remain here," he told the Indians, looking directly at the woman for a few seconds. "I shall be back soon. In the meantime, you shall pray for God's mercy on your heathen souls."

He went out, his long robe swishing on

the dirt floor. When he had gone the Indians sat in sullen silence. In the two weeks since they had been brought to the mission, an incredible change had been wrought. Before, their temescal and frequent bathing in the ocean had kept them clean. Now they sat in a stink of their own filth and perspiration, hair matted and uncombed. Once proud and care-free, they were now dull and dispirited.

They had been forced to kneel at gun-point while the padre had prayed over them, claiming them as the property of the Church and their souls for the Almighty. Thus "con-verted," they had become a part of the great network of laborers that toiled day and night to support the mission and increase its wealth. Those who resisted were whipped and sub-jected to lectures such as this one, on the virtues of obedience to the Church. Those who attempted escape were pursued and brought back by the soldiers to be publicly flayed as a lesson to the others. Some, the most obstinate and unbending, found free-dom in death.

The presence of her child had been a source of some protection for Claire. The cruelty of the mission fathers did not extend to whipping infant children, and as there was no one else in the compound to feed the child, the fathers had been faced with a choice of letting the child die or letting the mother live.

They had tried a number of remedies

for her defiance, including whippings and isolation from the others, to no avail. She remained a problem and an enigma.

The baby nursed energetically for a few minutes, then drifted into sleep, her lips still curled about the nipple. Claire waited until she felt the sucking cease. Then she gently handed her to the Indian woman seated beside her and went to the tiny window overlooking the yard. An elegant carriage, preceded by two soldiers on horseback, was just rolling through the mission's main gates. She watched the padre welcome the carriage's sole occupant, a tall, distinguished gantleman with grey hair and the most stylish suit she had seen since leaving England.

The thought gave her a pang. Little more than a year ago she too had dressed in elegant fashions instead of rags and rode in fine carriages. Once she had thought that her former friends would no longer recognize her. Now she scarcely recognized herself.

The two men outside had finished greeting one another. The Alcalde was obviously to be given a brief tour of the mission buildings.

Well, Claire thought, watching the gentleman nod his head in reply to some remark of the padre's, she had come west for one purpose, though it had long since dimmed in her eyes. She had been searching for her husband. If Peter had managed to survive the overland crossing and reach California, he might have gone to the pueblo of Los Angeles. She had learned from Lone Feather that it was the only town for hundreds of miles.

She was not unmindful that the same generality applied to Camden Summers. She knew that he was probably dead. After all, she had been in that river too and knew firsthand its dangers.

Still, she had survived, along with Morton. And Summers was a strong, resourceful man who had lived through many a harrowing experience. Looking back from the comfort of the tribe's camp, it had seemed to her at least possible that Summers might also have survived. If so, Los Angeles would have been a logical destination for him, too.

Though the mission fathers had decried her refusal to learn since she'd been their "guest," she had in fact learned a great deal just by listening. Next under the provincial governor, who ruled from someplace far north called Monterey, the Alcade was the chief governmental agent of each settlement, a combination of mayor, judge, and lawmaker. This Alcade, whom she'd heard referred to as Don Hernando, governed not only the pueblo of Los Angeles, but this entire region.

If anyone was likely to have word of Peter—or Summers—in this area it was the man just now stooping slightly to enter the low door of the chapel.

Claire had no illusions regarding the life that lay before her if she remained at the mission. Anger, and loyalty to Lone Feather and the tribe, had made her deny that she was white, but in so doing she had condemned herself to life as a slave. It was one thing to be sold to Lone Feather, he had treated her more as an honored wife than as his property; but it was another to be used, and misused, by the mission fathers and their soldiers for the rest of her life.

With a grim smile she slipped from the door of the shed used for a classroom. By now the padre and his guest had disappeared inside the chapel. Glancing around to be certain she was unobserved, Claire darted into the sunlight and ran to the wood-framed doorway of the chapel, her bare feet making whispering sounds on the dusty ground.

She was nearly there when the little party reemerged from the chapel, the Alcalde once again bending his head to clear the doorframe. Seeing her, the men stopped, startled. Padre Barragan gestured for one of the friars following him.

"Catch her," he snapped. "Take her..."

Claire had intended to throw herself to the ground at the Alcalde's feet, but at the last moment she caught herself. Instead she came to an abrupt halt, and, after a slight pause, dropped to a curtsy before him for all the world as if she were still properly gowned, and they were meeting in some London parlor.

"Don Hernando," she said, "please may I have a word with you?"

The fluent speech, after her weeks of

silence and Indian guttural, electrified the padre and his friars into silence. Don Hernando, approprately startled, demanded of no one in particular, "Who is this girl?"

Recovering, the padre took a step forwrd. "Just one of the Indians, sire," he said. "My apologies for this disruption."

He would have grabbed Claire's arm and dragged her away himself, but even as he was reaching to do so, Don Hernando cried, "Wait!"

He came forward himself, placing a bold finger under Claire's chin to tilt it upward. His eyes, dark and shrewd, raked her face.

"This is no Indian," he said angrily, and to Claire, "Who the devil are you?"

"Claire Denon, sir," she answered, "formerly of London and lately of the Malibu."

"But this is incredible. How did you come to be here, in the guise of an Indian?" the Alcalde demanded.

For the first time in weeks, she smiled. "I'm afraid it's rather a lengthy story," she said.

"Then we shall hear it at length." He turned to the padre, who had stood silently glowering at the source of his irritation. "Find us a place where the young lady and I can talk in comfort," he ordered. He turned back to Claire, but not before he had added to the padre's further discomfort, "And in private."

19

"This is the most remarkable story I've ever heard."

There was a tap at the door. "Come in," Don Hernando called gruffly. One of the friars slipped quietly into the room, lingering just long enough to refill their glasses from an earthen wine jug and steal a couple of curious glances at Claire, who at the moment was the source of rampant gossip throughout the mission.

When he had gone, hastened on his way by a dark scowl from the Alcalde, Don Hernando again took up the story. "And this other man, this Morton, he died in the mine collapse?"

"Yes," Claire answered. "After that I came to the coast with the Indians. I'm afraid there's not much else to tell. We were captured and brought here."

"But I don't understand. You've lived for the better part of a year an easy two days' journey from the village. A mere lark after what you'd already traveled. You could have made it on your own."

"I was exhausted from the ordeal," she said. "I needed time to recover, not only my strength, but my spirits, if you understand what I mean. And the Indians were very kind."

"So might the villagers have been, had you but given them the opportunity," he said with a certain asperity. "You make us Californios sound barbaric indeed."

"I have not fared very well at the hands of Californians," she said, fingering the tattered fabric of her dress.

"For which you must surely share the blame. When the soldiers came—or even when you arrived here at the mission—why didn't you let them know who you were?"

"I'm sorry, I didn't mean to offend," she said. "Your question is not an easy one to answer. I was angry, for one thing, at seeing people who had befriended me rounded up like so many cattle. Some of them were friends. There was one man in particular—and I had a child."

"By this 'one man in particular'?"

"Yes." She looked away from his sharp gaze. "When Morton died—that is, before he died—he sold me to this Indian."

"Dios mio," Don Hernando muttered, emptying his tankard in a gulp. "A pretty state of affairs. And what do you propose I do now?"

"I had thought, if my husband did reach California, you might have some news of him. Or even the Summers I spoke of," Claire said.

"Not a word," Don Hernando said, shaking his head. "But I only arrived in the territory three months ago. I suppose the best thing is for you to return to the pueblo with me. It's possible some one there may know something that they've simply not thought to mention to me."

"Then you have the authority to free us?" she asked hopefully.

"I have the power to free *you*, certainly."

Her smile faded. "And the others?"

"My dear girl," he said, as if speaking to a difficult child, "my government grants me the right to claim whatever I need of anything the mission produces, be it wine or grain or hides, but as to the souls they deliver to the Church, the mission fathers alone have authority over those."

"I should have thought there was an authority higher than theirs," she replied angrily.

"Perhaps," he said with a cynical smile. "But not one likely to answer to my petition. At any rate, what would you have me do? You could hardly bring an Indian lover and your child into the pueblo. Now it's no use looking daggers at me, I speak for your own well-being. I know those people; they'd never accept that. You'd be very likely stoned, or your house burned down. You know what people are like. And even assuming the best, what sort of life could this present your child? I've been here long enough to know that the lot of the half-breed is not an enviable one."

"Then I shall return to the Malibu," she stated flatly. "Surely that could cause no complaints."

"You must be joking," he said. "While it's true that the missions and the Spanish government are partners of sorts in the colonization of this territory, you are intelligent enough to see for yourself that the enterprise is not without its political intrigues. There is a great deal of jealousy and bitterness both ways. If it were generally publicized that I had permitted a white woman, an Englishwoman at that, to live with a miserable band of Indians—indeed, the purchased property of one of them—they'd have my head on a platter. And never mind that it was you who'd made the suggestion. If none of this had come up it would be one thing, but I'm afraid there are too many people curious about you already, including the good padre. I'm afraid it's out of the question."

"Am I to understand, then," she said, "that I am to be your prisoner rather than the mission's?"

He sighed and said, "I'd rather hoped you might see it a bit differently."

"I don't see how I can."

"This—this friend of yours—suppose I could procure his release, his and the baby's. Mind you, I don't say that I can, but just suppose they were free to return to their village, would you then come with me to the pueblo, where you belong?"

Claire hesitated for a moment. The offer was tempting. Freedom for Lone Feather and Shining Star, instead of a lifetime of slavery. And for herself a return to civilized life, all the comforts and amenities she had been without for so long. Even the wine they were drinking now had evoked all but forgotten memories of the past.

"You're asking me to abandon my child," she said.

"A bastard child, born through no wish of yours. And, I might add, one whose life will surely be better this way. She will be free to grow in the ways of her people. The alternatives, madame, are not attractive."

For a moment more Claire sat in thoughtful silence. Then at length she gave a toss of her head. "I'm sorry." She met his gaze evenly. "What you suggest goes against the grain of every mother's instincts. I cannot do it."

He came around the table at which they were seated, and, offering his hand, helped her to her feet.

"My dear," he said, giving her hand a fatherly pat, "I've had a long and dusty journey, which I must retrace tomorrow. I had looked forward to an evening's rest, and I think you might well benefit from the same. I will ask the padre to make a room available to you, and perhaps you'll be good enough to dine with me this evening. Tomorrow, well, we'll talk again.

After so long in the makeshift costumes of her westward journey it was an odd experience for Claire to be donning conventional wear once again. The friars, having shown her to a room, had brought an old sea trunk; it had been given them, they explained, by a sea captain whose wife, traveling with him, had died at sea. In it she found everything she needed to make herself presentable.

When she was dressed Claire examined her reflection in the mirror. She scarcely recognized herself. Her skin had acquired a deep golden hue, her hair was almost yellow-white. Her months with the tribe had erased the gauntness of the weeks in the wilderness, though her cheekbones remained stark and prominent.

There was a tap at the door. "Come in," she called. She heard the door open and close and turned to find herself facing Lone Feather. For a long moment he regarded her steadily, looking up and down the length of her borrowed finery. She realized with a faint reddening of her cheeks that this was the first time he had ever seen her dressed as a white woman.

"The Alcalde's invited me to dine with

him," she said, fingering the faded lace at her throat.

"He has spoken to me," Lone Feather said. "He has freed me and Shining Star to return to our village."

"Yes," Claire said. "He made the same offer to me. On condition that I not go with you."

"I come to tell you we are going."

For a moment Claire hesitated. Then she began to undo the bodice of her gown. "I'll come with you," she declared.

"No." Lone Feather put a hand over hers, staying her action. "I promised we would go without you. I come to say goodbye."

"But you can't. My daughter—"

"—Is half-Indian, half-white," he said. "With my people, she will be an Indian. I will treasure her, and she will grow to know the meaning of freedom. With you, she can know only pain and sorrow in a white man's world. It is better this way. You where you belong, us where we belong."

He smiled sadly at her. She felt the sting of tears at her eyes. It was the same argument the Alcalde had used, and its wisdom was undeniable. Still the tears came, and the heaviness in the heart.

"I'll come to the village to see her," she said. "I'll do everything I can for her."

He shook his head. "No. We will leave that place, move the tribe to another, where the mission will not find us. We are a dying people, but we will die in peace."

"Can't you tell me where you're going?"

"You would bring the white man," he said. "They would follow you and take more of our people until none were left. For my people's sake, for my daughter's sake, you must go from us, and forget."

"I will go," she said, speaking slowly. "But I will never forget."

He took her in his arms with surprising gentleness. She remembered his first embrace, so long before.

"When you came with the white man," Lone Feather whispered into her ear as he held her close, "I bought you from him, but you were never mine. Now I give you back to yourself. Go your way. If the old gods still hear our prayers, mine will keep you safe."

She tried to find the right words to say, but none would come. He kissed her briefly, his lips but brushing her own. She saw him leave through a veil of tears.

20

Claire had imagined that the pueblo of Los Angeles—or El Pueblo de Nuestra Senora la Reina de los Angeles del Rio de Porciuncula, as it was officially named—would be more or less comparable to St. Louis. Decidedly primitive by eastern standards, it would nonetheless provide a measure of civilized comfort and culture.

The reality was a shock. The village was nothing but a dusty cowtown. It sprawled without apparent plan or design over a shallow bowl of land formed by the low, encircling mountains. A grey mist from the ocean hung over everything like smoke. It softened the harsh realities of peeling whitewash and dusty streets where dogs lay lazily wagging their tails. Besides the guardhouse and the church, the town consisted of a handful of trading posts and a generous scattering of cantinas. A number of trails, most of them old Indian routes, led into the town. Along these various streets were scattered the homes of the residents: whitewashed adobe with low roofs covered in what she recognized as the same tar the Indians had used to waterproof their boats.

"How many people live here?" Claire asked the Don as the carriage swayed and jounced down what passed for a street.

"Somewhere between fourteen and fifteen hundred people," he answered. "It varies with the season. Sometimes, actually, with the time of day."

"Are all Spanish subjects?"

Don Hernando gave a little laugh. "On paper they're subjects of the empire. In actuality most of them have long since come to think of themselves as Californios. The *gente de razon*, they call themselves."

"Isn't Spain rather careless with her provinces?"

"Spain's empire is like a dying man," he said, not without a certain bitterness. He gestured with his hand at the sleepy village outside the carriage windows. "This is but the last faint reflex of the giant that was. There's less than four thousand non-Indians in the whole province, and a great many of those were born here. Perhaps three hundred soldiers to guard more than a thousand miles of coastline. If it weren't for the missions, grown

266

fat off the labor of the Indians, we'd be hard put to sustain ourselves. As it is the only real industry is the illegal trading with American and English ships."

"You make it sound like a land with no future," she said. From what she had seen of the pueblo, she was willing to accept that assessment.

"If it has one, it's not as a Spanish province, nor a Mexican one either," he said. The carriage slowed just then and he said with a cheerfulness that sounded forced to her, "Here we are. My wife will be delighted to see you, new faces are rare here."

While the Alcalde was handing her down from the carriage, a woman appeared in the doorway of the modest adobe structure. Claire thought she did not look in the least bit glad to see her.

"Ah, there you are," Don Hernando greeted the unsmiling woman. "May I present my wife, Doña Maria Isabella Marina Hernando. My love, this is Señora Denon. The Señora has found herself alone in our province through a lengthy chain of circumstances. I have offered her our hospitality until we can find suitable accommodations for her."

"Señora." Claire greeted her, dropping a curtsy.

Doña Maria did not return the greeting. She shot an angry look at Claire. Then wordlessly she turned on her heel and disappeared into the gloom of the house.

Looking only slightly ruffled, Don Hernando escorted Claire inside as though nothing untoward had happened. "Now, where's one of those maids? Ah, Teresa, there you are, will you see about a room for our guest? And inform the cook we will be three for dinner."

From the parlor off to their right Claire heard the clink of glass upon glass, as someone poured a drink. She thought of Doña Maria's cold welcome and wondered briefly if after all she might not have been better advised to remain at the mission.

Dinner was an uncomfortable experience. Though the Don filled the role of host with elegance and ease, his wife made no secret of her lack of enthusiasm for their guest's presence. She spoke only when asked a direct question, and then answered in the curtest, coolest terms.

Claire, several times looking up to find the Señora's hostile gaze resting upon her, noticed too that the Señora was rather fond of her sherry, a glass of which was ever filled at her place. As the evening progressed, the Señora's naturally florid complexion grew more ruddy and her black eyes glinted like polished stones.

Even Doña Maria's speech began to show the effects of the sherry she consumed, the few words she spoke becoming heavily slurred. Toward the end of the meal, in reaching for a salt cellar, she managed to topple her wine glass, spilling the amber wine across the fine lace of the tablecloth. Don Hernando rang for the maid, who appeared at once, cloth in hand.

"Let me be," Doña Maria snapped, brushing away the woman's efforts to wipe up the stain, and reaching instead to refill her glass.

"Perhaps, my dear, you should have some coffee," Don Hernando suggested.

"I'll drink what I like," his wife replied sharply, adding as she got a bit unsteadily to her feet, "And where I like."

With that she took her sherry and flounced from the room. A moment later they heard a door slam.

"I must apologize for my wife's behavior," Don Hernando said.

"I'm afraid my presence must be something of an inconvenience," Claire said.

Don Hernando gave a rather mirthless laugh. "You needn't trouble yourself on that account," he said. "My wife has far better motives for her resentment than your presence here."

He did not elaborate further and Claire thought it tactless to pursue the subject. They spent a rather desultory quarter of an hour sipping coffee and making idle conversation. She saw the Don's eyes drift occasionally in the direction in which his wife had disappeared, but he made no further mention of her or her behavior.

"But how thoughtless of me," he said at

last. "You must be wanting to retire. I'll have Teresa show you to your room. Tomorrow I'll make inquiries and find you a place to live."

"I'm grateful for all you've done," Claire said as the dark-haired maid came in. "I've a little money left that I held on to throughout my trip, and I can get more from London, though how long that will take is anybody's guess."

For the first time since dinner had begun he gave her a truly genuine smile. "We won't worry about that," he said. "The Alcalde's word should at least be worth some credit."

The room that had been provided for her was small and modestly furnished. Still it was luxury indeed compared to what she had known since leaving Virginia, and despite the coolness of her hostess Claire slept pleasantly. She dreamed that she heard the sound of the surf gently thrumming upon the wide white beaches of the Malibu.

The next day passed, however, and the next, and still the Alcalde found no other living quarters for her, though she would have thought it possible to canvass all of the town's inhabitants in less time than that. She began to wonder if perhaps in fact he was in no real hurry to move her out of his own home.

Truth to tell, had it not been for Doña Maria's churlish behavior, she would have been in no hurry to leave, as she found Don

Hernando most pleasant. His was the sort of intelligent, cultured company that she had missed for so long, and she enjoyed just sitting and chatting with him. It had been less than a year since he'd come from Paris where, she learned, he had been the Spanish king's ambassador, and he was filled with news and anecdotes of life in the French capital.

Strolling out into the primitive pueblo that was the Alcalde's current domain, Claire could not help but wonder what chain of circumstances had brought him from the glamour of Parisian life to this rustic station. Aside from the weather, which was nearly always warm and sunny, and the natural beauty of its location, she found that the town had little to recommend it.

As for Doña Maria, though she continued unfriendly, Claire actually saw very little of her. Only at dinner did she spend any time in the company of her husband and their guest, and this was invariably a repeat of the first evening's performance. Though Doña Maria did not always manage to spill her wine, she did usually reach the end of the meal in a state approaching inebriation.

It was not until Claire's fourth night there that the Señora's sullen anger and the incessant sherry combined to produce an explosion.

The Spanish residents of the town kept to that country's custom of sleeping through the warmest part of the afternoon. Claire, unaccustomed to the afternoon siesta, had taken to spending that time exploring, usually on foot, though Don Hernando had given her his generous permission to borrow a mount whenever she wished. She had taken advantage of that offer to visit one of the area's curiosities, a bubbling tar pit from which came the pitch that both Indians and settlers made use of. The black, shiny substance seemed to ooze up from the ground itself, not unlike some hellish mockery of a freshwater spring.

At dinner Don Hernando asked her impression of the pueblo, now that she had spent a few days there.

"I'm afraid it will never appeal to the idle traveler," she said frankly. "Though to be honest, I've been in worse places over the past year or two." She hesitated and then added, "But what of you? Surely this must seem a bit primitive to you after Paris and Madrid?"

Doña Maria made one of her few contributions to the conversation. "A refuse heap," she grumbled, draining her glass. "No decent person would set foot here unless forced to."

Don Hernando, ignoring the remark, said quietly, "In a month's time I'm to take over the duties of provincial governor, in Monterey, the capital. They say it's a lovely town and that life there is most pleasant."

"A provincial backwater," Doña Maria snapped. "To think that I, Doña Maria Isabella Marina Hernando, daughter of Spanish dons —wife of a Spanish don—" here she shot her husband a furious glance "should be reduced to living in this—this Indian village."

With an unexpectedly violent gesture, she seized her wine glass and flung it at a portrait of the Spanish king that hung over the mantel. The glass shattered, the wine running in bloodlike rivulets down the monarch's scowling countenance. Leaping up, Doña Maria fled from the room.

Claire expected Don Hernando to go after his wife, but he only sat staring sadly after her. He did not even seem concerned with repairing the damage to the painting, though it had the look of a valuable piece.

"Once again I'm sorry that I seem to be an additional burden for your wife," Claire said.

"You needn't be," Don Hernando replied. "Her behavior is no different from what it would have been. My wife is not a happy woman, as you no doubt have observed for yourself."

"It must have been a difficult change for her, coming here from the places you've been," Claire offered, wanting to be charitable.

"Difficult indeed," he said. Rather abruptly he added, "I suppose you've wondered how we came to be here?"

"Don Hernando, I—I wouldn't wish to intrude."

He ignored her reply. "You must have noticed my wife is rather fond of her sherry," he went on. "She has been for many years, though less conspicuously than now. We were in Paris. I believe I told you, I was ambassador there. One time one of the King's chief ministers came on a visit. He told me that there had been some talk regarding my wife. The king was embarrassed."

"How awkward for you," Claire murmured, uncertain why she was being told these things.

Don Hernando scowled at her from under lowered brows. "It was more than awkward," he said. "The man insisted that my services were valuable to his majesty, particularly as the two governments were trying to conclude some difficult negotiations in which I had figured prominently. On the other hand, there was this embarrassment. Oh, let me not spare myself, there were some outside activities on my part that they were aware of. I'm not the sort for celibacy, I'm afraid, and my wife long ago ceased to be interested in certain aspects of a marriage. I hope this is not distasteful for you?"

"I lived for a long time without many of the social niceties," Claire replied.

"Yes, of course." He was thoughtful for a moment before continuing. "He told me—the king had nothing in this, you understand, it was the minister's own idea—he said there was an easy solution. If my wife were to have an accident I could pursue my interests without hindrance. I could serve the king without embarrassment for myself or him."

Claire was shocked and could think of no suitable reply.

"I threw the man out bodily," Don Hernando concluded. "After that, well, less than a month later, we'd been assigned here. I believe

I explained, this is only temporary, until I take over as provincial governor in Monterey." He took a long sip of his wine, regarding her over the rim.

"Don Hernando, why are you telling me these things?" Claire asked.

"Because I want you to come to Monterey with me," he said.

"But to be frank, I hardly think your wife would welcome my company," she said.

"I wasn't thinking of my wife."

"Indeed, I'm certain you were not."

"In Paris, in other places we've lived, it was easy to make outside arrangements. People don't much mind a man having a mistress as well as a wife, assuming everything is managed discreetly. But here in this primitive settlement even if it were possible to arrange, the few women here are married. I would not choose to sully another man's marriage."

"But I am married too," she said.

"Yes, of course." He looked away. "I'm afraid I've offended you."

"Well, I—I'm flattered, certainly, but this is so sudden."

"My dear, you are a beautiful woman who at the moment is rather in need of a friend, and I—let me be blunt—I am a lonely man. Forgive me if I have been hasty in making my offer, but I did not feel that time was a commodity I could afford to squander."

"Yes, I see your point." Claire hesitated. Though she had protested that she was a married woman, she could see that her marriage, if such it still was, had long since been sullied. She had gladly taken Summers for a lover and learned to love him. Morton had taken her by force. Lone Feather had purchased her from the trapper, but he had not had to force her, and if she had never come to love him, she had regarded him affectionately as a friend and had come to give herself to him gladly enough.

Why then hide behind the tattered shreds of her marriage now? Her situation, if not as desperate as it had been at times in the past, was hardly enviable. She could no longer depend even upon the protection and support of Lone Feather and his people. She was truly alone in this great wilderness, and she had just been offered the protection of an intelligent, cultured aristocrat. Nor was Don Hernando unattractive, if she would be honest with herself. She took him to be forty or thereabouts, but though he was older than she, he remained handsome and trim, and he was an undeniably pleasant companion.

Still she hesitated. Rising from the table she said, "I'm afraid some of that precious time will have to be squandered, after all. I shall use it to consider your offer."

He rose too. Coming about the table, he took her hand and raised it gently to his lips. She found herself thinking of Peter's proposal to her. He had fallen to his knees to pray. Summers had taken her without asking, as naturally as the sun takes its piece of the sky.

Morton had been a beast. Lone Feather she had had to teach to be tender.

And Don Hernando? Supposing she said yes to his offer. How would he differ from the other men she had known?

He released her hand to look into her eyes. She blushed, due to the course her thoughts had taken.

As if reading them, and wishing to reassure her, he suddenly smiled broadly, tenderly. "I shall be patient," he said.

21

Don Hernando's assessment that the few women in the settlement were all married was an entirely accurate one. Claire had quickly learned that she was the only woman of age who was without the company of a husband, and this had proven to be something of a problem, as the unattached males vied for her attention. For the most part these attentions were innocent, the lonely gestures of womanless men, but there were some among the Angelenos who pressed their suits more forcibly.

She understood then that when Don Hernando spoke of her needing a friend, he was offering his protection not only from the dangers common to the settlers, but from some of the settlers as well. This point was brought home to her on the day of the fiesta.

Don Hernando told her of it shortly after their frank conversation. "You have never been to a California fiesta?" he asked. Claire shook her head. "Then you are in for a special treat." He grinned. "This fiesta is at the rancho of the Ramierez family, and everyone comes."

"But are you sure I'm invited?" Claire asked.

To her surprise Don Hernando laughed. "Invited? To a fiesta? My dear Claire, one does not send invitations to a fiesta, one only announces where and when. The Californios love a big party, any excuse will do. And," he added, "they come from all parts of the province. It is possible you may hear news of your husband. Or even this other man, Summers, if he still lives, if he reached California. Much news is exchanged at a fiesta, and much gossip."

The prospect of a party brightened Claire's spirits considerably. Not since London in the days before Richard's tragic accident had she been to a full-scale party, the sort that had once been like lifeblood to her. She supposed that the primitive society of the Californios would not afford a very grand affair, but at least it would be fun to be where there was music and laughter and gaiety.

She found a dress among those she had been given, and with the help of Doña Maria's maid, Teresa, she was able to transform it into something suitable for a party. It was of a deep emerald-green velvet that set off her pale hair and her dark eyes. She wished that she had some of her old jewelry. Richard had given her a pendant that would go very nicely with the dress, but of course it was in Virginia, and for all she knew she might never see it again. She settled instead for the gold nugget that Lone Feather had given her, replacing the leather thong with a ribbon that matched the color of her dress. Though it was an unusual adornment, she was not displeased with the effect. Certainly it seemed appropriate to a California fiesta.

Doña Maria herself would not be attending the fiesta, Teresa informed her. "She never goes to the fiestas," the maid said, her expression making it clear what she thought of such foolishness.

Don Hernando had announced that they would depart for the fiesta at midday, as it was several hours' travel from the pueblo. As the time of departure approached, the entire household seemed to bustle with preparations. Claire had just finished dressing when Teresa knocked and came into her room.

"From Don Hernando," Teresa said, handing her a small box.

"Thank you," Claire said, ignoring Teresa's curiosity and setting the package aside. Teresa's face clouded with disappointment, but the ringing of a bell sent her scurrying elsewhere.

When she was alone Claire opened the box to find a stunning brooch of a large topaz in a setting of gold filigree. For a moment she hesitated; this was not the sort of gift one should accept from a gentleman, particularly one who had recently asked her to be his mistress.

She pinned the brooch to the bodice of her gown, just intending to see how it looked. The effect was so striking that she decided she would wear the piece to the fiesta at least. Later she could return it to Don Hernando with her thanks, and no real harm would be done.

Shortly before time to depart, Don Hernando himself came to her room. It was her intention to thank him at once for the brooch, and explain her plan to return it to him later, but he was so evidently preoccupied that he did not even seem to notice that she was wearing it.

"I'm afraid there's been a change in plans," he said without any greeting. "My wife has decided after all that she will attend the fiesta. She's dressing now."

"I see," Claire said, wondering whether her presence had played any part in Doña Maria's change of plans.

"I've taken the liberty of making arrangements for you," he went on, his expression a wordless apology. "You will travel with the Delgados. They shall arrive for you soon."

"That's very kind of you," she said. The two exchanged a long look, neither of them putting into words what both were thinking. If she accepted the Alcalde's proposal, this would always be her lot. She would be "the other woman" in his life. His wife must ever come first.

"It doesn't matter," she said, putting a hand on his arm. "I've met the Delgados, they're a charming couple, and I mean to enjoy the fiesta to the fullest, as I hope you do too."

"Thank you," he said, briefly kissing her hand.

"And I think it's a good thing that your wife is going," she added. "It may be just what she needs to lift her spirits."

"Perhaps," he said, but his eyes held no confidence.

The Delgados were among the few families in the pueblo who owned carriages. Claire rode in comfort with Señora Delgado, a round-faced creature only slightly older than herself and already the mother of five children. The younger children traveled with their mother inside the carriage, while the oldest boy, already nearly a man at twelve, rode with his father alongside.

Many of the pueblo's residents rode horseback, horses as richly caparisoned as their riders. Others traveled in oxen-drawn carretas, crude farm carts on wooden wheels, decorated for the occasion with gaily colored ribbons.

They traveled in a steady stream over the gently rolling hills, often shouting or laughing

as they passed one another. Those who had
traveled the greatest distances had stopped at
other ranchos along the way. Many were gaily
dressed, but some had come in everyday
clothes, planning to change on arrival.

A bright and colorful scene awaited them
at the Ramierez rancho. The first guests had
arrived just after dawn, bringing some rabbits
they had caught along the way to add to the
food supply. Already there was a line of carretas
on the outskirts of the rancho and a dozen or
so horses at the hitching rails. Some vaqueros
with guitars were playing and singing with
more enthusiasm than skill, and the women
bustled to and fro with excited cries and
much happy laughter.

Señora Delgado informed Claire as they
alighted from the carriage that soon the dancing would start, and then she would see something special: the fandango of the Californios.

"How excited the young girls look," Claire
said. It was the first time Claire had seen the
gracious life of the California ranchos up
close. She had to admit it was quite different
from the impressions she had formed beforehand. The men were as colorful as the wom-
en in their velvet suits with wide-bottomed
slashed pants, or tanned suits of white buckskin.

The food was astonishing in its diversity
and quantity. There was fresh game and fish
and mountains of the thin, flat pancakes the
Californios called tortillas. A huge table was
laden with fresh fruits, and pots of beans

steamed temptingly. Whole sides of beef turned on spits over great open fires, their juices spitting and sizzling as they fell onto the coals. And everywhere wine flowed. It was the tart, faintly bitter wine made by the missions, and no doubt commandeered by Don Hernando himself, in the name of the King, Claire thought with wry amusement.

It was far from what she had known in England, but not so different from the parties thrown on the Virginia plantations, with dozens of guests traveling from afar.

She could not help noticing that an army of servants toiled to provide this pleasure for the others. Only here the servants were Indians and not Negroes. She found herself thinking of the people she had lived with at the Malibu. They had been reduced to just such servitude. She had come close to such a life herself.

Soon the dancing began, the milling crowd forming a rough circle about the first couples. A couple, whom she later learned were the Ramierez, danced first. Claire found the dance a disappointment. The gentleman was lithe and graceful, but his partner could scarcely have been seen to dance at all. Her skirt touched the ground so that not a hint of her feet could be seen, and she glided soundlessly about with her hands straight at her sides and her eyes down. She might have been taking part in some sacred ritual.

Soon, however, they were joined by other couples, spirited young men and women who danced with elegance and verve. Though the dances were unfamiliar to her, Claire found herself tapping her heels in time to the incessant beat, and humming one or two airs that sounded familiar.

She saw Don Hernando at a distance throughout the afternoon, his wife at his side. To Claire's surprise Doña Maria, who was usually so dour, seemed actually to be making an effort to be gracious. It was the first time Claire had seen the Señora out of the confines of her own home, and certainly the first time she had seen the woman smiling. It only added to her uneasiness over the Alcalde's proposal, seeing the two together looking like any married couple.

While she was watching, Claire saw Don Hernando turn from his wife to speak to another gentleman. At almost the same moment a passing vaquero, another of the Ramierez, Claire thought, handed Doña Maria a glass. For a moment the Señora seemed about to refuse the glass. Then, with an almost furtive glance in her husband's direction, she lifted the glass to her lips and took a first, tentative sip.

Frowning, Claire turned away from the scene. She did not live to tend to another's business. Still she had seen the effect that drinking spirits had on Doña Maria. She could only hope the Alcalde's wife would not be an embarrassment to him. Such a fine, kindly, sympathetic man deserved... With a start Claire realized that her attitude toward Don Hernando was becoming possessive. It was as if—but she did not let herself finish that thought.

A handsome young man in buckskin asked her to dance. Though she was unfamiliar with the dance, she nodded anyway and moved with him into the crowd, forcing a smile to her lips.

Foreign though it was to her, the dance was not difficult. She had learned from the Indians something of giving oneself to rhythm and movement and could follow the lead of her partner easily enough. It was evening already, the day having sped by, and bright lanterns had been strung about the patio, holding the darkness at bay. For a few minutes Claire forgot herself, forgot all that had happened in the past two years. For a brief span of time she was young and carefree again, with nothing more serious to worry about than music and dancing and a handsome man smiling at her in a flirtatious manner.

She had forgotten Doña Maria too, and was unaware that the Señora had spotted her dancing and had moved closer through the crowd, her dark brows drawing together in a disapproving scowl. Her bearing was as stiff as ever, her chin held high. Only a brightness to the eyes and a faint tremor in the hand holding the wine glass might have indicated to the observer that she was less than sober.

"Thief!"

The sudden cry startled Claire from her reverie, though it was not until she saw heads

turning in her direction that she realized it
had been directed at her. She looked around
and saw Doña Maria standing only a few feet
from her, her face contorted with jealousy
and rage.

"Thief!" Doña Maria cried again, pointing
an unsteady finger. "That's my brooch. You've
stolen it."

Claire felt her cheeks burning crimson.
Worst of all, she could think of nothing to say
in her defense. No doubt when Don Hernando
had given her the brooch he had been
expecting his wife to remain at home for the
day and later he had been too preoccupied to
notice; but that would hardly satisfy the ring
of Californios quickly forming around them.

"I'm sorry," she stammered. "I had nothing to wear. Don Hernando graciously loaned
me this. I'm sure he meant no..."

"Liar!" Doña Maria cried. "Liar and thief!"

With relief Claire saw Don Hernando
approaching through the crowd. Her relief
was short lived, however, for in the next moment Doña Maria had flung a glass of wine at
her, the red liquid splashing across her face
and her bosom. Stunned, Claire stood motionless as the Señora dashed forward and seized
the brooch in her bony fingers, literally tearing it from the dress.

"Stop this outrage at once," Don Hernando
demanded, stepping between the two women.

Claire did not wait to see what might
happen next. Covering her face with her hands,
she turned and pushed her way through the

crowd, tears of humiliation streaming down her cheeks. Once through the throng, she hitched up her skirt and began to run, paying little attention to where she was going. It mattered only that she hide herself in the surrounding darkness from all those staring eyes.

She ran past the spits where the sides of beef were still roasting, past the hitching rails where horses and oxen alike stood patiently waiting. Gradually the noise of the fiesta faded in the distance. She slowed to a walk, the cool night air helping to restore some order to the turmoil of her thoughts.

The fiesta, which she had been enjoying immensely, had been ruined for her. Worse than that, she knew that Doña Maria's drunken accusations would brand her forever among the arrogant Californios of the pueblo. They would believe tht she had truly attempted to steal Doña Maria's brooch. Either that, or they would take it for granted that Don Hernando was her lover. Why else would a man give another woman his wife's jewelry? Either way her reputation was bound to suffer in the close-knit community of the pueblo.

So intent was she on her own thoughts that she was unaware for some minutes that she was being followed. She had come into the open fields beyond the rancho's buildings. Before her a wide valley lay shrouded in darkness. The fiesta was but a vague murmur of sound in the distance. She found herself thinking of the Malibu, where the music was the wash of the surf upon the beach, and the incessant rhythm of mortar and pestle as the women pounded acorns into flour. How peculiar life was, that among her own people she should find herself longing for the simplicity of life in an Indian village.

A twig snapped somewhere nearby. She paused, glancing around, and saw someone approaching. She waited, not truly frightened, her first thought that Don Hernando might have followed her.

The moon, tangled briefly in the branches of an elm, floated free, its pale light showing her the face of the approaching cowboy. She recognized him. Though she did not recall his name, she had seen him about the pueblo, usually going in or out one of the many saloons. Once or twice he had spoken to her. She had returned his greetings, while pointedly not encouraging his interest.

She waited now in silence for him to walk up, noticing as she did so that drink had made his gait unsteady. He hesitated a few feet from her; then, with an ingratiating smile, he came up to where she was standing.

"Evening, m'am," he greeted her.

"Good evening." She did not return the smile. "Is there something you wanted?"

"Ugly business back there," he said, shrugging his head in the direction of the fiesta. "Doña Maria looked fit to be tied. And those other old biddies, well, their tongues won't stop wagging for a month of Sundays...."

"Please, I wanted to be alone," Claire said.

He took a step closer. In the moonlight she could see that a bead of spittle had run from one corner of his mouth. She found her gaze drawn to its gleam.

"It's not good for a woman to be alone," he said.

She remembered then. He was one of the womanless men. His wife had died a year or more ago. Some said from one of the many beatings he had inflicted upon her.

"Woman needs someone with her," he said, coming yet another step closer. "Needs a man to look after her."

"I think I'll go back now," Claire said, attempting to step around him. "If you'll excuse me."

He reached out and caught her wrist. "No need to run off," he said. "I thought maybe we could get better acquainted. Ain't no one going to see what we do clear out here 'cept maybe one of those young couples already sneaked off for the same thing."

"I'm afraid there will be nothing for anyone to see. I really must be getting back."

He pulled her close. "Now don't go getting grand on me," he said.

"Stop it."

"A woman that's had a buck for a lover's got no call to go getting grand with a real man. There's lots of men wouldn't even look at a woman's been laying with an Indian, you ought to be grateful."

"Let me go," she said, struggling in his embrace.

"*Si señor,*" a voice said from the darkness behind him. "You will please let the señora go."

The cowboy let her go so suddenly that she nearly fell. She took a step backward, gasping with relief, and turned toward her rescuer. He was a stranger to her, an elegantly dressed vaquero in richly embroidered trousers, wearing a wide-brimmed hat. At the moment he held a six-shooter in one hand, a lighted cigarette in the other.

"Mind your own business," the man with Claire said.

For an answer the vaquero cocked the hammer of his revolver. The cowboy hesitated for a moment. Then, with an angry growl, he stepped away from Claire.

"Wasn't doing no harm," he muttered, starting back toward the fiesta.

Claire watched him on his way. When he was all but out of sight in the semidarkness, she turned her attention to the vaquero, who had not moved except to follow the cowboy's progress with his eyes.

"I must thank you for your assistance," she said.

"You are free to go now, señora," he said, speaking in a thick accent. "He will not trouble you further, I think."

"But who are you? And why did you come to my rescue just now?"

He returned the six-shooter carefully to

his gunbelt and dropped his cigarette to the ground, grinding it out under the heel of a splendid leather boot.

"I am paid to see that no harm comes to you," he said. "Please, señora. This is no place for a woman alone. It will make my work much easier if you return to the fiesta."

"Paid...? But I don't understand, why would anyone pay you to see...?"

He tilted his head back, revealing a brutally scarred face to the moonlight. "I am in the employ of Don Hernando," he said. "Now, *por favor*..." He made an impatient gesture with his hand in the direction of the distant lights.

She went past him. When she had gone a few yards she looked back, thinking to find the vaquero following her, but he had vanished somewhere among the shadows. Yet when she had stood for several minutes contemplating this new turn of events, a discreet cough from somewhere not far distant reminded her that she would be safer elsewhere, and she once again resumed her walk.

She was both flattered and surprised to know that Don Hernando had made arrangements for her safety. She was, as he had pointed out, in need of protection, and he had seen to it discreetly. In more ways than she had realized, she was in his debt. Perhaps he was right. Perhaps the cowboy who had just tried to assault her had been right. This raw land was no place for a woman alone. On her own she would remain the prey of every lustful, lonely man who was without a woman. She could find herself the victim of another Morton, or worse. As Don Hernando's mistress, she would be both cared for and protected. It would be so easy.

And yet there was the humiliation she had just suffered. She would know the same fate in a hundred different, often subtle, ways. Even those who accepted her position—and she was sophisticated enough to know that there would be those who would toady to the province's governor, regardless of their private opinions—would find ways of reminding her who and what she was. In London she had seen other powerful, rich men and their kept women ostensibly accepted, but in fact slighted and spurned at every opportunity. She herself had laughed with the others behind the women's backs.

Was she now to join their ranks?

22

By the time she had returned from the fiesta, Claire had reached a decision that she would find other living quarters for herself, rather than continuing the friction with Doña Maria. She soon found, however, just how much damage had been done by the scene at the fiesta. Although she personally called upon most of the pueblo's families in the next few days, she found no welcome. Most were polite, though some of the women were noticeably cool; but none had room to spare, or if they did, they had some other reason for being unable to help her just now.

After several days of making inquiries, Claire rose early one morning and without rousing the servants saddled one of Don Hernando's horses. She did not want to be followed on this occasion by Don Hernando's vaquero, and instead of riding out by the gate she led the animal around the stable and walked him some distance from the house before mounting up and beginning to ride.

It was a ride of two, perhaps three hours, through the low mountains that ringed the village and toward the ocean. Lone Feather had given her a pretty good idea of the relative locations of the pueblo and the Indians' village, and at any rate, once she had reached the water's edge, she had only to follow it until she found the camp.

At last she spotted a familiar-looking cluster of hills, beyond which she was sure the village lay. A few miles beyond she saw the village itself.

Her excitement was short lived, however; even as she drew near she was conscious of the lack of activity and noise. Always the first thing one heard on approaching, sometimes long before the village could be seen, was the pounding of the acorns. This silence was eerie and unnerving.

The village was empty. The tipis of mud and leaves still stood in their random pattern. Even the temescal looked unchanged, except that no smoke rose from its central opening. She rode among the structures, calling the names of those she remembered, but no greetings came in return, no children came to gaze in wonder, no dogs barked at the horse's hooves.

Dismounting, she wandered disconsolately

through the empty camp and finally to the beach, where the waves pawed restlessly at the sand.

The Indians had gone, as Lone Feather had promised. She stared out over the water at the distant horizon. He had spoken of islands that lay offshore, just far enough to be invisible from the beach—invisible to the dangerous eyes of the white man, the mission fathers. Had they gone there? Or had the mission come for them again, taking everyone this time?

She thought of her child, Shining Star, whom she would never see again. Her daughter would grow to womanhood unknown to her. And Lone Feather had been kind to her. Was he gone now forever from her life?

At last, seeing that there was nothing in this place for her, she mounted again and began the ride back to the pueblo of Los Angeles.

As she rode she thought of what lay before her. Don Hernando would be leaving soon for Monterey, to assume his post as provincial governor. She would be friendless without him if she stayed.

But there was nothing to stay for. Since arriving at the pueblo she had questioned those Californios who had come from other areas. There was no word of Peter, nor of Camden Summers. If either of them had reached California, they had not come to the town of Los Angeles.

To Monterey, perhaps? Or to Yerba Buena, which she had been told lay still farther to the north?

Don Hernando himself, hearing her approach, came out to meet her as she rode up. "We were worried about you," he said, helping her down from the horse. "My man said you had simply vanished. I didn't know what to think."

"I'm sorry," she said. "There were things I needed to do. Don Hernando, there's something I want to say."

"Yes?" He prompted her.

"I've made up my mind, I will come to Monterey with you, if you still desire it."

He smiled, the leathery skin about his eyes crinkling into myriad tiny creases. "I would be delighted," he said. "Delighted indeed."

PART III

The Californios

23

"Señora, your horse is ready."

"Thank you, Redwing." Claire stepped from the shade of her open doorway into the morning sunlight. Don Hernando was already mounted, waiting patiently for her. He turned to smile down at her as she came out.

"Sorry to be late," she apologized, checking the girth herself although the Indian servant had already done so.

"I'm afraid there's going to be more delay yet," said the Don, now the provincial governor.

She followed his glance. Though his own impressive house was in the center of the town of Monterey, he had provided Claire with a rather simpler one on the outskirts at the end of the main street. Just now a cart was traveling the street in their direction, leaving a cloud of dust in its wake.

"Doña Magdalena," Claire said with a grimace, recognizing the cart's driver. "What do you suppose that old hen's come to gossip about this time?"

"Nothing flattering to us, you can be certain of that," Don Hernando replied.

They waited for the cart to pull up alongside them. Doña Magdalena, who thrived on keeping the small community's gossip circulating, did not attempt to climb down, a task made difficult by the combination of excessive weight and voluminous petticoats. Instead she greeted them from the driver's seat with a kittenish grin.

"*Buenas dias*—I've picked a bad time to call, it appears."

"We were just going for a ride," Don Hernando replied.

"I've been wanting to explore those hills," Claire added. "Of course, if I'd known you were coming—"

"Now, no need to trouble yourself over *me*," Doña Magdalena said. She paused, and with an innocent lift of her eyebrows, asked of Don Hernando, "And how is your wife these days? We've hardly seen her since she arrived."

"My wife, as I thought everyone knew, rarely leaves her room," Don Hernando said. "Her health, you understand."

"Indeed I do." Doña Magdalena dropped

her lashes discreetly, but only for a moment. "I suppose you've heard all about the new man over to the mission? Friar Hidalgo, I believe he calls himself."

"Something of a firebrand, from what I've heard," Don Hernando said.

"Fire and brimstone," Doña Magdalena agreed. "He's simply got no use for the lifestyle of us Californios. Wicked and indolent, he calls us. And of course it's all too true." She paused again, grinning slyly, and said to Claire, "He's had a bit to say about you, but I suppose you've heard all about that."

"No, I'm afraid I haven't," Claire said.

"I think we should go now," the Don suggested.

Ignoring that, Claire said, "Tell me, what has this Friar—Hidalgo, is that the name?—what has he said about me?"

"Well, I don't want to carry tales," Doña Magdalena said. She waited for someone to insist, but the other two regarded her in cool silence. Undeterred, she went on. "Mind, he hasn't mentioned you by name, though he might not even know that. He's just made mention several times of the new governor's whore."

"That will do," Don Hernando snapped.

"I'm only repeating what people have told me," Doña Magdalena protested innocently. "That's why I drove out, if you want to know. I thought you'd be grateful to hear it from a friend."

"As indeed we are," Claire said, mounting with the ease of an experienced rider. "And we thank you for your trouble."

"But I haven't... There's more, you know," Doña Magdalena cried, seeing that the two were reining their horses about, preparatory to riding off.

"I think we get the general drift," Don Hernando said. "And now, if you will excuse us." Without waiting for a reply, he rode off, Claire close at his side. Doña Magdalena, feeling cheated out of half the satisfaction she had anticipated, glowered after them until the dust from the horses' hooves settled over the cart.

They rode out of town to the southwest, climbing the hill through pine woods. Don Hernando rode ahead, following a sandy track that seemed to lead them nowhere in particular. The sound of the sea followed them upward, not so much breaking the silence as haunting it.

She had fallen in love with the California capital from the first day of their arrival. The houses were the same whitewashed adobe that had been common in the pueblo of Los Angeles, though here many were green with moss, or hung with bougainvillea, evidence of the town's greater age. The better houses had outside stairs that rose to second-story balconies and roofs of red tile.

It was the ocean that she loved most,

though, reminding her of the Malibu. It was grander here, with rocky lagoons and the amethyst-tinted bay itself. The town was virtually built on the white sand of the beach.

Some days the wind blew down from the forests that were green splashes on the ochre-colored hills, and then the air was redolent of pine resin. More often it came in from the sea, with its almost magical tang that seemed to quicken the senses. Throngs of ducks and seagulls hovered, and troops of sandpipers ran to and fro after the retreating waves, crying in chorus.

One was never away from the sound of those waves. It roared in the rooms of her house as in a seashell.

It was an easy place with which to fall in love, an easy place in which to be happy. Certainly her life was far more comfortable than it had been for a long time, free of the sort of danger and hardship to which she had become all too accustomed.

She could not, however, forget Doña Maria. Since the day of the fiesta at the Ramierez rancho, the señora's condition had worsened steadily. Sharing their home in Los Angeles, Claire had been an unwilling eavesdropper to the quarrels between the Don and his wife.

From Los Angeles they had journeyed northward along El Camino Real, the so-called King's road. Little more than a trail worn by the agents of the hide and tallow trade, it was at least well marked by the pale yellow of mustard plants. The plant's seeds had been carried in the wool of the sheep driven by the Franciscans in their journeys to establish the missions.

Here too husband and wife had clashed. Doña Maria had threatened, pleaded, connived, and even asked for a divorce to get her husband to let her return to Spain, to no avail.

At length, having arrived in Monterey, the Doña had given up the fight. On their first day there she had withdrawn to her own room, from which she had scarcely emerged since.

Had Claire been able to disregard the needling of her conscience, this might have been a blessing. There was little question that it made her role as the governor's mistress easier. Though many of the Californios might turn their noses up at her in private, Don Hernando had rightly predicted that they would not risk snubbing her openly. With Doña Maria living in nearly total seclusion, Claire functioned openly as the Don's hostess and companion, performing most, if not all, of the wifely duties.

Still she was never totally forgetful of her place, nor of the woman living her drink-blurred life behind the closed doors of her bedroom.

Which was why Doña Magdalena's remarks rankled so much. "Who is this friar Doña Magdalena mentioned?" she asked aloud.

"Friar Hidalgo?" Don Hernando grimaced. "Something of a fanatic, from what I've been told. I've heard of him since I've been in the province, though I've not yet met him. Spends his time wandering from mission to mission, scourging the locals."

"Do you think he really said that about me?"

"I shouldn't be surprised; it's a natural for him. Oh, don't look so unhappy, my dear. I doubt if he truly cares who you are or what you do. It's me he's after. Me and the entire government. They've got a great deal of the wealth of the province firmly in their hands— the best lands, the most cattle, the most servants. While we try to establish a handful of outposts such as Los Angeles, they've already got a string of them, running from south to north, already firmly established. The crown wants to share in their wealth. They want to keep what they've got. I represent the crown. So..." He shrugged.

"But the crown, with its vast resources..."

Don Hernando gave a coarse bark of a laugh. "Spain is bankrupt, its coffers empty, its notes worthless. They came here looking for treasure. All those legends of gold. Cities made of it, streets paved with it. They wanted that gold. They needed it."

Claire, who had herself seen the gold of Lone Feather's tribe, asked, "Have they never found it?"

"Not a scrap. The fools. While they've scrabbled for nonexistent gold, they've ignored the real treasures."

"I don't understand."

They had ridden to the crest of a hill and suddenly before them lay a dazzling vista that stretched from wooded hills to the great white plain that was the beach, and beyond that the vast imponderable ocean.

"There," Don Hernando said, gesturing with a free hand. "And there. And there. How long have you been here in California? Surely you've looked about you? Surely you've seen for yourself the great diversity? The soil is rich, far richer than the soil of Spain. Anything would grow in this soil. The climate has sun the year round, and gentle rains, and ocean breezes to keep it all pleasant, never too hot, never too cold. The forests. The streams, the oceans. The wildlife. The mountains, what might lie in their valleys, on their peaks? It's California that's the treasure, and they've ignored it while they prattled about their cities of gold. Someday California will be a colony to rival all of Spain, to surpass her even. But she'll be someone else's colony."

"Do you think England has designs on California? So many of the local people talk that way, but I'd never even heard of California when I was in England," Claire said.

"England?" Don Hernando gave a disdainful snort. "The English are like those birds that steal nests from others instead of building their own. They're no good at starting from scratch."

"But there's scarcely anyone else here. An occasional Frenchman. Some Russians up north."

"The Americans," Don Hernando said.

"The Americans?" Claire repeated, astonished. "But they're barely able to manage their own affairs, let alone deal with distant colonies. They're like children."

"Very rambunctious ones. A few years ago—well within the lifetimes of men living—that was a wilderness much as this. Look what they've done with it in no time at all. They've defeated the greatest military machine in the history of man. They've got their independence now. They're feeling their muscles, looking around for new conquests. That's a powerfully addictive drug, conquest. And California is here, at their back gate, so to speak."

"But it's not. It's so very far. It's impossible to journey from there to here."

He smiled patiently at her. "You made the journey. And you're but a woman."

"I survived a journey in which two men perished, but that only means that I of all people know how arduous an undertaking it is."

"It is always hardest for the first. A worn trail is easier to follow. But come, let us return. For the present, it is Spanish California that we must deal with, and the lazy, unproductive Californios living in their grand ranchos, self-satisfied, waited on hand and foot by Indian slaves. It will all go soon enough, swept away by winds of change."

He reined his horse about, but he paused to look eastward. "But mark my words, the winds will blow from that direction," he said.

24

Though Claire found it difficult to agree with much of what Don Hernando had said of California and its future, it was certainly true that the life of the Californios was a lazy, indolent one. The *gente de razón,* or people of reason as they liked to style themselves, claimed to be aristocrats, but theirs was an aristocracy quite unlike what she had known in England. For one thing, in England the purity of one's bloodline was an issue. Most of these people were unashamed to admit that theirs was mixed blood—some Spanish, some Negro, some Indian.

For another, the California aristocrats defied most of the rules by which the upper classes of other countries such as England defined themselves. An Englishman's place in society could be ruined by the knowledge that he had broken the law. The Californios blithely ignored laws and trade regulations, and dealt freely with any foreign vessel or traveler that happened their way. How else, they argued, were they to obtain the simple necessities of life, which the Spanish government, regulations notwithstanding, was unable to provide.

Even their manners, which could be painfully elaborate, bowed to the necessities of the moment. Though a young maiden was not permitted to enjoy a gentleman's company without the presence of a duenna, or chaperone, it was not at all unusual to see the same ladies pause in their progress along the streets to relieve themselves when the occasion demanded.

Still it was an easy and gracious life, wedded to the horse of necessity. The Californios were proud people of almost innocent arrogance, even the men displaying an astonishing physical grace. Their hospitality was enormous, and if they thrived on gossip, as people will who are cut off from the mainstream of events, they were at least egalitarian in that practice, pricking big and little alike with their barbs, and as quickly forgiving those who gossiped about them. Though actual cash may have been in short supply, those things necessary for life's enjoyment were not. The result was that amusement had become the real purpose of existence.

It almost seemed at times as if every day was a holiday of some sort. Every Sunday was a fiesta, and feast days, weddings, and birthdays provided almost endless excuses for merrymaking. With virtually no industry but illegal trade, and with an army of Indians to attend to manual labor, with a climate that occasioned no hardships, and the bounty of ocean and earth at their fingertips, the Californios were able to devote themselves almost exclusively to the pursuit of pleasure.

That pursuit sometimes took what Claire regarded as barbaric routes. The Californios engaged in a number of activities that Claire felt certain would have been banned in most civilized countries.

For one, there was the bull tying. For this, a mounted vaquero took a position at either side of a gate in a stone corral near the plaza. A bull was driven from the enclosure, and when he had run a short distance along the street, the vaqueros galloped after him. The first one to reach the bull would seize his tail, turning it around the pommel of the saddle. In this manner, by guiding his horse a little to the side, the vaquero could throw the bull completely off his feet. In an instant the vaquero leaped to the ground and with a piece of rope, tied the bull's legs together. The vaqueros were so skilled at this sport that the contest went as a rule to the one with the fastest horse, who could reach the bull first.

Yet another pastime was the so-called

cock race. A rooster was buried in the ground, with only his head showing, and the head was covered with grease. The vaqueros, perhaps half a dozen of them, would race toward the unfortunate creature, each man bending low from his saddle. The winner was the one who succeeded in pulling up the bird by the head, which sometimes separated from the body.

To Claire's mind, the cruelest of all these events was the fight between bear and bull. When she first heard that one of these was to be staged, an occasion for considerable excitement among the Californios of Monterey, she declined to attend. However, Don Hernando took offense at her condemning something she had never even seen, she'd reluctantly agreed to accompany him to the event.

"It's not much different, after all, from a bull fight," he assured her.

Claire, who had never seen a bull fight, found little comfort in the comparison. As there was no arena as such, the fight was to be staged in the same corral used for the bull tying events. Don Hernando and the town's leading citizens watched from the porch of the adobe hotel. The others found places where they could, on porches, roofs, and even fence tops.

A cheer went up from the crowd when a huge grizzly was dragged into view by three vaqueros on horseback.

"A fine specimen," was Don Hernando's verdict. Claire could not help a shudder as she saw the beast's mammoth paws and long, menacing teeth.

From one of the ranchos came a huge and powerful looking bull, his head set low on thick and powerful shoulders. The bull pawed the earth, straining against the ropes that held him.

Finding themselves in the same pen, the two beasts might have avoided one another, but the vaqueros, anticipating this, fastened them together by a long chain before freeing them from the restraining ropes. The chain, fastened about the leg of each, meant that the animals must soon interfere with one another's movements, assuring that a fight would ensue.

Another cheer went up as the bull began the fight by charging the roaring grizzly. For a moment the two combatants vanished in a cloud of dust.

The grizzly evaded the initial charge, but the chain held him to the bull. The grizzly's efforts to escape brought the bull to his knees, bellowing loudly.

On his feet again, the bull charged once more. This time, seeing escape was impossible, the grizzly met the charge with a great blow of his paw, which was not enough to stop his enemy's advance.

Bull and bear went to the ground together, rolling over and over in the dust. The spectators called out to one or the other of the animals, cheering them on.

"The bear's got the best of it now," Don Hernando said. "On his feet, the bull's a menace, but he's not built for wrestling in the dirt like this."

Claire, holding a lace handkerchief to her nose to prevent sneezing on the rising dust, watched the battle with morbid fascination.

As Don Hernando had said, the advantage had now gone to the grizzly. Despite his sheer bulk and the fact that he was badly gored, he twisted and writhed about with the agility of a cat. In a moment he was on his hind legs, and had managed to get his teeth into the bull's neck, forcing the hapless creature once again to his knees.

The bull gave a bellow of pain and by sheer brute force managed to get to his feet, throwing the grizzly off, but the bull was so weakened and terrified that instead of continuing to fight, he struggled desperately to escape. In his efforts, he actually dragged the enraged grizzly for several feet before that animal was able to right himself, and leap upon the bull's back, bringing him to the ground once again.

The bull now kicked and thrashed in sheer panic, to the disappointment of the crowd. The small boys atop their fences shouted disparaging remarks, and some began to hurl stones and debris at the beasts.

At last the bull, numb with terror, ceased to fight at all, though his sides could be seen heaving in and out with the effort of his breathing.

With disgusted expressions and loud oaths, the vaqueros entered the corral and dispatched both beasts with their guns. It had been, judging from the reactions of the onlookers, a disappointing bout.

Claire could not help a sickish feeling in her stomach as Don Hernando escorted her to his carriage. As he was handing her in, one of the rancheros spoke to him. Don Hernando stepped aside to talk with him for a moment.

A minor commotion broke out nearby as someone pushed his way through the crowd toward the governor, and a voice called out, "Is this our noble governor?"

Claire, still queasy from the spectacle she had just witnessed, sank back against the cushions, only half-listening to the conversations outside.

"I am Don Hernando," she heard. "What can I do for you? And who are you, might I ask?"

"Friar Hidalgo, at your service."

At once Claire sat forward, peering through the windows. The friar had managed to position himself so that his back was to her. Even so, he looked like some Biblical prophet, dressed in a toga-like robe fashioned of some animal skin. His hair was long and filthy, and a bushy beard moved as he talked. Like a prophet, too, he carried a long, rough-hewn staff.

Don Hernando came toward the stranger. "Well, we've heard a great deal of you," he said.

"And I of you," Friar Hidalgo replied, laughing coarsely. The voice, with its peculiarly accented Spanish, had a familiar ring to it. "And your whore, whom I'm told is beautiful. I only regret arriving too late to see her before she hid herself in your carriage."

"Sir," Don Hernando said indignantly.

"That's all right," Claire said, more curious than angry. "If the good friar wants to see me, I don't mind."

She stepped down from the carriage without waiting for assistance. "I'm afraid you're mistaken, señor," she said. "I have nothing to hide."

Friar Hidalgo turned slowly toward her. For a moment she did not recognize him. The elements, or perhaps some great trauma, had aged him incredibly, making him look ancient though he was but a year or two older than herself. The matted hair and beard concealed part of his face, too. Only the eyes, burning with a feverish intensity that had merely been hinted at before, told her who he was.

"Claire," he said, so softly that she barely heard her name.

She tried to speak his, but no sound would issue from her throat. Shaking her head to and fro in disbelief, she took a faltering step toward him, then another.

The shock was too great for her, however.

The heat, the blinding sun, the squeamish stomach—all combined against her.

She heard Don Hernando cry, as if from far away, "Catch her, someone!"

The earth tilted and slipped beneath her feet, and the next moment she had succumbed to an enveloping darkness.

25

She woke in the familiar surroundings of her own bedroom. Two of the local women were bathing her forehead with cool, damp cloths.

"In a moment, señora," one of them said when she tried to sit up. Firm but gentle hands restrained her. "Rest now, *por favor.*"

She sank gratefully into the pillows, glad for a moment to collect her scattered thoughts. She had a vivid memory of the stone corral, of a bear and a bull fighting viciously, the smell of blood sickening the air.

One of the women went out. There was a commotion at the door; she could hear whispered voices arguing inaudibly.

Suddenly she was aware of someone else in the room. She turned to watch him cross toward her. The shutters had been closed against the glaring sun so that the room was in shadow, but it was not hard to distinguish the animal-skin robe, or the immense beard.

He paused by the side of the bed, familiar ice blue eyes staring down at her.

"Peter," she said, staring back. "It is you, then. I thought perhaps I'd only dreamed that." She struggled to a sitting position. Both the women who had been with her had disappeared. She heard the bedroom door close softly, but she was too occupied with her long vanished husband to spare attention for anyone or anything else.

"I wish I'd only dreamed this," he said with a toss of his head that took in not only the room but the entire house as well. "If you only knew how often I've prayed for your safety, your well-being. Only to find you here, like this—the governor's whore."

"Stop it." She swung her feet to the floor and got up. He made no move to help her. His eyes followed her, accusing her.

"I left you in Virginia."

"Yes, that's it exactly. You left me in Virginia," she snapped. "Nothing to do but wait and worry. You stopped writing. I had no way of knowing what had happened, whether you were alive or dead."

"There's no way to write from out there." He made a gesture toward the great plains. "If you'd ever been there, you'd know."

"I know," she said. "I've been there too."

"You?" He stared, aghast. "What do you mean?"

"I came looking for you," she said. "I thought, I don't know what I thought now. It's all so long ago and far away. I felt that I'd driven you away, I was guilty. And I suppose, if I'm to be honest, I was bored too, and restless. Maybe I'd heard the same siren's call you heard, only I didn't recognize it."

She paused. There was a bottle of sherry on the table by the window. She went, silently offering him some, and pouring herself a glass when he declined with a shake of his head. He waited for her to go on.

"I journeyed to St. Louis," she said, the sherry helping to clear her head. "I found some men there, trappers, who told me they'd taken you west."

"Morton and that scummy sidekick of his," Peter said with a disgusted grimace. "They're swine. I hope you steered clear of them."

"I hired them to take me where you'd gone."

"I can't believe you escaped Morton unstained," he said. His eyes narrowed sharply. "Or, more likely, you didn't, I suppose?"

She sighed. "Whatever crimes they committed, they've paid for them," she said.

"They're dead?"

"Leblanc was scalped by the Pawnee," she said. "Morton almost made it here. He died in a cave-in in the desert east of the pueblo of Los Angeles."

"East of—you and Morton crossed the plains, the mountains?"

"There was another man with us, he drowned in a river. Morton and I managed to survive. After the desert we met up with some Indians. They brought me to the ocean. From there I made it to Los Angeles."

"It's incredible. I can hardly believe your surviving out there," he said. He came closer to her, his eyes glittering with what might almost have been sexual arousal. "That wilderness."

"You survived it too," she said.

"That's different. But a woman." He came still closer. The ice blue eyes looked her up and down. She felt other memories stirring within her, ugly, hateful memories. She thrust them aside.

"How did you manage?" she asked.

"The Indians," he said.

"They helped you?"

He turned from her, seeming to force his eyes from the pale expanse of her bosom. "I prayed with them," he said. "They saw that I was a holy man. I told them I was seeking a sort of paradise. In the desert, I ..." He paused, looking for the first time embarrassed. "You know about Christ, and his ordeal in the wilderness. It was the same. I was alone, it must have been a month, maybe two. I had visions. He appeared to me."

Remembering the desert, the burning, merciless sun, she realized that he must have suffered hallucinations as she had. With his religious bent, his would undoubtedly have been of that nature.

"You might have died," she said.

He had been gazing into the distance, but now he looked back at her. He was smiling, as if in the throes of some remembered ecstasy.

"Maybe I did," he said. "I thought I was going to, I remember fainting, and when I woke, he was there."

"You saw someone?"

"Not exactly." He frowned suddenly. His eyes darted to and fro, as if seeking something. "There were voices. Many voices, and then one voice." He shook his head, passing a hand before his face as though a curtain hung in his way.

"Some more Indians found me," he said. "I lived with them. I don't know, a long time. They said I performed miracles, I can't remember. The voices, they were there all the time, no one else seemed to hear them, they told me things."

He stopped, silent for so long that she thought he had forgotten her and his story both. Finally he said, "They brought me to one of the missions, in San Diego. I don't remember much. I was in a fever, they thought I was dead for sure. Suddenly the fever was gone. Since then I've traveled from mission to mission. I came here because—" Again he paused. When he looked at her, it was accusingly. "I came here because of you. When they spoke of you, they gave your name the Spanish pronunciation, Clara."

"But they must have said I was from the east, that I was searching for my husband. Everywhere I've gone, I've asked about you. Surely you must have suspected it was I."

"Not in the least," he said, shaking his head thoughtfully. "Who would have dreamed you'd be here? When I'd remembered you, it was, I don't know how to say it, it was like remembering someone I'd dreamed of a long time ago. I'd forgotten that you were flesh and blood. When I was in the desert, when the voices came to me—you won't understand this—I cleansed myself of all that. Of you, and of the old fires that used to burn in me. They were consumed in a greater fire. I scarcely remembered you at all."

After a moment, to his surprise, she laughed. The sound annoyed him in some way he couldn't define. "What's funny?" he asked.

"Us. Everything," she said, still laughing. "You crossed a wilderness, an entire continent, looking for treasure. I crossed it looking for—I don't know, absolution, I suppose. And here we are. You in animal skins, looking like Elijah, and I...?" She shrugged.

"Seeking absolution? In a man's bed? A married man's bed? You find that amusing?"

For a moment she looked at him as if seeing through him. "And yet," she said, speaking slowly as if searching for words to express her thoughts, "and yet, we found what we were looking for, didn't we? We found California."

"I don't know what you're talking about." The blue eyes blazed angrily.

"California," she repeated. "The treasures—the mountains and the trees and the ocean, treasures all, everywhere you look. And absolution, too. Peter, it's a different world here. Virginia's gone, and London too. The lives we used to live. Your brother. The quarrels and pains, they've been left behind in that other world. We've got another chance. California's given us absolution. It was California we were searching for all the time."

She came to him and put a hand lightly on his arm. "Peter, I know we didn't do very well at it, but we are married. And this is a new life for us. Perhaps if we both tried."

He shook off her hand. "I'm not Peter," he said harshly, "I'm Friar Hidalgo, and I'm married to the Church now."

"But what about me?"

"I came here because of you, though I didn't know who you were. I came to chastise you and your paramour for your sinful lives. Look at you, you talk about being married to me, about wanting another chance, and here you are, another man's mistress, living in his house, shameless." He looked around and, spying a stole lying across a chair, he snatched it up and threw it at her. "Your breasts are half-bare, señora, cover yourself in the name of decency."

He started from the room. "Peter!" she cried.

"Hidalgo," he corrected her, "Friar Hidalgo. And I will be back, señora, never fear. The Church is my marriage now. I will not rest until she is yours as well."

26

It was the biggest excitement the town of Monterey had had in ages. It was far more thrilling to its residents than the disappointing fight between bull and bear, which they thought it resembled. If Don Hernando could be cast in the role of the bull, for which his stubbornness, if nothing else, suited him, it was not difficult to see the wild Friar Hidalgo as a bear. But would his claws triumph over the bull's strength?

For days the Californios could talk of nothing else but the discovery that Friar Hidalgo—here, it was agreed, for the sole purpose of chastizing the Don and his mistress—was none other than the long-lost husband of the lovely Clara herself.

What a juicy scandal! The Don's wife,

Doña Maria, drinking wine in the unbroken privacy of her bedroom; the mad friar, a modern-day John the Baptist who even went so far as to hold a baptismal service at the beach; the handsome new governor, an austere Old World aristocrat of the sort rarely encountered in raw California; and the aloof, though admittedly lovely Claire herself. Clara, as they invariably called her, turning her name Spanish. While the women laughed and chattered in the cool shade of their parlors, the men gathered in knots along the town's streets and in the cantinas to pursue the same subject.

In the days since her meeting with Peter— she could not bring herself to call him Friar Hidalgo—Claire had become nearly as much a recluse as Doña Maria, rarely venturing outside her house. She discouraged all those visitors who came to call, thinking to pick up fresh tidbits to add to the stew of gossip. Only Don Hernando, who after all had provided her the house in the first place, was permitted inside. Even he found the reception a cool one.

"You must see how this changes everything," Claire pointed out.

"My darling, I know what a shock this has been to you," Don Hernando said, coming to her and attempting to put his arms about her.

Claire turned from him, shunning his embrace. "It's different now," she said. "My husband..." She let her voice trail off lamely.

"That madman? You're no more married now than you were a day ago, a week before that. Less, maybe. At least in your memory he was a real husband, not a Biblical patriarch. And what of my wife?"

"I've been thinking of her, a great deal, in fact," Claire said. "Which we ought to have been doing before this."

"You're letting his filthy accusations taint your thinking, Claire."

"Please, Don Hernando." Claire pressed her hands to her throbbing temples. "I must have time to think. I don't know what to do."

"Well, I do," Don Hernando said angrily. "I'll have that scoundrel whipped in the streets for the things he said. I'm governor here. Mission or no mission, he's got no right to insult decent people."

Claire gave a mirthless laugh. "I'm afraid our 'decency' is rather in dispute at the moment, wouldn't you say? And anyway, you can hardly have the husband of your mistress whipped in the streets. That would really give the good señoras plenty to talk about."

"Damn them all." Don Hernando poured himself a drink and downed it quickly. "Has he come back to see you?"

"He will. I know Peter. Excuse me, I mean Friar Hidalgo."

"What if he does? What then? Will you don animal skins and join him in his search for sinners?"

Claire met his gaze thoughtfully. "I don't know," she said. "I just don't know."

Don Hernando's heart ached as he gazed back at her. When he'd first laid eyes on her at the San Fernando mission something had happened inside him. He'd blamed it on her eyes. There was something about the way she had of looking at you; it played tricks with a man's good sense. He'd known long before he suggested it just how his wife would react to his bringing this beautiful stranger home with him, but he had been unable to help himself. Nor had he planned on making her his mistress. Even when he had finally suggested that to her, he hadn't dared to dream that she would agree. Indeed, he would have been content to have her about, to be able to see her when he wished, to know that she was happy.

For perhaps the first time in his aristocratic, well-organized life, Don Hernando was in love. He was not a man accustomed to displaying his emotions. Since his earliest childhood he had been trained to keep them locked securely within himself. No enemy had ever seen his fear. He was known to have a temper, but the full depth of his anger had yet to be measured. He had married for political and social reasons and taken mistresses in answer to physical urge.

In myriad ways, significant to himself, he had attempted to demonstrate his feelings for her. He'd hired someone to protect her from unwanted advances, had given her gifts, and had even brought her with him to Monterey, despite his wife's misery and the inevitable gossip of the local people. In every indirect way he had tried to tell her what it was impossible for him to say directly.

What was he to say now that would not add to her confusion and unhappiness? If it would have helped, he would have tried to go deep within himself, to reveal his innermost feelings to her, though it would have violated all of his experience and character. But he was wise enough to see that it was too late for such a declaration, that it could only make things worse.

He turned from her so that she could not see how difficult the suggestion was for him and asked, "Do you wish me to stay away?"

Her silence was so lengthy that he actually dared to hope she would say otherwise, but after a while she sighed and said, "It might help to still their tongues a little."

He did not say goodbye, nor tell her that she had only to send for him if she needed him. That much at least she surely knew. He gathered his hat from the hook by the door and went out without a backward glance. A moment later she heard the sound of his horse's hooves fading in the distance. He did not ride toward the town, she noticed, but up into the hills where he would be alone.

From outside came a puzzling murmur of voices, punctuated by a childish giggle. Claire, going to the window, saw that a group of the town's children had gathered across the way to watch her house. She supposed that they had heard their parents hint of the dramatic events expected to occur. The children had come to be an audience.

She did not scold them, but carefully closed the shutters over the windows, plunging the interior into darkness. Then she seated herself to await the call Peter was certain to make.

But Peter did not come. The days passed slowly for Claire as she waited in the sheltered gloom of the house Don Hernando had given her. The children ceased to sit across the way, finding nothing to amuse them in a still house with closed shutters. The townspeople ceased to invent excuses to stroll by the out-of-the-way location. The hours inched more slowly than the snails that frolicked by the cistern. And still Peter stayed away.

At first she was puzzled, but as the days succeeded one another she thought she began to see the point. She knew the ways in which Peter's mind worked, and the long hours of waiting gave her the time needed to see things from his point of view.

Peter's return had been sufficient to put a halt, at least temporarily, to her relationship with Don Hernando. Peter was clever enough to see that the criticism of the townspeople would effectively separate them. As provincial governor, Don Hernando was not completely above censure. As for herself, it was one thing to be the wife of a man missing and presumed dead. It was another altogether to be the wife of a religious man very much on view in the community. What might have been forgivable, if maliciously noted, in one set of circumstances became quite scandalous in another.

But for Peter it would not be enough simply to interrupt her liaison with the governor. Peter's thought processes were such that he would expect her to suffer some punishment for her misdoings. She strongly suspected that by ignoring her now he was in a way punishing her. After all, she was as effectively isolated as if she had taken the vows. Indeed more so, for at the mission she would have had the company at least of other penitents. Here she saw no one but the two Indian servants Don Hernando had hired for her, neither of whom conversed with her in more than the most essential monosyllables.

Her home had become a prison. She was guarded by her gossiping neighbors. Locked in by her own guilty conscience.

With realization came anger. Trapped in the confines of four small rooms, Claire began to pace as she had once paced the grandly elegant rooms she had occupied in Virginia. Who was Peter to manipulate her life in such a calculated manner? Granted he was her husband, but he was a husband who had abused and misused her during their time together. A husband who had married her as a result of treachery toward his own brother. A husband who had left her in a foolish quest for fortune in the west. A husband who, having reached California, had made no effort to inform her of his whereabouts or his well-being.

Indeed, in every effective way, her husband had divorced her long before she had become Don Hernando's mistress.

From room to room and back again she went, each pace fanning the anger smoldering within her. At night she heard the sounds of merrymaking from the town. Music from fiestas and cantinas, and young people calling to one another happily. There was laughter and shouts, and the strumming of guitars.

At last she could bear her isolation no more. It was the second of October, and Doña Magdalena's feast day. For weeks the Doña had planned a grand party to celebrate the occasion, and Claire had been invited long ago. Of course, it had been supposed that she would come in the company of Don Hernando. But the invitation had not made this mandatory, and late on the afternoon of that day, Claire decided that she would attend the party after all, but alone.

Almost the first thing she had done upon arriving in Monterey was to have several new dresses made, and now she searched through them for just the right outfit for the occasion. She had all but forgotten a gown of red satin, picked only because Don Hernando had thought the color striking on her with her golden hair and deeply tanned complexion. Now it seemed exactly right for her mood of defiance. Her jewelry was still minimal, but Don Hernando had given her a pair of gold hoop earrings, which she wore. An embroidered shawl completed the effect.

Though the rainy season had officially begun, the minimal rains that had fallen had not yet managed to turn the dirt streets into seas of mud, as she had been warned would happen soon enough. Shunning horse and buggy, Claire decided she would walk to Doña Magdalena's house, which was near the center of town. She knew that Don Hernando would have expected her to send a message to him, letting him know her plans. He would expect to take her, but that was only certain to fan the flames of gossip, and she had decided to brazen it out on her own.

Doña Magdalena's house being judged too small for such a crowd, the party was being held out of doors, becoming as it progressed more or less a community affair. Wooden planks had been put down for a dance floor and around these were arranged wooden benches for the ladies. A makeshift band had been assembled. Claire could hear their lively music competing with the hum of conversation and the click of heels on the planks as she strolled purposefully along the street. Balls of pitch had been set atop tall poles, providing a flickering illumination.

The party had begun before she set out, and most of the townspeople, always eager for fun, were already there. She met no one along the way and had moved through the crowd to the very edge of the dance floor before her arrival was generally noted.

She was not unaware of the stir she caused. Anger had added color to her cheeks and, while the women whispered rapidly behind their fans, a number of the local swains, seeing her without an escort, hurried over to greet her.

Claire threw herself into the festivities. Scarcely a person present had not witnessed the scene when she had recognized Friar Hidalgo as her missing husband, and those who hadn't seen it had certainly heard every detail. But they were wrong, she thought grimly, if they supposed she would hide herself forever from observation.

Fortunately the scene was made easier by the fact that Don Hernando was nowhere to be seen. For his own reasons, and no doubt assuming she would be absent, he had chosen not to attend the party. She was grateful, as her mood of defiance did not extend to him. She had no illusions regarding their relationship. She was not in love with the governor. He had proven himself a good and reliable friend, however, and she had no wish to hurt or embarrass so fine a man.

The unattached gentlemen, seeing she was receptive to their invitations, flocked to ask her to dance. Her smile never wavering, she danced waltzes, polkas, and the Spanish fandangos, barely pausing for breath between them.

It was while she was dancing the fandango

that Don Hernando, made restless by the sounds of music drifting from the party, left his house and came to make an appearance.

He stood at the edge of the wooden floor watching her and thought she had never looked more beautiful, nor more unobtainable. He understood as the others did not that her brazen manner was largely bravado. He knew that inside she was hurt and frightened, but she was too proud to display such feelings.

At last, unable to bear the ache in his heart, he stepped forward, meaning to claim her for the next dance. Before he could do so, however, he became aware of a commotion back in the crowd and he paused, craning to see what was happening.

Someone was approaching. The crowd parted to make way, and Don Hernando had a glimpse of a wild-eyed figure clad from head to foot in animal skins despite the night's warmth.

"Harlot!"

Until she heard Peter's cry, Claire had been completely unaware of his approach. Only a minute before she had glanced about and found herself gazing into Don Hernando's eyes.

The music whined to a stop, the other dancers melting back from her as the friar advanced onto the dance floor. Even Claire's partner of the moment seemed to vanish in a twinkling, and she suddenly found herself alone facing Peter.

She tried to smile, though her legs were

trembling so badly she half-feared she might fall. "Peter," she said with false cheer, "how nice to see you again."

He ignored her efforts to remain friendly. "Whore!" he cried.

"Sir!" Don Hernando would have stepped forward, but two of his friends gently restrained him.

"Peter, I—it's a party." Claire spoke in a low voice, coming toward her husband. She put a placating hand upon his arm. "Let's not spoil it by making a—"

He did not wait for her to finish, but raised his hand and struck her with such force that she was sent crashing to the wooden floor.

Don Hernando gave a cry of anger and would have leapt upon the friar, but his friends intervened, grabbing his arms and preventing his interference.

"He's her husband," several of them hissed at once.

For several seconds Claire lay stunned upon the floor, her jaw aching where Peter had struck her. Shame, rage, humiliation washed over her like the waves of the nearby surf. She looked around and saw a wall of people, staring at her, some with pity, some with scorn, a few even with amusement. She saw Don Hernando, his arms pinioned, his face contorted with frustration and rage.

The silence of the crowd was eerie, so complete that the ocean sounds could be heard clearly. Not a person moved or spoke, but remained frozen as if in a tableau.

Slowly, favoring an ankle that had been twisted under her, she got to her feet. Fixing her gaze straight ahead, she limped off the floor. The crowd, still silent, parted before her like the waters before Moses' rod. No one moved to help or impede her progress. Even Peter seemed stunned by what he had done and stepped aside to let her pass. Still walking with a painful limp, she passed through the throng and disappeared along the darkened street.

Watching her go, Don Hernando felt his face burn with shame. Even when the men holding him released his arms, he made no move to follow her. He felt as if he could never face her again.

After a long moment someone ran their fingers over the strings of a guitar, unleashing a cascade of liquid sounds. The crowd gave a great collective sigh, beginning to talk all at once.

Down the street Claire heard the grumble of their voices like the threatening growl of some dangerous beast.

27

It was late when she woke the next day. She lay abed, listening without knowing just what it was she was listening for. Something was wrong, though she couldn't quite put her finger on it.

She had it at last. There were no sounds of activity about the house. Surely by now the two Indians who acted as servants, Redwing and his wife, should be up and about their chores.

She got up and dressed quickly, then went in search of them. There was no sign of either. She went through the kitchen and out the back door to the shed that served as their quarters.

Neither of them was there; nor, she realized after a moment of glancing around, were their belongings. Blankets, pots, ornaments, all were gone. The shed was empty. The Indians had left sometime since the night before without a word to her.

It was the first sign. The second occurred when, seeing that the Indians had left nothing for her breakfast, she set out for the trading post. She had walked only a short distance when Doña Magdalena drove by in her cart and pointedly snubbed her.

It was then she realized that she had become a pariah, an outcast. The Californios might gossip and laugh about the friars of the missions, and they might connive with the government of Spain to rob the missions of their hard-won wealth; but their blood was Spanish, however mixed with the blood of the new land. In their veins ran the Spanish awe for the Church and its representatives.

It was not her husband, Peter, but Friar Hidalgo, Franciscan, who had branded her a harlot. He had proclaimed her sin for the entire town to witness. Before, they had viewed the contretemps with amused detachment. His actions had forced them to take sides, with or against him. And firebrand and fanatic though he might be, he represented the Church. Though she had been an outsider, though they had clucked their tongues at her relationship with Don Hernando, they had nonetheless suffered her presence in their midst. Now the doors were closed to her.

Yet such was the nature of things that

even as the townspeople brought the weight of their censure to bear upon her, they still regarded the situation as one of their chief sources of entertainment. Those same people who had turned their heads and averted their eyes as she passed along the street watched the unfolding of events with unabated relish. They might well be prepared to snub this English woman who had somehow found her way to their town, but they had by no means lost interest in her.

As a result, Claire was perhaps the last person to know when Peter paid a call upon her, the others having observed his progress toward her house for a considerable distance.

He came in without knocking, entering from the front door. She was just coming in from the rear, her arms laden with wood for the cookstove. For a long moment they contemplated one another. The unaccustomed load made her arms ache, and she had to turn away to drop it in the box by the stove. Too, events had unnerved her more than she wanted to admit. She found she had difficulty meeting Peter's coldly disapproving stare.

"Would you like some coffee?" she asked, lifting the pot and weighing its contents.

"I'm surprised you learned to cook for yourself," Peter said. "You were always used to having everything done for you."

"You might be less pleased when you've tasted this," she said, handing him a steaming mug. "I learned it over a campfire. The only

345

real requirements, though, were that it be as strong and as hot as possible. I think you'll find this qualifies nicely."

To her surprise, he clasped her hand and turned it palm up, studying it. Once she had been inordinately vain over her hands; now they were calloused and burned, and there was a nasty-looking splinter imbedded near the thumb. Unexpectedly he lifted her hand to his lips.

The gesture made her uncomfortable, and she took her hand from his. "I'm afraid they're not very pretty," she said, turning away and pouring a cup of coffee for herself.

"Have the Indians gone?" Peter asked.

"Like everyone else, driven away by your Old Testament rantings," she said. She lifted the lid of the stove and thrust a length of wood inside.

Far from being offended by the remark, he seemed to find it amusing. Grinning, he glanced about the tiny kitchen. "Did he provide this house for you?"

"Yes," she said. She turned back to him. "Does that make you uncomfortable here?"

His grin faded. "You can't stay," he said.

"I've nowhere else to go."

"You'll come to the mission to live. In time you can take vows."

"No!" She all but shouted the word at him. She turned from him again and went to stand at the back door. His suggestion had roused a storm of unpleasant memories within her. Thoughts of Lone Feather and his tribe, of her daughter, Shining Star, whom she would never see again. She thought of the morning the soldiers had come to the village, rounding up Indians like so many cattle and taking them to the mission for their "conversion." She thought of the indignities and the cruelty suffered at the mission, cruelties she had escaped only by revealing that she was a white woman. For others, however, they could end only in the mercy of death. The very suggeston of going to live at the mission filled her with dread.

"I cannot go there to live," she said.

"You cannot remain here, it's indecent," he replied. "I've already arranged for a room for you at the mission."

She sighed and turned back to the room. "Peter," she said, "I don't wish to quarrel with you, truly I don't. So much has happened, it's difficult to say who's to blame. But we are still married. It may seem peculiar to you, but that is a fact I've never forgotten. And we are finally together once again. Perhaps if we both made a special effort, we could still make a success of our marriage. At least we could try. Why don't you come here to live? Don Hernando won't mind, I'm certain he won't, he's really a very nice person."

For an answer, Peter threw the cup of coffee against the wall. It shattered noisily, leaving a vivid stain. "Have you no shame?" he demanded in a loud voice.

He strode angrily to where she was standing and, seizing her wrist in a violent grip, yanked her toward him, thrusting his face into hers.

"The Church is my bride now," he said, "as she will be yours. I swear by Almighty God, I will not rest until you have seen the sinfulness of your ways and taken the vows."

Staring into his gleaming eyes, she thought, not for the first time, that Peter was a little mad. Perhaps he always had been. A bead of sweat inched its way over his brow. She was aware of some passionate emotion boiling within him, threatening to erupt. She would not have been surprised if he'd attempted to throttle her.

Instead, after a moment in which the only sound was the rasp of his labored breathing, he flung her hand away from himself as if its touch dirtied him.

He dashed from the house. Claire, rubbing her bruised wrist, stared after him in dismay. She was terrified at the prospect of going to live at the mission. What was she to do? Alone and friendless, she could hardly remain where she was indefinitely.

Tears forming in her eyes, she sank to her knees on the hard floor and rested her cheek against the wood of the kitchen cupboard.

What was she to do? Where was she to turn?

It took the better part of the day to journey on foot to the mission, separated as it was from the town by the brown hills. It was evening by the time Peter returned there, the vespers ringing as he let himself through the front gates.

He was not a social person, and the brothers of the mission had soon abandoned their efforts at making friends with this firebrand who had come to them out of the California wilderness. His zeal was both a challenge and an embarrassment to them. They had no doubt that he was of a truly holy character. In the short time he had been among them, he had attracted a small but enthusiastic band of supporters.

The more moderate members of the mission, however, saw Friar Hidalgo as a danger. The missions of California stood in a state of siege, set upon not only by the greed of the crown, but by the very colonies for which they had paved the way into the wilderness. It was dangerous, the moderates among them argued, to further antagonize the townspeople. At times such as these, the argument went, it was wise to attract as little attention to themselves as possible, since the attention they would get was unlikely to be friendly.

Peter had remained steadfastly aloof from all such discussions. Like the fanatic that he was, he saw things in a simplistic vision, everything black and white and with no grey areas to raise questions. Let others debate. He had come to ferret out sin, and he would not rest until victory was his. And God's.

As he passed through the gardens of the

mission grounds, some of the friars greeted him. Others steadfastly ignored his arrival.

Near the wine shed one of the Indians was being whipped. Peter interrupted his progress to investigate.

"Caught stealing wine," the soldier explained when Peter asked why the Indian was being punished.

Peter glanced down at the kneeling figure. The man's back was crisscrossed with welts, some of them fresh, others already faded into lifelong scars. The punishment in this case was not severe, twenty lashes, and it appeared to be almost over.

"Carry on," Peter said. He was about to turn away when one of the soldiers administering the punishment gave a yelp and clapped a hand over his eyes.

"What's wrong," Peter asked.

"Someone's thrown a rock," the other soldier said, stooping to retrieve the stone. His companion's eye was bleeding.

They looked around, but though the compound was busy, no one else seemed to have noticed the incident. Nor was the culprit easily identifiable. A dozen or more Indians worked within throwing distance. The soldier looked alarmed.

"These blasted Indians—" he started to say.

"Are our children," Peter finished for him. He took the stone from the soldier's hand and tossed it into the bushes. "Continue with the punishment."

Peter turned and continued on his way, dismissing the incident. There were always some few among the Indians who could not be subdued. It had aroused yet another controversy in the mission when he had suggested that such troublemakers ought to be put to death as a matter of course.

His thought quickly returned to Claire. Since the moment of their confrontation in town, he had been unable to banish her from his thoughts for more than a minute or two.

Alone in his cell he extracted a rosary from the pocket of his robe. The room's single decoration was a rosary of cut tin upon one wall. He knelt before this and began to pray in earnest.

But try though he might, he could not erase from his mind the image of Claire as she had looked earlier, when he had gone to her house. His suggestion that she move to the mission had frightened her, though he was at a loss to understand why. He had a vision of her as she had looked when he had drawn her close to him, her eyes wide with fright, her lips trembling. The bodice of her dress had been cut low, revealing the fullness of her breasts and the dark, richly scented valley between them. In his mind's eye her breasts seemed to grow until they were enormous, dwarfing him. His pulse began to pound in his ears.

With a low groan Peter sank forward on the hard dirt floor. He was physically aroused by his memories of her. The arousal shamed him and he tried to will it gone, but like the breasts of his vision his erection seemed to grow until he was unable to ignore it.

Suddenly he sprang to his feet, tearing his robe from his body. Beneath it he wore what at first glance appeared to be a tunic of armor, but which in fact was made of tin and pierced like a grater so that it lacerated the flesh at the slightest movement.

Carefully Peter removed the tin shirt. His back and chest were bleeding in a hundred places from the lacerations. He had made the shirt himself specifically to wear when he called on Claire. The pain had been intended to purify his thoughts, but it had failed. He had been unable to control the lustful visions that had tortured him since their reunion.

Flinging aside the tin, Peter knelt and withdrew from under his bed a scourge made of several lengths of rope braided together and tied with numerous knots. Still kneeling, he raised the scourge over his shoulder and began to beat his already torn back with it, the knotted ropes streaking his flesh with new welts.

While he thus abused himself, he tried to direct his thoughts to prayer. To his dismay, the image of Claire returned to haunt him. Feverishly he lashed at his back with the scourge.

28

For a brief period of time the town's attention was diverted from Claire's situation by the occurrence of an ugly incident. A soldier from the presidio, coming drunk from one of the cantinas, happened upon a family of Indians from the mission. Thinking to have some fun, the soldier approached the squaw, and when her husband objected, knocked the man to the ground. Seeing his wife being dragged behind a building, the Indian picked up a rock from the roadway and crushed the soldier's skull. In a panic at what he had done, the hapless brave fled into the pine forests.

Of course the matter could not go unpunished. The Californios were not likely to forget that some forty years before the Yuma

Indians had risen up against the first of the Alta California settlements, killing more than thirty soldiers and four priests. Though the Pacific Coast Indians were regarded as generally harmless, it was universally agreed that any threat to the status quo needed dealing with quickly and sternly.

An enormous posse was formed from the local men and those from the outlying ranchos, who were equally eager to keep the Indians in line. Nearly sixty men searched the forests with a fine-tooth comb, and after only a single day's efforts the brave was flushed from hiding and brought back to the town.

Claire, watching from her front door, was dismayed to see that the brave was Redwing. He and his wife had fled to the mission in the wake of Peter's demogoguery.

The Indian was hanged. Afterward his head was removed and placed atop a stake at the edge of town as a warning to others.

Claire could see the grisly sight from the window of her parlor. It seemed to her to symbolize all the horror she felt at the treatment of the Indians. She knew, as no other white woman in the town could, what degradation and abuse the Indians suffered at the hands of the white man. A white man in the same position of defending his wife would have been regarded as a hero. Redwing had been murdered.

On the third night after the hanging Claire was awakened by a peculiar sound from outside. Puzzled, she went to investigate and found Redwing's widow, Summer Meadow, dragging an enormous woven basket along the street. It was obvious that the basket's contents were quite heavy, for the Indian was struggling mightily.

Claire quickly donned a dress and went out. Summer Meadow, hearing her approach, stopped and stood at the end of the basket, watching with wary but grief-reddened eyes.

"Will you let me help you?" Claire asked, indicating the basket. The Indian had never spoken more than a few words of English, and Claire was not certain if she had been understood. She put a hand on the basket and made a pulling movement.

For an answer, Summer Meadow stepped around and lifted the lid from the basket. Claire gave an involuntary gasp as she recognized Redwing's headless body. She took a step backward. Summer Meadow carefully replaced the lid.

Summer Meadow picked up the rope with which she had been dragging the basket. Flinging it over her shoulder, she began to strain against it, once more inching her heavy load along the rutted street.

Claire's initial horror gave way to comprehension; Summer Meadow was taking her husband's body to bury it. The officer of the presidio had waited until late at night to give her the body, thus avoiding offending the townspeople.

With an angry toss of her head, Claire came forward and took hold of the rope as well. Summer Meadow gave her a brief, unreadable glance, then resumed her own efforts.

It was easier for the two of them. They passed the last house and Summer Meadow turned into an open field. After another fifty yards or so they came to a mound of dirt, beyond which lay an open grave.

The two women rested at the graveside, getting their breath back. Staring down into the hole that Summer Meadow must herself have dug, Claire wondered how they were to lower the heavy basket into it, but apparently Summer Meadow had already taken this into consideration. She took hold of one side of the basket, gesturing for Claire to do the same. Together they managed to tilt the basket on its edge over the yawning grave until the body within had tumbled out and into the hole with a loud thump and the loosening of some dirt. The basket, empty now, went in on top.

It was macabre and frightening, and Claire would have been glad to take the shovel lying nearby and begin at once to fill in the dirt, but Summer Meadow indicated that there was something more to be done, and when she started back across the field Claire followed.

They came to the stake on which Redwing's head rested. Claire, her nerves already taut, could not look at the grisly sight but Summer Meadow, with no show of emotion, brought a crate and, clambering upon it, reached down her dead husband's head. Without even looking to see if Claire was following, the Indian started back toward the gravesite. Claire for once would have welcomed the quiet and solitude of her parlor, but the sight of the hapless woman carrying the severed head to its grave unnerved her and she went too.

They took turns shoveling the dirt. Claire's back and arms ached from the unaccustomed exertion and her hair lay in wet tendrils over her brow.

At last the job was done. Claire stood rubbing the small of her back with one hand, the other resting upon the shovel's handle. She had no idea what to expect now that the burial was finished. She waited for a cue from Summer Meadow.

For several long minutes Summer Meadow stood in silence, staring at her husband's grave. She might have been praying silently or simply remembering a happier past. At last, without a thank you, without even so much as a final glance in Claire's direction, Summer Meadow turned and began walking away in the direction of the mission.

Claire watched until the Indian had disappeared into the darkness. Then, feeling oddly let down, she herself tossed aside the shovel and made her way over the uneven ground toward her house.

It seemed as if she had spent the entire night at their eerie task, but the distant sound of music from the cantinas told her it was not so late after all, perhaps midnight or a bit later.

She had left the front door open, as was common during the warm nights. As she came up to it, she thought she heard a sound from within, and she hesitated, wishing she had taken time to light a lamp before she went out.

She chided herself for being foolish. No one had come here in days except Peter, still trying to persuade her that she must come to live at the mission. And she had continued to resist.

She stepped into the deeper darkness of her parlor. As she did so there was the unmistakable sound of a match being struck. From her bedroom came a quick flare of light as someone put the match to a candle.

She stood spellbound in the front doorway, unable to will herself to move. Her legs ached from the work of hauling the heavy funeral basket and the bending necessary to fill in the grave hole.

A man appeared in the bedroom doorway. His back was to her, and the lamp, which he held in front of him, cast him in a silhouette.

She found her voice at last. "What are you doing here?" she demanded.

Her voice startled him. He whirled about too quickly. The candle went out. She had a glimpse of him starting toward her.

Genuinely frightened now, for she had

seen enough to realize that he was not dressed like the local vaqueros, Claire turned and tried to run away. She had gone only a few feet when he caught up with her. She was caught in a powerful embrace and lifted from the ground, her feet still churning.

"Claire—it's really you," a familiar voice said.

She stopped fighting against him and threw her head back, staring wide eyed up into the face of Camden Summers.

He carried her back into the house to her bedroom. She clung to him, kissing his mouth, his throat, his chest where the shirt lay open. She was too dazed at seeing him again, too thrilled by the long-remembered feel of his arms about her, to question how and why. He was here. It was enough.

It was not until she was lying upon the bed, her clothes gone, watching him shed his own with practiced speed, that she remembered Peter.

It cast a dark cloud over her pleasure. "I think I ought to tell you..." she began hesitantly.

He kicked aside his trousers and came to kneel naked over her, lowering his mouth to the upturned tip of one breast.

"What?" he asked in a muffled voice.

A shiver of excitement rippled through her at the touch of his tongue. His hand glided over one impatient thigh.

"Nothing," she murmured, lifting her arms about his powerful neck.

"How on earth did you ever find me here?"

He sat on the edge of the bed, fishing in his pocket for a tobacco pouch and a rolling paper, sifting tobacco through his fingers, deftly rolling it into a cigarette. She ran her eyes like loving fingers down the hard expanse of his back, savoring the stark relief of musculature, the ridged spine, the cleft that disappeared under him where he sat. She had forgotten, perhaps had never fully known, how a man's body could excite and stimulate her. At least, this man's body could.

"I looked around some," he said, lighting the cigarette and blowing the acrid smoke out his nostrils. "Asked a few questions."

He looked down at her, letting one hand rest lightly at the base of her stomach, barely touching the fringe of red-gold hair.

"We thought you had drowned."

"Thought so myself for a while," he said. "Finally got to the bank, but my leg was broke. Didn't even know it was till I tried to stand up. I waited around a few days, thinking maybe there'd be some sign of you. Finally I figured you must have drowned or been washed farther down than where I was. So I tied myself to a log and started downriver. Found a place where you must have camped, but that was as close as I got. Morton must have taken good care of you."

He glanced at her face. "Morton's dead," she told him.

"You kill him?"

"No. His greed did it for me."

He nodded, knowing Morton well enough to recognize the probable truth of what she said. The rest he didn't ask about because he already knew what it would have been for her with the man, and he didn't want to hear. If Morton had still been alive, he would have found him eventually. It was just as well Morton was dead. It saved him the trouble.

"When I got out of the canyon," he went on, "I had to wait around a while for my leg to get better. Then I set out west, figured if you made it, you'd be in one of the settlements. When I got to Los Angeles, I heard about an English lady who'd traveled north to Monterey in the company of the governor and his wife. Figured that had to be you."

She was silent for a moment, thinking how badly things had worked out. If only Summers had come a little sooner; she would gladly have ridden out of Monterey with him, gone anywhere at all that he wanted to go; and she need never have encountered Peter again. She could have married Summers, believing her husband dead, and no one would ever have known the difference. A husband lost in the wild reaches of the west would have had little occasion to haunt them. But this man down the road, tormenting her for her "sinful ways," he could not be so easily dismissed.

"You look thoughtful," Summers said. "You're not sorry I found you?"

She smiled and stretched lazily, reaching to run the fingers of one hand down the broad expanse of his back.

"No, I'm not sorry," she said.

Later she would have to find some way of telling him about Peter. But not now, she thought, as he lowered his mouth to hers. Dear Lord, not now.

29

She told herself that it was a fool's paradise in which she was living. The local people could not have helped seeing Summers. It could only be a matter of time before one of them told him the truth. Worse yet, Peter himself might appear on the scene.

A score of times and more she tried to tell Summers about her husband, and each time her courage failed her. This was too good, this interlude that had unexpectedly been granted her. For the first time in her life, she was in love, she was loved, and reveling in it. He made love to her day and night, seemingly inexhaustible.

She rose in the early mornings, hurrying about the town. Eggs from Señora Albego, who kept chickens and goats, flour for tortillas from the general store, fresh fish down by the water. If she could but keep him there, within the confines of her house. It was like an enchanted cottage. So long as he did not step outside its sheltering walls, the spell could not be broken. She cooked and hurried back to bed. She cleaned and joined him once again. He took her and rested, and took her again. Ate and slept, and took her once more.

And the hours passed.

For two days she kept the world at bay, each moment more precious than the one before, for she knew that they were dwindling.

On the third morning she came home to find him gone, the bed empty. There was no note, no explanation. Had he simply gone for a stroll? Or had he somehow found out? Perhaps Peter had been there, or one of the local gossips.

She dropped into a chair, her purchases forgotten. She waited, her eyes bleak with the knowledge that the spell was ended.

He had gone out for some air, unused to being confined for long, and thinking he would find her along the town's main street.

He saw nothing of her, but the noise from one of the cantinas made him think of a cool beer and he went in. Like most loners he was sensitive, even in a crowd, to his isolation from others. When he went into such a place, it was his custom to sit alone, for he did not often seek companionship.

He found a small table off to itself and sat there nursing his beer and ignoring the unwelcome attention he was receiving from the other patrons. Some curiosity was commonplace. Strangers were not an everyday sight in towns such as this, and the convivial Californios could be counted on to welcome a newcomer, not so much for his own sake as for the new contribution to the endless merrymaking that they pursued. But this, he knew instinctively, was something more than that. Though their faces were different, he had known these men before, he had met them in frontier towns, in mountain camps, along the trails that already had claimed the importance of being named. They too were loners, and such men understood, as others might not, that Solitude was a whore who, having once gotten a man in her embrace, did not easily relinquish him. They knew that there were men who wanted to be alone, and some, a few, who were doomed to loneliness, want it or not. They left them alone, partly because they respected such needs, and partly because it was often dangerous to do otherwise. Frontier men learned quickly—or sometimes too late—that it was wise to leave such men alone.

Sipping his beer, tilting his chair back so that it rested precariously against the wall behind him, Summers observed that his entrance had made a stir something more than that afforded a mere stranger. He interested them in some way. He was someone they had talked about, perhaps had been talking about when he came in, for some of them had that embarrassed air men have when caught at common gossip.

But why, for Heaven's sake? He was nothing to them. Not much different, surely, from others who passed through.

It occurred to him suddenly. It was Claire that interested them, not him. It was unlikely that his coming would have been unnoticed in a town this size. A beautiful widow, a foreigner to boot, living alone. No doubt every unattached man in the place kept one eye on her house. And they would notice and resent his appearance on the scene.

Satisfied that he had found his explanation, Summers lowered the legs of the chair to the floor. He finished his beer and would have gone, except for the stranger who entered just then.

Though the newcomer was dressed little differently from anyone else in the place, he nonetheless wore a quiet air of authority about him. There was nothing of the dandy about him. Such a man as that wouldn't have lasted long in the west. Yet he was unmistakably an aristocrat.

The governor, Summers thought, seeing the deferential manner in which the other men greeted him, not obsequious but guardedly respectful.

And handsome. That discovery gave Summers pause. Claire had traveled northward in the company of the governor and his wife.

Where was the governor's wife?

So intently was he studying the man just inside the doorway of the cantina that it was several seconds before he realized the man was looking for him.

Someone told him I'm here; that's why he's come, Summers thought, waiting.

As if to confirm his intuition, the man's gaze stopped when it found him. After a moment's hesitation he made his way across the room in Summers' direction. Summers saw one or two of those at the bar cast quick glances over their shoulders, while trying to pay no attention.

"You must be Summers," he said, pausing before the table.

It gave Summers an eerie feeling to be addressed by name by a stranger in this distant land to which he'd never before traveled.

"What makes you say that?" he asked aloud.

The stranger smiled, a not unfriendly, but slightly condescending smile. "Claire's spoken of you often," he said. "Though she thought you were dead. You're the only likely candidate to be visiting her here."

The way he said her name, something that happened in his eyes for a brief second or two—so that's what happened to the wife, Summers thought.

The stranger paused, waiting for some reply. When none was forthcoming, he extended his hand, saying, "I'm Don Hernando, provincial governor here in Monterey."

Men did not customarily shake hands in places such as this. It made a man vulnerable to a swift knife stab or the bullet of a left-handed gunslinger. Summers' hesitation was automatic, but he did shake the governor's hand.

"I was wondering if we could have a few words?" Don Hernando said.

"Talk away. I'll listen," Summers replied.

Don Hernando's eyes flicked toward the bar, but he did not turn in that direction. He must have been aware that theirs was by now the only conversation taking place in the cantina, and that all those men paying such fierce attention to their drinks were straining to hear all they could.

"My office is in my home," Don Hernando said. "Just a short distance from here. I've got some real brandy, if you'd like a drink. Save it for occasions."

Summers hesitated a moment more before pushing his chair back noisily and standing. "This must be one," he said.

They went out together, Don Hernando graciously stepping aside to let the plainsman precede him. When the news had first reached him that a stranger had arrived in town and was staying at Claire's, Don Hernando had guessed that this must be the man Summers of whom she had spoken frequently. Summers was supposed to be dead, but it was never easy to be certain in the wilderness, and anyway she herself had never fully given up hope or she wouldn't have continued asking about him. And who else could it have been? Her husband was accounted for, the other men who had started west with her were inarguably dead.

Don Hernando had left word about that he wanted to speak with the stranger, should he venture out alone. Summers had no more than set foot inside the cantina than one of the vaqueros had rushed off to Don Hernando's with the news.

When he had first come into the cantina, however, Don Hernando had thought for an awkward moment that he was mistaken. The man looked like an Indian. He thought of the Indian who had purchased Claire and brought her to the Malibu, but had dismissed the notion at once. No Indian would have gone to live with a white woman in a Californio town and stepped out into broad daylight afterward. It would have been inviting a lynching.

A half-breed. To a man of Don Hernando's untainted blood that was even worse. Grand God, the man looked like a savage. He moved along the rutted street like a stalking puma.

Still Don Hernando needed no reminding that this was a different world from that of Madrid and Paris. There were worse qualities here than looking dangerously fierce. Soon after his arrival on these shores, Don Hernando had been treated to a lesson on the relative unimportance of bloodlines in this new world. Disregarding the warning sounds, he had stepped too close to a rattler, who in turn had disregarded Don Hernando's genealogy and struck as democratically as if the blood invaded had not been blue.

Don Hernando was a snob but he was no fool. He had come here in political exile, but he had fallen in love with California almost at once. And he was shrewd enough to know after less than a year here that in the taming of this land men like this half-breed would count for far more than men like himself, however useful he might be in some spheres. This did not in any way diminish Don Hernando's opinion of himself. Don Hernando knew who and what he was, as well as what he was not.

Don Hernando's house was cool and dark inside, shutters closed against the midday heat. There was no sound of activity. The maid had taken to spending much of her time in Doña Maria's bedroom. Some days Don Hernando saw no one in his house but the unspeaking Indian who served his supper.

The two men had spoken little since leaving the cantina. Don Hernando's office was on the second floor with a balcony and outside stairs leading to it. It was here that Don Hernando ushered his guest.

"The brandy's from Paris," Don Hernando said, pouring two glasses. He lifted his own and sniffed tentatively at the amber liquid. Summers half-drained his glass at a gulp.

"What's this all about?" Summers asked. He was sure now that Claire and the governor had been lovers. One part of his mind shrugged off that discovery. This was a hard land, and those who survived it learned the art of doing what had to be done.

There was another part of him, however, that bristled at the thought of the intimacy the two must have shared. It was a new experience for the plainsman. In the past he'd taken women where and when he found them. Why then this need to be with Claire, whom he should have long ago forgotten? His curt account of his search for her had told her nothing of the mental agony, the uncertainty he had suffered, not knowing whether he was actually following her trail or moving farther away from her at each step. He'd wondered endlessly if she had survived, not only that river, but Morton and the desert and all the rest.

When he'd heard of her journeying northward with the governor it had been like a man finding a new soul. He had traveled here almost without rest.

I should have headed east after all, he thought angrily. Just who he was angry with he wasn't certain. Better yet, I should have stayed in St. Louis.

"It's about Claire," Don Hernando answered.

Summers finished off the rest of his brandy. It was good, far better than the Indian beer he sometimes had on the plains, or the rot-gutting home brew that was commonplace around St. Louis.

"What's she to you?" he asked sullenly.

"I'm in love with her," Don Hernando said. "The same as you are."

"What makes you say that?"

"Aren't you?" The question earned him a piercing glance but no reply. "You've followed her halfway across a continent to be with her. That ought to be enough to convince any man."

Summers continued to glare at him.

Don Hernando went on, uncomfortably aware that the man facing him was as dangerous as any rattler. "The difference is that while we both love her, she only loves one of us. You."

"Bull." Summers turned away and went to one of the windows that overlooked the town. In the distance he could glimpse the sunlight glinting off the ocean.

Love. How the hell had it come to that? A man fucked a woman not because she meant anything special to him, just because she was there and no one else was. Nothing you planned, just something that happened.

Though he had to admit, it was something he'd thought about a long time beforehand. And she was different. Not just the sex, which had been different, too, in some way he couldn't explain. But it was the rest of it. The way she'd come to look at the mountains.

And the times when he'd finish making love to her and find her staring up at the sky. Not like she was dreaming or thinking of something else, but actually looking. At the sky, at the whole, endless, beautiful sky above. For Christ's sake, who ever heard of a woman doing that?

For the first time in his life Summers had a sensation of falling, of drowning, as if he had stepped into something too deep and it was pulling him down.

"You've got no ties back east, isn't that right?" Don Hernando was asking. "Nothing in the States?"

"Ties?"

"Family. Wife. Children. Business investments?"

"I've got nothing like that anywhere."

Don Hernando came to the desk and picked up an official-looking document from its surface. He handed the paper to Summers, who looked at it curiously.

"That's the title to a land grant," Don Hernando explained. "It was originally given by the King to someone here he owed a favor to, but the man died before the gift was given. It's within my power to give it to anyone I choose."

"Why tell me?"

"It's good land, more than two thousand acres in the great central valley. Out there," he added, pointing inland. "It would make a great ranch. A fine home for the right people."

"Me?" Summers asked, surprised. "Me and Claire?"

"This is a land of promise."

Summers tossed the title onto the desk again. "I'm a plainsman," he said. "I come and I go, like the dust on the plains."

"She'll let you go," Don Hernando said. "And you'll make yourself come back."

With a quick, angry movement, Summers snatched up the document again, peering at it. "What's all this about, anyway?" he demanded. "What's in it for you?"

"All men aren't like you," Don Hernando said. "I'm not ashamed to admit that I love her."

"Then you go. Start your goddamn ranch yourself. Leave me out of it."

Don Hernando made no answer to that. The answer was too painful for him to dwell on and already known to both of them.

As if reading his thoughts, Summers asked, "What makes you so sure she'd go with me, anyway?"

"Her husband..."

Summers interrupted him. "Her husband's dead," he said. "Her and me traveled a thousand, maybe two or three thousand miles. Her husband could have been buried anywhere along that trail. Or anywhere else in that damned emptiness out there. What are you looking at me funny for?"

Don Hernando was indeed staring at him strangely. It hadn't occurred to him. The man had been with her three days. Hadn't she told him yet?

"Her husband..." he started again and again paused.

Summers swore and crossed the room to him in two quick strides, seizing the front of Don Hernando's lace-trimmed shirt in a fierce grip.

"Spit it out," he said, his eyes flashing like sparks off an anvil. "What are you trying to say?"

30

She was pumping water at the rust-reddened pump. He took the handle from her and pumped with a vengeance, filling the bucket and splashing water over their feet.

He stopped all of a sudden. The pump handle stood out horizontally then descended slowly earthward, unnoticed by either of them.

"Why didn't you tell me?" he asked in the voice a little boy used when hurt and bewildered. It was like the stab of an arrow in her breast.

"I was afraid."

"Afraid of what, for Christ's sake? Afraid of me?"

She nodded, tears brimming in her eyes as the water had filled and overflowed the forgotten bucket at their feet.

"Afraid you'd leave me again," she said.

"You're goddamn right I'm leaving." He turned from her and strode into the house. She followed him into the bedroom, where he seized his saddlebag and began cramming his things into it. Unable to speak, she stood in the doorway, watching him and crying noiselessly.

"Two things I never took before," he said without looking at her. "Another man's horse and another man's woman. Those are my rules."

"I was married before!" she cried, wanting to run to him, to fling her arms around him, and afraid to move, afraid he might drive her from him with blows. "I was married all the time."

"I thought he was dead!" Summers fairly shouted at her. "I figured the worms had eaten him. How the hell was I to know he'd turned into some sort of mission saint? Lady, that's too rich for my blood, me and a saint's wife. You got any idea how that one's gonna look in the good book when they start tallying things up?"

He buckled the saddlebag and threw it over his shoulder. "I'm going and that's that," he said.

"I'll come with you!" she cried, clinging to his arm as he pushed past her.

"Not with me," he said, shrugging off her hand. He turned to face her. His voice was angry but his expression was one of pain.

"Not with me. You married him. As long as he's alive, that makes you his woman. The law says so. The Lord says so. And I say so."

She began to sob, unable to hold back.

"Damn," he said. "Double damn." He whirled about and left, vanishing through the open front door.

She tried to cry his name but it wouldn't come. She ran after him. Summers had paused going down the path. Peter was standing by the street. The two men regarded one another silently for a long moment. Then wordlessly Summers went past him and along the street. Peter looked after him for a few seconds before starting toward the front door.

Claire fled into the kitchen. Sinking into one of the wooden chairs, she buried her face in her hands and wept with a fierce anguish.

There was a footstep nearby and she glanced up to see Peter standing a few feet away, watching her.

"Go away," she said, covering her face again. "Go away and leave me alone."

For an answer he came closer, pausing for a moment to stare down at the trembling of her shoulders. From where he stood over her he could look clearly down the front of her dress between the ripe fullness of her breasts. His hand reached out, seemingly of its own accord. His fingers brushed lightly over her upper arm.

She jerked away from the touch and jumped up so abruptly that the chair fell crashing to the floor. She snatched up a deadly looking kitchen knife and held it menacingly before her.

"Leave me alone or I'll kill you!" she shrieked.

Fear flickered briefly in his eyes then vanished. He smiled, an almost beatific smile.

"Like a snake molting its skin," he said. "You shed one lover and put on the next. A born whore."

He started for the door but paused to turn back. "It's no use, you know," he said, still smiling. "The Church will be your lover. You will come to see that I am right."

He went out. She stood sobbing for several minutes, still holding the knife before her. Finally it slipped from her fingers and fell with a clatter. She dropped to her knees in an attitude of supplication, but no prayer came to her. Slowly she sank forward until she lay sprawled upon the cool floor.

Doña Maria Isabella Marina Hernando woke with a start. It was night. The light seeping through the closed curtains at her windows was silver and pale.

Her head throbbed, as it often did when she woke, and her mouth felt dry as cotton. She sat up, feeling across the bedside table. The decanter was always there, and her glass, for when the thirst woke her. She drank, grimacing at the first sour taste, sighing as the wine seemed to wash the cotton from her mouth.

There was a gentle sound of snoring from the adjoining alcove, where the maid, Teresa, slept nights, ostensibly to be close to her mistress. Though once asleep, Teresa was not easily wakened.

Doña Maria got up from the bed and went to one of the windows, pushing the curtains aside and staring out at the moonlit garden. As she watched an owl, returning from some hunting flight, swept down straight as a dagger into the heart of the olive tree behind the house. It vanished with a rustling sound among the leaves and branches.

Doña Maria waited, holding her breath, half-expecting to see the tree begin to bleed. After a long moment she began to think of herself, of the pain that pierced her own heart. Like the tree, it did not bleed, though the wound went deep.

Finally she turned from the window and, without turning on a light, she began to dress. From a drawer of her dresser she took a sheathed dagger. It was old, hundreds of years old. An ancestor had brought it back from one of the first Crusades. Its handle was encrusted with precious stones. She drew it, tossing the sheath aside. Its blade was long and slender, the sort of blade that could glide almost unfelt between a person's ribs, plunging without pause into a heart.

She flung a cloak about her shoulders

and, clutching the dagger close to her bosom, stole from her room. In the alcove Teresa snored on.

In his own room Don Hernando turned on his bed, the latching of a door adding a bizarre twist to his dreams: Did someone go out? It was the King. Let us all dance.

In the parlor, which she had scarcely visited since their arrival in Monterey, Doña Maria grew confused. She bumped into a table, nearly toppling it, and was then unable to remember the way to the front door. For an uncertain moment she stood in the center of the room, turning slowly about.

She spied it at last, the door, and in another moment she was gone, the heavy folds of her cloak whispering a ghostly encouragement.

Claire, too, slept fitfully. The parting with Summers earlier in the day was like a scene from a play. She saw it enacted again and again. Each time she tried to bring it to a different end, and each time she was foiled by her own fear and guilt, by Peter's arrival, by Summers' anger.

She got up and made her way to the water pail in the kitchen, drinking thirstily. It seemed for a moment as if something moved outside the window and she stepped closer to see, but everything appeared still. In the distance a mockingbird unleashed a torrent of silvery notes, rushing so quickly that they spilled and tumbled over one another in their progress down the scale. It was warm; the night air was thick with dampness and the heady smells of ocean and flowers and pine, the scent of California.

She went back to her bed, but sleep, like a reluctant lover, held himself away from her just out of reach. This way and that she tossed and turned, and when the noises came finally, they were lost in the creak and groan of her bed as she moved upon it.

Only pale moonlight illuminated the room, but it was a shadow that warned her, some deepening of the darkness that was sensed more than seen. Someone had crossed the threshold of her room.

Her first thought was that it was Summers, come back to her. A deep weight within her seemed to take wing and soar.

She moved to toss aside the bedclothes and sit up, and as she did she saw a shadow move toward her, gliding soundlessly, and the joy died within her, impaled on fear.

"Who…" she started to say, but at that instant the moonlight glinted off something different, and she recognized it for the blade of an upraised dagger. At almost the same moment Doña Maria threw back the hood of her cloak, revealing her face.

For a moment Doña Maria hesitated, head cocked as if she were listening. With a whimper of fear, Claire tried to scramble from the bed. Her feet caught in the twisted bedclothes and with a cry she tumbled head first onto the floor. She had a glimpse of Doña Maria's feet as the woman rushed toward her and the gleam of the dagger, lifting, lifting, coming down at last.

Someone else was in the room. Claire had a dizzying view of feet, two people who crazily seemed to be dancing, bodies writhing, twisting together. The dagger fell to the floor, so close that it almost slashed her cheek. From the corner of her eye she could see the steel vibrating ominously.

There was a crash as someone was thrown across the bed. Then someone was kneeling, hands were gripping her shoulders, freeing her from the hindering tangle of bedclothes.

"Are you all right?"

"Don Hernando?" Claire blinked, unsure if she recognized the familiar face.

"I'm sorry," he was saying, helping her to her feet. "She must have woke me going out, but it was a few minutes before I thought to go along to her room. When I saw the sheath to that old knife, I knew where she must have gone. I was afraid of being too late."

He was out of breath and she realized he must have been running. After a second details began to fall into place. Doña Maria had attacked her with a dagger, had meant to kill her. Don Hernando had saved her life. Not for the first time.

She freed herself from his embrace and stepped back from him to glance toward the bed. Doña Maria lay in shadows, a motionless heap of garments, with one hand lying free as if reaching for her in supplication.

"Is she—?"

"She must have fainted," Don Hernando said. "I had no idea the woman was so strong."

Despite her recent terror, and her gratitude that he had saved her life, his remark grated. "...the woman," he had called her. But the woman was his wife, a pathetic creature gone mad on jealousy, frustration, unhappiness.

Don Hernando tried to put his arm about her again; again Claire moved away from him, frightened of the security his embrace had inspired in her, a security to which she was less entitled than the unconscious woman on the bed.

"Please," she said, wiping her brow, "a light..."

He struck a match, lighting a candle from it. In its flickering glow Doña Maria looked as if she were sleeping. Her lips had formed into a half-smile, and the deeply etched lines that made her look so shrewish when she was conscious had faded. She might have been a young girl, dreaming of some swain.

And perhaps, Claire thought, glancing at Don Hernando, perhaps she is.

"I'm sick about his," Don Hernando said. "It won't happen again, I promise you."

"But it will," she said. "It will all happen again. Over and over. Your wife, the people here, my husband. I'll have to leave here. I can't stay in this house."

"Leave? But you can't. A woman alone, there's no place you could go."

"There is one place," she said. "The mission. Perhaps Peter is right after all."

"You're hysterical," Don Hernando said, making a dismissing gesture with his hand.

"Perhaps." She leaned toward the mirror over her dressing table. She did indeed look a trifle hysterical, with her hair falling about her face in an uncombed tangle and her eyes gleaming feverishly. It would have been easy to assume that she was mad and Doña Maria a sleeping innocent.

"I forbid this," Don Hernando said.

She turned to face him. "Neither the decision nor the responsibility are yours," she told him.

His face turned red, but he stood his ground. "I love you," he said.

"And she loves you," Claire said, indicating his wife.

The statement startled him. "Doña Maria? Ours was an arranged marriage," he said.

To his surprise, Claire laughed. "Men are such fools," she said. She saw in his eyes that he too had begun to wonder if she were a little mad. He took a step toward her, but she put up a hand as if to ward him off. "Please, leave me alone," she said, adding spitefully, "you've been willing enough to do that till now."

"Claire..."

"Please."

"There's so much still to be said."

"And all of it ugly," she replied. "Or painful."

She saw him make the effort to regain his aristocratic aloofness. He pulled his shoulders back, his chin tilted ever so slightly upward. He went to the bed and gathered his wife up in his arms.

"I'll take her home," he said.

"Don Hernando," she said and hesitated briefly. "Please—if you do love me—for my sake—be kind to her."

He shook his head wonderingly. "She just tried to kill you," he said.

"Yes, I know. Any woman who's been in love knows that feeling," she said.

He studied her as if unable to decipher her meaning.

"If you could send someone in the morning, early," she said. "To help me."

"I'll see to it," he said.

31

She was awake soon after dawn, having slept badly, and began the work of packing up the belongings she had acquired since arriving in California, surprised at how they had accumulated.

She heard someone outside and called, "Come in," thinking it was someone sent by Don Hernando to help her move. When she looked up, she found Summers standing just inside the door.

"I couldn't leave without coming to say goodbye," he said, remaining where he was.

"Where will you go?" she asked.

"Los Angeles pueblo, for now," he replied.

"There are boats stopping there from time to time," she said. "It shouldn't be too hard to get back east."

He grinned briefly. "Never fancied myself a sailor," he said. "You saw what happened last time I tried to handle a boat."

She managed the ghost of a smile herself.

"What about you?" he asked.

"I'm moving to the mission." His smile faded, and she went on quickly, feeling the need to justify her actions to him, "It's only temporary. I've got to live someplace, and it isn't really safe for me in this house. Or very comfortable, as long as I'm facing the truth. I've become something of an outcast."

He did not reply. "Anyway, I may follow my own advice, and look for a ship to take me back east," she added.

"If that's your plan," he began and hesitated.

"Yes?" She was sure he meant to suggest they travel together; and she would go in a minute, forget Peter, forget Monterey and California, forget everything else.

"Nothing. I'd better go."

"Will I see you again?"

He stared at her for a long minute, as if memorizing her features. "It's a big place," he said.

She had been kneeling by her trunk. She got up, unsure whether or not she should go to him. He seemed to sense her confusion because he moved toward her. It was foolish and yet somehow she felt if he only held her again, kissed her once more, all of this would vanish and it would be simply the two of them together, never again to be parted.

"Hello." It was Don Hernando's voice calling from outside. Summers halted abruptly, a pained expression appearing briefly on his face. A moment later Don Hernando came in, stopping short when he saw the other man.

"Forgive me, if I'm intruding," Don Hernando said.

"I was just going, Summers said. He turned away from her, glancing back at the door to say, "Take care of yourself," and with that he was gone.

"I'm sorry. I've come at a bad moment," Don Hernando said.

Claire shook her head. "Like he said, he was just going anyway."

Don Hernando had brought a horse for her, and for her things, a carreta driven by one of the Indians who worked at odd jobs around the town.

Claire finished packing and the Indian carried the trunk out to the carreta. With Don Hernando at her side, Claire went through the house. It was the closest she had come to a home of her own since leaving London. Since her father's death, in fact. In London she'd been a glorified house guest. The house she had shared with Peter in Virginia counted for very little in her memories.

They came out the front door, to find the carreta loaded, the oxen munching disinterestedly at the grass, and the Indian nowhere in sight.

"The scoundrel," Don Hernando fumed, peering up and down the street. "I've never known him to run out on a job like this. He's always been one of the more dependable ones."

"They've their own reasons for fearing the missions," she said. "Maybe he just didn't want to go there."

"I'll drive you myself," Don Hernando said, but she put a restraining hand on his arm.

"That won't be necessary, I can manage," she said.

"You shouldn't be driving around the countryside by yourself," Don Hernando said.

She smiled. "I've traveled through far worse," she reminded him. "I really think I prefer to be alone. Anyway, I'll probably find the Indian along the trail. He might just have gotten impatient and started out."

Don Hernando looked as though he would like to argue, but she climbed into the driver's seat and it seemed the argument was already settled.

"Take this, at least," he said, handing her one of his revolvers. She put it on the seat beside her.

"I'll come to see you tomorrow," he said.

"It will be like a reunion, won't it? We met in a mission, if you remember."

"I'll never forget it," he said.

She pretended not to see the moisture threatening to spill from his eyes and gave the oxen a flick of the whip that started them slowly forward. When they had gone a few feet, the carreta creaking and clanking over the rutted surface of the street, she glanced back to wave to Don Hernando. Then she fixed her gaze forward toward the nearby hills, beyond which lay the mission.

Don Hernando watched until she was all but out of sight. Finally, moving like a man stooped with exhaustion, he started back toward his own house.

He had almost reached there before he became aware of a crowd of people gathered around the front of the house. Some of those in the group spotted him, and one of the men ran out to meet him.

"Don Hernando!" he cried while still at a distance, "your wife!"

"Doña Maria? What's happened to her?" Don Hernando demanded.

The man started to answer, then shook his head, pointing toward the waiting throng.

Don Hernando began to run. The crowd, seeing him approach, parted to make way for him. He dashed into the house, following the line of people along the corridor to his wife's room at the rear, the room from which she had so rarely emerged. Her little maid stood weeping in the doorway.

Don Hernando pushed the maid aside and went in. This room too was crowded with people. He had a glimpse of a rope hanging

from one of the ceiling beams and an overturned chair on the floor beneath it.

The doctor was kneeling by Doña Maria's
bed. At the sound of Don Hernando's entrance he rose, turning to face the Don with a
sorrowful shake of his head.

"Dead," was all he said.

Claire was almost to the gates of the
mission before she noticed the unusual quiet.
The fields, normally manned by an army of
Indians, were virtually empty. Within the mission walls too she found things unusually still,
with only a few Indians to be seen.

She asked to speak to the padre. She had
met him from time to time in Monterey and
had found him kindly and pleasant company.
Today, however, he seemed preoccupied.

"What can I do for you, my child?" he
asked when she had been shown into his
office.

"I wish to be permitted to stay here for a
time," Claire said.

"Yes, Friar Hidalgo asked us some days
ago to prepare a room for you," the Father
said. "Will you be with us long?"

The knowledge that Peter had made arrangements for her arrival before she had
even reached a decision to come here annoyed
her.

"Only for a few days," she replied, adding,
"Just until a ship comes in."

He nodded his approval and seemed to

dismiss both the matter and her. She saw that he was nervous, and on an impulse asked, "Father, is something wrong?"

"Wrong?"

"Here, I mean. You seem disturbed. And I noticed that the Indians seemed to have vanished."

He gave her a quick, reassuring smile. "They are the children of the light," he said, coming to take her arm and escort her to the door. "Try though we might to elevate them, they still sometimes revert to their pagan ways. A great many of them have disappeared for the moment. Perhaps some festival in the hills, some pagan ceremony. They will be back, rest assured. We are their fathers. We have brought them the truth."

Claire, who knew firsthand the truths taught the Indians by the missions, made no reply to this. A friar was summoned to show her to the tiny room that had been made ready for her.

She was no sooner alone than there was an imperious knock at the door and, without waiting for permission, Peter opened it and came in.

"So," he said, his eyes gleaming triumphantly, "you have come."

"I'm afraid for the moment I have no other alternative," she said. "But I mean to stay only until I can catch a ship to the east."

He came closer. "You will never leave here," he said. "I will be your conscience."

"I have one already."

"Tainted. Corrupted."

"Tainted and corrupted perhaps, but my own, and no concern of yours," she replied evenly.

He seized her wrist in a sudden and fierce grasp. "I have wed us to the Church," he said, leaning his face close to hers. "Just as surely as you and I were wed in the past. You will be mine forever, mine and the Lord's."

For the first time it occurred to her that Peter might be more than just a religious fanatic, that he might be truly mad.

"Let me be," she said, jerking her hand away from his. "I came here because I had no place else to go, because I was afraid to stay on where I was, but I owe you nothing."

"Do you think to divorce me?" he asked.

"It was you who divorced me. You said yourself you all but forgot I existed. You even have a different name from the man I married. For all intents and purposes my husband is dead."

He seemed to weigh this possibility. She expected an argument, but instead he turned to go. "I will be back later," he said.

"I'll be busy later."

"I'll wait," he told her, going out with a final, chilling smile.

Despite the knowledge that Peter would be close at hand, she had expected the mission to provide a haven of rest and peace of mind. This day, however, there was something in the air, a tension that few wanted to acknowledge but that seemed to permeate everything regardless.

A few of the Indians continued at their jobs. During the afternoon a few more drifted back from wherever they had been, but most of the mission's slave population remained absent. Nor would those who were on hand offer any explanation, steadfastly insisting on their ignorance.

Despite his promise, Peter did not return to her room that day. Claire went to bed soon after dusk, only to be awakened sometime later by the gentle shake of a hand. She sat up, angrily thinking that it was Peter after all, come to molest her. Instead she saw that her visitor was an Indian woman.

"You must wake up, señora," the Indian said, shaking her shoulder.

"What is it? Who are you?" Claire demanded, peering through the darkness at the face near her own, a familiar face, but one she couldn't identify at the moment.

"I am Redwing's widow."

Claire remembered then. She had helped the woman bury her husband only a few nights before. She shook her head sleepily, trying to make some sense out of what was happening.

"I don't understand," she said.

"You must flee here now," the Indian said. "You must run into the hills and hide until the soldiers come."

"The soldiers...? But it's the middle of the night, why on earth..."

"Blood will be shed tonight," the Indian said. "White man's blood."

Comprehension dawned with a stab of fear. "Indian uprising?" she asked.

"Go now, at once."

Claire scrambled out of the bed, fumbling on the bedside table for matches. She had been assured in Virginia that Indian uprisings were a thing of the past in the United States, but here in California the situation was far more primitive. Though these Indians were generally docile, she had heard tales of an earlier uprising in which settlers and military alike had been slaughtered. It was the unspoken fear of all the Californios, for all their arrogance in dealing with the Indians.

"I'll only take a moment to dress," she said, striking a match to the candle. A gust of air all but extinguished the flame, and she turned to find the door standing open, the Indian gone.

"Wait!" she cried, running to the open door. She had just reached it when the night air was rent by a shriek of agony, followed by another, and yet another. Shots rang out, at first in an almost orderly succession, and then a deafening volley, punctuated by more and more cries and screams. Someone was swearing in Spanish, and she heard the unearthly war whoops of the Indians. Shadowy figures dashed to and fro across the darkened grounds.

She could see that she would never be able to cross the grounds and escape the mission without being spied. Better, she thought, her heart pounding, to put out the light and hide where she was.

She closed the door of her room and started back to the candle, but before she could reach it to extinguish it, the door was flung open with a crash.

With a muffled cry she whirled about, to find herself facing two Indian braves. Their faces were vaguely familiar and she supposed she must have seen them working around the mission or the town, but the night had transformed them. They were naked, having shed both their servants' garments and their docile manner. One carried a knife and the other a gun, and as she stared wide eyed at them, their eyes raked over her body hungrily, reminding her that she wore nothing but the flimsiest of nightdresses.

"What are you doing here?" she demanded, assuming an air of bravado she was far from feeling. "Get out."

For an answer they advanced a few steps into the room. It was not necessary to read their eyes to see what they were thinking. Their sweat-glistening bodies gave evidence of their reaction to her own near nudity.

She remembered her reticule, pushed carelessly under her bed. In it was the revolver Don Hernando had given her earlier in the day. If she could only reach that.

"I'm going to see the padre," she said, starting toward the bed.

For a moment she thought her bluff might work, for the Indians let her almost reach the bed. Then suddenly the heat within them exploded in a flurry of motion. As if on cue they rushed at her, seizing her as easily as if she had been a rag doll and threw her across the bed, knocking the air out of her. Stunned, she tried feebly to slap their hands away, but a brutal blow from one of them all but knocked her unconscious. In a daze she felt her flimsy garments being torn from her until she lay naked and helpless beneath them.

Grinning crazily, the bigger of the two threw himself upon her.

32

Her knees were forced apart. Pinned helplessly beneath him, Claire closed her eyes, praying for unconsciousness.

Suddenly there was a commotion from the door and Claire opened her eyes again, looking past the Indian's shoulders to see Peter and one of the younger friars burst into the room.

Her first thought was that they had entered a deathtrap, for both the Indians were armed, while Peter carried nothing but a rawhide whip.

To her surprise, though, the sight of Peter brandishing the whip as if he were the avenging angel quite unnerved the Indians, so ferocious a moment before. Abandoning their own weapons, they retreated in terror from the whip's lash. They circled the tiny room, cringing as the rawhide strands cracked about them. Finally, seeing their opportunity, the two braves shoved past the younger friar and ran into the night.

"Stop them," Claire gasped. "They may hurt someone."

"The soldiers will capture them," Peter said, not even deigning to glance in the direction of the door. "The uprising's over already. We were expecting something of this sort."

She realized then that the sounds from without had changed. There were fewer gunshots, and the cries and screams were in the Indians' tongue.

"Thank Heaven," she gasped, rubbing the bruise left where the Indian had struck her. "Peter, please, I . . . my clothes . . ."

She tried to sit up, but to her surprise Peter leaned over the bed, seizing her shoulders so that she could not rise. His eyes, no less feverish than the Indians' had been a moment or two before, moved slowly up and down the length of her body, lingering like a malevolent caress at her thighs and her breasts.

"You," he said, his words emerging slowly and with great effort. "You—just as—I dreamed of—you—all these nights, night after night . . ."

"Peter, please," she said, struggling against him, "I must cover myself . . ."

"No!" He shoved her backward upon the bed. "I'll have you," he said, his breath rasping hoarsely. "I'll have you as I've had you in my dreams, those cursed dreams."

"Peter, in the name of God..."

He tore at the skirt of his robe and she had a glimpse of his member, swollen and red with lust. The young friar stared in horror. He was one of those who had revered Friar Hidalgo since he had emerged from the wilderness, looking upon him as a modern-day prophet.

"Friar Hidalgo!" he cried, running forward. "You're beside yourself. It's the excitement..."

"Get away!" Peter shouted, cursing and striking out at the young man.

The young friar struck at Peter's shoulders with his fists. With a snarl of rage Peter shoved him away. "Leave us alone," he ordered. "This has nothing to do with you."

"Please," Claire sobbed, tears streaming down her cheeks, "help me."

The young man came at them again. The Indian's gun had fallen to the floor by the bed and with an oath Peter snatched it up and in one swift movement aimed and fired. The young friar's face seemed to explode, and he fell across the foot of the bed, landing across Claire's bare feet. She felt the gush of warm blood and screamed in horror.

Peter slapped her. Then he was upon her again, forcing her knees apart as the Indian had done, and she felt the tearing pain as he entered her brutally.

She turned her head and found herself looking at the bloody face of the dead friar. She began to sob and retch all at the same time, while Peter's body pummeled hers mercilessly.

It might have lasted minutes or hours, she couldn't say. At long last she felt the stiffening of his body, followed by the wet warmth within her. He sank heavily down.

For several long minutes they lay motionless. Finally he rose, slipping from within her. She closed her eyes, unable to bear the thought of looking at him.

"You witch," he said, flinging the words as violently as he had wielded the whip earlier. "You demon. You've broken my vows."

"Your vows were a mockery," she said, opening her eyes after all.

"I ought to kill you," he said, snatching up the gun again.

"No, you ought to fall on your knees and beg forgiveness. Not mine, but your Maker's," she replied.

He lifted the gun, placing the barrel against her temple. She felt the kiss of the cold steel and knew that in a second or two more his trembling finger might squeeze the trigger and all would be ended.

"Go ahead," she said, not taking her eyes from his. "Kill me. It will not erase your shame. Nothing will ever undo what you have done."

"Whore."

To her own surprise and his as well, she suddenly smiled. "Far worse than that, Peter, you are a fool. I traveled across an ocean as your bride. I crossed a continent at the constant peril of my life, trying to find you, not because I loved you, but out of guilt, because I thought I'd driven you to your death, and out of a sense of duty, because I felt that I owed you something. Owed you? For using and abusing me, for taking me at your will, and often even more cruelly than tonight. And still I came, and would have been your wife again, if you had wanted me. And there you were the fool, Peter, because you did, and you tried to pretend otherwise. I was a fool too, because I must have known, and I too tried not to see. I forgot, we both forgot, that beneath that holy robe there is still a man, still the same man who was willing to kill his brother for the sake of a woman. And now, for the same reason, you've killed any remaining vestige of affection or respect I might have felt for you. Kill me if you wish. I shall join my husband. My husband, who died somewhere in the great western wilderness."

She waited, expecting at any moment the explosion, wondering if there would be pain, or if it would be too swift for feeling.

With a sudden cry, as if of great pain, he flung the gun aside. He turned from the bed, stumbling like a drunken man, and staggered from the room into the night.

She waited, half-expecting that he might return. The sounds from outside had dwindled to an occasional shot and a muted babble of voices.

She got up, flinging a blanket about herself like a robe, and went to the door, staring out. The soldiers had herded the Indians into a ring, like cattle. As she watched, a brave dashed toward the gates and was shot in the back, falling lifeless to the ground. The uprising had been brief. Its consequences for the Indians would, she was sure, be far worse than anything they had inflicted upon their captors. Even now, even with what she had suffered, she could understand, for she knew of their frustrations and agonies.

Two soldiers dashed by. Seeing her, they paused briefly. "Are you all right, señora?" one of them asked.

"Yes, I'm all right," she replied. They ran on.

She turned back into the room, closing the door and leaning wearily against it.

It was true. Despite what she had suffered, she felt a lightheaded sense of relief. She knew that she had spoken the truth to Peter: it was over at last. The debt, the duty, the fear, even the need, whatever it had been. Most of all the guilt: for what she had done to Richard, for not loving Peter, for driving him from her.

Whatever happened to her, whatever happened to Friar Hidalgo, Peter was gone, as dead to her as if she had thrown dirt upon his grave.

At last—for perhaps the first time in her life—she was truly free. Not simply of others, but of the toll she had exacted of herself.

33

"You're sure this is the right decision?" Don Hernando asked.

Claire indicated the ship riding the waves in the bay. Nearer, at the beach, a small boat was waiting for passengers.

"There's no telling how long I might have to wait for another ship if I miss this one," she said.

"Would that be such a dreadful thing?"

She smiled wryly. "I'm afraid it will take the good people of Monterey a considerable period of time to forget that I came here as your mistress. And of course that unfortunate business of your wife. No matter how we try to excuse it, the major share of the blame is at our feet."

"Still you don't have to leave California

altogether. That land grant I gave Mister Summers, he said he had no use for it. And I'm certain he'd want you to have it."

"And I'm to live alone out there in that boundless valley?" Claire asked. "Build my own house, fence the land, and what, do you suppose? Raise cattle? By myself?"

"Spain's grip on this land grows more feeble with each passing season," Don Hernando said. "I suspect I'll soon be out of a job."

"My dear friend." She took his hands in her own, stretching up to kiss his cheek. "I have an abiding affection in my heart for you, and for California as well. But I've known a great deal of pain and unhappiness here, and at the moment, I'm pretty much at loose ends. I don't know just what I want, or what I'm seeking, or where I belong. I thought if I returned to our place in Virginia I might get a better perspective."

She paused, looking past him toward the hills that bordered the town, and beyond to the uncharted wilderness that was California.

"Do you think I'll see him again, ever?"

He did not answer directly, unsure of just which man she meant. Reaching inside his jacket, he brought out a folded document.

"At least I've made a free woman of you," he said, handing the document to her. "This officially makes you a widow. It may serve to avoid some complications at some future date in your life." She hesitated before taking it. "There may be another man for you someday," he added. "There's no reason to let the past stand in your way."

"So far as we know, Peter is alive," she said, still not taking the document. There had been no word of Peter since the night of the Indian uprising. He had been seen running into the hills. When it had been learned that it was he and not the Indians who had killed the young friar, the soldiers had joined a search for him, but he seemed to have vanished on the wind.

"No, you're mistaken," Don Hernando said. "Peter, the man you married, is dead, just as I've stipulated in this paper. He died somewhere out in the great desert. This man, this Friar Hidalgo, he's not your husband, he's someone else entirely. Even if he lives, and in this land a man alone in the wilderness has slim chances, he's nothing to you."

Claire was less certain of Peter's chances. He had survived once before against incalculable odds. But then so had she, much to her own surprise. Don Hernando's words only echoed what she herself had thought when Peter had fled. After a moment she took the paper, thrusting it into her reticule.

"I think the point is rather moot," she said, smiling. "If I can't marry the one man I love, and I can't love you enough to marry you, well...." She shrugged. "What more is there to say?"

A man from the waiting boat hallooed for her. They were impatient to be on their way out to the ship. Once again Claire stretched up on her toes to kiss Don Hernando. This time their lips brushed lightly.

"Goodbye, dear friend," she said, the tears in her own eyes rendering his invisible.

"Claire . . ."

She turned from him and started down the beach. There was a crowd of townspeople watching, as there always was when a ship came in or left. One or two of them called farewells to her. She waved her hand at them, not trusting her voice to answer. Don Hernando watched as one of the sailors helped her into the boat, another taking her reticule.

A moment more and the small boat had pushed off, tipping forward and back in the swell of the surf. Don Hernando watched until he could no longer make out her features. Her hair had become a speck of yellow against the blue horizon. Finally he turned and made his way back toward his own house.

He was drinking a glass of sherry when he heard the sound of a horseman approaching, riding hard. He paid little attention until he realized that the rider was reining in his horse just outside.

Don Hernando's office was on the second story of his house. He stepped out to the balcony in time to see Camden Summers leap from his mount.

"Where is she?" Summers demanded, seeing the governor on the balcony. "I've been to the mission, her house. Not a sign of her. Do you know?"

For a few seconds Don Hernando experienced a churlish resentment. The woman he loved had just turned him down, and this man was the reason she could not return his love.

As quickly as it had come the jealousy faded. If Summers were here, Claire would stay as well. Perhaps not as his mistress, but his at least to see, to know, to love even. Here, and not a world away from him.

"The beach!" Don Hernando cried aloud, racing down the stairs. "Come with me, quickly."

"Where...?" Summers started to ask, but Don Hernando waved his questions aside.

"Hurry," was all he said.

The two men ran along the muddy street, causing passersby to stare after them curiously. Summers, running with the ease and grace of the plainsman, had a hundred questions he would like to have asked, but the governor was breathing so hard with this unaccustomed exertion that he plainly had no breath left for answering questions.

Summers had been camping in the great central valley when a chance encounter with a trapper had brought the news of the Indian uprising. Since then he had traveled day and night, tortured by his fears for Claire's safety. He'd been a fool to go away without her. He should have taken her with him. He had

411

waited all his life to find this woman. What right had anyone to stand in his way now?

In the long, arduous hours of his journey he had sworn that nothing would separate them again.

Beside him Don Hernando came to a sudden stop, his chest heaving with his labored breath. Summers stopped too. Before them lay the beautiful white sand, the sandpipers playing catch-me with the surf. Far out upon the water, just clearing the bay on its way to the open sea, rode a sailing ship, its sails taut in the steady breeze.

"She's gone," Don Hernando managed to gasp.

"Gone?" Summers felt as if the world were dropping from under his feet. Something inside him seemed to burst with a sharp stab of pain.

The governor lifted a trembling hand and pointed in the direction of the sailing ship. "Gone," he said again.

The two men came back through the town at a slower pace, walking dejectedly with their heads down. There was no conversation. The questions that each might have asked had been rendered pointless by that one glimpse of a distant ship.

They came by the trading post. Summers, thinking to ease the pain gnawing at his innards, turned away, crossing the street toward the cantina.

Don Hernando was at the door of the trading post when Claire came out. The owner's son followed her, balancing her portmanteau and a bag of supplies as well.

Don Hernando stopped dead in his tracks, staring in astonishment. She smiled, an almost apologetic smile.

"I couldn't leave," she said. "I watched the town getting smaller and smaller, I saw the hills and the pines, and I thought of what I was leaving, and what I was going back to. I paid the sailors to row me back. I was just going to..."

She stopped then, looking past him. Don Hernando did not have to turn and follow her gaze to know the cause of that sudden leap of joy in her eyes.

He stepped aside, refusing to acknowledge his own fresh pain as Claire took a faltering step, then another, and another until she was running, laughing and crying all at once, toward the man standing in the middle of the street.

ROMANCE...ADVENTURE...DANGER...
by Best-selling author, Aola Vandergriff

THE BEST OF BESTSELLERS
FROM WARNER BOOKS